SKIN DEEP

A DETECTIVE MARCY KENDRICK THRILLER

THEO BAXTER

INKUBATOR
BOOKS

Published by Inkubator Books
www.inkubatorbooks.com

ISBN (eBook): 978-1-83756-334-0
ISBN (Paperback): 978-1-83756-335-7
ISBN (Hardback): 978-1-83756-336-4

1

SHE'S ALMOST PERFECT
KILLER

Police Detective Third Class Marcy Kendrick of the Homicide Special Section Unit has made headlines once again for executing yet another purported serial killer. This time for the assassination of one Jackson Martin, age 35, who allegedly kidnapped, raped, and murdered six people in the Brentwood Park area over the last eight months.

The killer, dubbed the Brentwood Rapist, has been linked to the deaths of Jesslin Saunders, age 17; Carrin Mayberry, age 18; Sara Michaels, age 17; Diane Fontane, age 19; Sam Hunley, age 18; and Lisa Karp, age 18.

According to my source in the Los Angeles Police Department, Detective Kendrick discovered a tenuous link between the victims and Mr. Martin, which led to a police chase and the eventual killing of Mr. Martin in an alleyway by Detective Kendrick.

I ask you, is this the kind of cop we want on our streets?

One who takes the law into their own hands and murders suspects before they receive due process?

In my opinion, Detective Kendrick is a vigilante cop with a vendetta against the good people of our community, and we should all be wary of her. I look forward to Internal Affairs getting involved and finally getting her off our streets. I'll keep you all posted on what's going down with the corrupt cops in the LAPD, so keep your eyes plastered here for further updates.

I smiled as I reread the LAPD Copwatch Blog. It was my favorite of all blogs to read because the blogger usually focused on my favorite homicide detective, Marcy Kendrick. She'd always been one to push the boundaries on the job. Her history was quite fascinating to me. As a child, Marcy had witnessed my mentor's murder of her mother.

It was quite a loss when Lemuel St. Martin stopped killing after that. Some people deserved death. Especially women who perverted themselves. Whoring themselves out for fame or money. Not my Marcy though. I felt she was more like me than she was probably willing to admit. I was pretty sure she enjoyed killing. I knew I would enjoy it when I finally made my first real kill. I just needed to find a woman who matched all of my criteria so I could begin.

I'd been searching for a long time now, wanting to ensure everything was right. The woman I had in mind had to meet some pretty high standards. Not just Lemuel's, whom I strove to emulate, but my own conditions as well. With that in mind, I'd practiced with surgical tools so I could be as adept at removing skin as he had been. It wouldn't do for me to make a mistake and ruin my trophy.

I'd spent a few hours a day working at it for the past several years. Of course, I wasn't able to use real women to practice on. Not because I couldn't, but I might have gotten caught before I was ready. So I'd settled for animals and the occasional corpse I'd managed to get my hands on in the morgue where I'd taken a job as a nightwatchman. I had access to all of the deceased, but I usually chose to practice on the homeless nobodies most people didn't care about. Over time, I felt I'd perfected my skills, and I was ready for the real thing now.

I clicked off the blog and logged into Instagram. There were several women I'd had my eye on. I'd even found a few who lived here in Los Angeles, ones I'd been able to surveil. I would probably investigate them further in the future, but my first had to be special. I scrolled until I found the account I was looking for. Michella Graves. I kept coming back to her.

She had the right look, as she resembled the first woman that Lemuel, the Face Flayer, had murdered all those years ago. Michella was tall, with curves for days. She had burnished red-gold hair, and green eyes, which sparkled in the images she posted for the adoring public to consume. I followed all of her social media and was able to track everything she did by her photos because she was dumb enough to leave the location attached to them. Through those photos, I'd discovered where she lived, which was right here in LA. Convenient. It was as if she wanted me to know where to find her.

I'd done my research on her, as I'd done on all of the women that I'd been keeping tabs on. I knew nearly everything about her. I knew where she shopped for clothes, where she bought groceries, and whom she brought to her bed. Funnily enough, they weren't men. That was why I considered her only *almost* perfect.

Well, that and the fact that Michella was rather obnoxious and full of herself. Thought herself better than every guy she encountered. She used men for money, having them pay for her attention, which made her no different from the whores on the corner who offered sex for money. Actually, it made her worse. The guys got nothing real out of it, and they were left with drained bank accounts because of her. She got their money, and they got what? A picture of her tits? That was bullshit.

After considering all my options, I decided that Michella would be my first.

The thought of killing her excited me, but I was getting ahead of myself.

I had always been prone to playing with my food before eating because it made it taste so much sweeter. Likewise, I wanted this beauty to *know* that I had her in my sights. Michella being frightened of me turned me on. Though it was the idea of killing her while I had my way with her that really got me going.

Michella would be the beginning move of my game with my soulmate, Marcy.

I couldn't wait for the game with my beloved to start, but I had work to do.

I had to make Michella aware of me.

With that in mind, I grabbed the car keys from the counter and headed out the door. I glanced down the hallway but didn't see anyone, which I was grateful for. I didn't like talking to neighbors. I wasn't a big fan of people in general. They were pretty useless overall, as a species. Only a few were worth my time. Some because I could use them, others, like Marcy, because I felt a kindredness with them.

Michella would be heading out any time now. She'd said in her latest Instagram post that she was going to the Venice Boardwalk to do a meet and greet and take selfies for her page. She seemed to fancy herself as an Instagram model, but all her photos were self-taken. She didn't have a photographer following her around. No security. She did have a hefty following though, over a million subscribers, and usually got pretty good interactions on her posts.

Her popularity made this all the more enticing for me.

I took the shortest route I could to Michella's place, but it still took me twenty minutes to get there. I hoped I wasn't late as I pulled into the parking lot of her apartment complex and searched for her little, pale blue VW Bug. It was still in the lot.

Good.

I parked nearby and waited.

I had spent hours surveilling her apartment building, as well as her, without letting myself be seen. I hadn't wanted Michella catching sight of me until I was ready to begin.

A few minutes later, I watched as she strutted her way across the parking lot in a pair of bright pink, ass-hugging shorts that barely covered anything and showed off her tanned legs, with a matching pink bra-like top, and four-inch, pink heels. Her long hair—one of her best features—hung in glorious curls down her back, and it swayed as she walked.

She flipped those tresses over her shoulder with a practiced toss as she climbed into the car. I had to admire her beauty; after all, that was one of the reasons I'd chosen her.

Lemuel had chosen women not because of their beauty, but because they were simply whores. I wanted the women I chose to be part of my collection to be stunning, yet still match his requirements. It had taken a long time just to find Michella. There weren't a great many redheads who met my needs in the LA area.

Excitement for what was to come filled me as I turned the car on and pulled out of the lot a moment behind her. Not that she'd noticed. She was too self-involved to realize she was being followed, so far anyway. She'd be aware of me soon. I'd make sure of that.

I stayed with Michella all the way to the boardwalk and parked in the same lot she did. I followed her throughout the day, making eye contact with her any time she headed to a different section. After the third time our eyes had connected, I could see it in her gaze. She was apprehensive. Each time we made contact, I'd leer and drag my gaze over her, letting her know what I thought of her. It was a fun game.

The fourth time Michella's gaze aligned with mine, I noticed she was becoming increasingly nervous. That sent a thrill through me. I watched her from a distance for a bit after that. She looked over her shoulder constantly as she moved through the crowds, as though she could feel my eyes on her. I waited until she got to where she was going and calmed down some before once again letting her see me watching her. She glared and turned her back to me, but I could tell that I'd rattled her.

I continued my game until she made her way back to her car. I quickly entered the lot from the other side and got into my own car. When she pulled out of the lot and onto the street, I was just two car lengths behind her. As we maneuvered in traffic, I pulled into the lane next to her and stared at her, waiting for her to realize it was me. Her eyes widened with fright. As soon as the lights changed, she pressed on the gas, speeding off ahead of me. Her little bug of a car had probably never gone so fast.

I chuckled as I moved through the intersection, keeping my eyes on her car. I didn't want her so upset that she got into an accident before I was finished with her. My plans for her were too precious. I moved into her lane and stayed a few cars back, tracking her. Her car was pretty distinct, so it wasn't as if it was hard to follow. Besides, I was pretty sure I knew where she was going. It was nearly time for her to stop for her favorite iced coffee. She pulled into a Starbucks and headed inside. I parked in the lot and watched her through the glass. As soon as she had her drink in hand and was heading for the door, I was there waiting for her, pulling it open as she fumbled for her keys.

I enjoyed the way she jumped when she realized it was me again. I smirked at her.

"Asshole. Stop following me!" she muttered, her cheeks turning slightly pink.

I watched her hurry to her car with her iced coffee in her hand. I greatly enjoyed how anxious she was now. I'd done that to her. It was exciting to watch her hands shake as she tossed nervous glances in my direction.

As soon as she'd pulled out of the lot, I returned to my car, watching her again as she headed down the street. I knew where she was going just by our location. Michella was pretty predictable. We were close to her apartment now. She was headed home, probably to change for a night out with her girlfriends. That was her typical routine. Being a Saturday, she would either hit a club or a bar with those girl-friends she liked to hang out with.

I'd let her have fun for a little bit before I made myself known again. Only when she was alone, of course, I didn't want her friends to ID me. That would end my game too soon. Not my game with Michella, which was indeed fun, but the game I intended to play with my beloved.

I parked a few spaces down from her Bug. I could see her disappearing inside, still looking over her shoulder. Scaring her sent a tendril of excitement through me. I couldn't wait for the fun to begin for real. But that would come later.

I spent the evening in the same bar as Michella and her friends, and when she went off to the bathroom, I made sure to "accidentally" bump her shoulder. The look in her eyes, the absolute terror that resided there, excited me. I grinned, baring my teeth at her as she hurried on to the bathroom.

For the next two weeks I played a very intense game of cat and mouse with my intended victim. Michella behaved exactly as I expected. Frightened beyond reason, jumping at every little thing... it was glorious to watch. She'd attempted to take my picture a few times, but I hadn't allowed the opportunity. Anytime she fumbled for her phone, I'd turn and move behind another person or just disappear from her view.

Now her time was nearly up. The game was starting to get dull, and she had begun to show signs of weariness in her face, and that wouldn't do. I had plans for that face.

Tonight would be the night. I was ready. Everything was in place. I followed her again, this time to a friend's house, which was her typical Friday night activity, and I sat out in my car, waiting for her to leave. For a moment I feared that she'd planned on staying, so I'd gotten out and peeked through the window to see what she was up to. They were merely drinking and watching a movie I didn't recognize. Rolling my eyes, I returned to the car.

An hour later, Michella tipsily made her way to her VW Bug. I followed her to her complex, parked a few spaces down again, and got out of the car with my bag of toys in hand. It was late, and there were no other people around. As soon as she entered the building, I caught the door behind her so I could follow her in. I already had the chloroformed rag ready. I couldn't afford for her to scream. That wouldn't be acceptable despite the fact I would have loved to hear her crying out for me.

As she put her heel on the first step—her building didn't have an elevator—I wrapped my gloved hand around her head, making sure to get the rag over her mouth and nose. She whimpered as she struggled against me, but suddenly went limp, dropping her keys to the ground.

Smiling, I pocketed the cloth, bent down for the keys, then lifted her in my arms before carrying her up the stairs to her apartment on the second floor. I unlocked the door as though I'd been there before and belonged. That was the key, acting like you belonged. I'd studied the building intensely in my first week of surveillance and knew everywhere the building had cameras.

I was wearing a black hoodie, pulled up over my head, thin gloves—the kind doctors wore—a black gaiter covered my mouth and nose, along with aviator-style sunglasses. I knew I was unrecognizable, but I didn't want to give them anything they could use, so I kept my back to all the cameras.

Once inside, I maneuvered to the bedroom and laid Michella down on the bed. I wanted her awake for what I was going to do. However, I didn't want her screaming or attacking me, so I opened my bag of toys and pulled out a ball gag. It was perfect for her. I opened her mouth, set the ball in place, and fastened it to the back of her head.

I stripped off the minidress she was wearing and her heels. I wanted her in sexy lingerie for this. Once she was adorned in a pair of lacy blue panties and bra I had brought for this occasion, which accentuated her curves to perfection, I pulled out my padded Velcro cuffs and attached them to her wrists, then to the decorative, brass headboard. She wouldn't be getting out of them; they were pretty heavy duty. I did the same to her ankles, not wanting to be kicked. There wasn't a footboard, so I had to improvise and use some of her scarves that I'd knotted together to secure her feet to the bed legs.

Once she was ready, I headed back to the living room and made sure to lock the main door. I didn't want anyone coming in and interrupting us. Michella woke thirty minutes later. The look in her eyes when she realized her predicament nearly made me come. I'd removed my sunglasses, hood, and gaiter. I wanted her to know it was me. That I'd gotten to her. That I'd have her.

"Hello, Michella. You're excited to see me, aren't you?" I leered down at her.

"Mmmf!" She attempted to speak through the ball gag, but it was quite effective in its job.

"No, you're right, you can't speak. Isn't the quiet lovely? So much less annoying than the sound of your voice." I chuckled.

"Et... Mmm... gggaahh!" She jerked her arms, but they weren't moving.

"Now, now, the fun is just beginning." I flicked open a

knife and moved toward her. "I've been looking forward to this for a very long time. I had to find the right girl to start with, and while you aren't perfect, you are nearly so. Almost the perfect girl. So why you, you might ask?" I tilted my head and sat down beside her. "Well, it was time for me to choose. You see, I have a game to play with a particular, trigger-happy detective. Which meant I needed to settle for my near ideal. The one who matched most of my criteria." I touched her nose, almost gently, and gave her my most sinister smile. I had practiced it for just this moment. "That would be you."

Michella jerked her head away from my touch.

I gripped her chin, not too hard though, turning her face back to me. "Now, that wasn't very nice. It's a good thing I don't want to harm your face." I touched the knife to the delicate skin of her chest, drawing blood. I chuckled at the terrified look in her gaze. "I think it's time to unwrap the goodies, don't you?"

Michella tried to scream and struggled some more against her bindings.

"Now that's lovely."

Michella's eyes were wide with fright and pain, and her breathing picked up.

"That's it, beautiful." I enjoyed seeing her fear. "Exquisite."

I played with her for a while as she attempted to scream, which made it more thrilling for me. I wanted to remember this first kill, to savor it. Michella laid out before me, bleeding from the cuts I'd given her, terror in her gaze as I fondled her, would be forever locked into my favorite memories.

"Time for us to say goodbye now, my sweet Michella," I

murmured against her ear. I wrapped my gloved hands around her neck and squeezed.

Her eyes bulged, and her body shuddered.

"Yes!" I cried as she gasped her final breath.

She'd been exquisite.

I couldn't have chosen better for my first kill. Everything had gone exactly as I'd envisioned. I'd planned and executed it perfectly. I stroked her face, wishing I could enjoy the actual feel of her skin, but I didn't dare take off my gloves.

After another moment of basking in my kill, I knew it was time for me to take my trophy and set the scene for my beloved.

Turned out, Michella actually was perfect.

Who would have guessed?

I smiled in contentment as I removed my bloody gloves and traded them for a new pair. I packed the bloodstained pair in my bag with all my other things, made a few adjustments to her, and then checked the room to be sure I was leaving nothing behind that I didn't want to be found. I didn't want any trace of me left. Finding nothing of importance, I put on my sunglasses, pulled up my hood and gator, and left her apartment, leaving the door unlocked behind me.

2

LUCK IS NOT ON MY SIDE

MARCY

I left the hospital where my partner, Detective Second Class Angel Reyes, had just come out of surgery. It sucked that he was going to be out of commission for a while. I really hoped the captain, or worse, Jordan, wouldn't assign me some rookie to work with.

I had finally been cleared of the Brentwood shooting by IA a week earlier and was heading back to work. I hated that I'd had to shoot the guy, but he'd given me no choice. Honestly, it had been more a case of suicide by cop. Angel had thankfully been there and backed me up. He'd even taken a shot, but of course it was my bullet that had taken the guy out, not his. Not that Angel wasn't a good shot, he was, but I was better. And no, I wasn't bragging.

I'd been shooting since I was legally allowed to hold a gun. With my past, there was no way in hell that I'd ever be without protection. *If only—*

I shut down that thought real quick. I didn't like thinking of it. Of that night. I shook my head and cleared my mind as I made the short drive from the hospital to the precinct.

Angel had been in a terrible car accident the day before, which was what landed him in the hospital. He'd had surgery, and I had wanted to be there to make sure he made it through. I hadn't actually gotten to talk to him, he'd been sedated after the surgery, but at least I knew he was going to be all right, eventually.

I parked in my usual spot and headed inside. I steeled myself because I knew I was going to be seeing Jordan. The man I'd been married to for ten years, who'd subsequently cheated on me and was still pissed off at me because I'd divorced him six months ago. Of course, he hadn't wasted any time getting remarried to the hot little number he'd cheated on me with. I rolled my eyes and gritted my teeth as I entered the building.

I kept my eyes down as I made a beeline for my desk. I wove my way between my colleagues, hoping that Jordan was in a meeting somewhere. But no luck. As soon as I put my purse in my desk drawer, I heard him.

"Detective Kendrick!" he bellowed.

I turned and glared at him. "Lieutenant Brasswell." Oh, yes, and on top of everything, Jordan had just been promoted to my immediate superior. Not that he was superior, far from it, but the brass had given the promotion to him over me because I'd been tangled up in that IA investigation, which I was pretty sure wouldn't have lasted as long as it had if Jordan had kept his fat mouth shut.

"I can't believe IA allowed you to come back to work." Jordan sneered, his hands on his narrow hips, his brown suit jacket open.

"What is your problem with me, Lieutenant?" I was impatient to get this over with and started tapping my foot. I couldn't believe that we'd been married as long as we had.

He was a pompous ass then, and he was even worse now. Promoting him had just made his ego swell even more.

"My problem, Marcy, is that you are too damn eager to kill our suspects!" Spittle flew from his mouth as he spoke.

Jordan had always hated the fact that I was a better shot than him. I was better at most things than him, and yes, this time I was bragging. Still, that hadn't helped when it came down to the promotion. In the end the brass had chosen Jordan. Yes, I was irked about it.

Still, I kept my voice down and even pleasant. "IA cleared me, just as they did for the two other shootings. I had just cause to shoot. Would you rather I allow the suspect to kill me and Reyes? I thought he was your friend?"

Jordan and Angel had been in the Academy together and had been friends ever since, though from what Angel had said, that relationship had been a bit strained since Jordan's and my divorce. I wasn't sure why though. Angel would never say.

"Of course that's not what I want. Don't be ridiculous. I'm your lieutenant now, and I have a duty to make sure all of our officers are following the rules. I can't play favorites."

"As if I would ever be your favorite." I snorted.

"You were at one time," he replied.

"Maybe before wifey found her way into your pants—" I sucked in a breath. I had told myself I wasn't going to do this. I wasn't going to play this game with him. "Look, all of that is behind us. You made your choice, and I made mine. We still have to work together, and I'd like to be civil."

"That would be a first. You haven't been civil to me since before the divorce."

"With good reason," I snapped, starting to lose my cool again.

"Detective Kendrick, my office!" Captain Jack Robinson called from his doorway.

"Yes, sir," I replied and tossed Jordan a glare before I headed for the office.

As soon as I entered, Robinson closed the door behind us. "Have a seat, Detective." He gestured toward the chairs in front of his desk.

I was a little worried about why he'd called me in here, but I did as he asked. "What's going on, Captain?"

"A couple of things. First, how's Reyes?"

I smiled and arched a brow at him. "You weren't on the phone talking to them right after he got out of surgery?"

Captain Robinson had always been a caring man. He cared about his officers, and he was fair when it came to issues between us. He wasn't hot-headed or sexist like many other precinct captains that I'd heard about. So it didn't surprise me at all that he started by asking about Angel.

"Of course I was, but you saw him. How is he?" He seemed anxious and a bit nervous, and that had my concern rising.

I shrugged and studied him. "As I'm sure the hospital told you, he'll live to fight crime another day. Shattered his leg in a few places, so he'll be in traction for a while."

"Good. That's good. Well, not that he'll be off duty for a while, but that he's going to be okay." He sighed and dragged a hand over his haggard face.

"Sir? Are you okay?"

"Just been a long night, and this morning has been something else."

"Oh?"

"Meetings all morning after what happened to Reyes—"

I interrupted, "Please tell me you aren't assigning me a rookie."

"No, unfortunately, we don't have any rookies to assign, and everyone else is already teamed up. Looks like you're going to be on your own until Reyes recovers. You okay with that?"

A feeling of relief flooded through me. "Of course, sir. Actually, prefer it to working with anyone else. I know I can trust Reyes to have my back."

"Good, now, I've got something else to discuss with you. I almost gave the case to Hummel, but then I heard you out there with Jordan. Is that going to be a problem? Do I need to have you reassigned to another precinct? Tell me now before we get going on this next case, because I have a feeling it's going to be a hard one."

"No, sir, please don't. I can handle myself with Jordan."

"Good, see that you do. Now the case, I need you to head over to the Windfair Apartments. Apartment 25. We've got a victim, but it's not pretty, Kendrick. And because of your history, I want to be sure you can handle it."

"I'm not sure what you mean, sir. I've handled plenty of crime scenes. What's so special about this one?" I had to wonder because I'd been at this job for several years now, and he'd never asked if I could handle a case before. Though, his previous words had me thinking that this one might be dealing with a possible serial killer. It was too soon to know that, wasn't it? Usually, we had to wait until there were several murders.

Robinson took a deep breath and replied, "The vic's skin was flayed from her face."

A shudder went through me at his words, and I knew I was probably three shades paler than I'd been when I'd walked in here, but I wasn't about to give up the case. Not this one. Not when it could be *him*. Him being Lemuel St. Martin, the Face Flayer. The man who murdered my mother twenty-six years ago.

I swallowed hard and nodded sharply. "I'm a professional. I can handle it."

"You're sure? Because I need my best and brightest on this case." He narrowed his eyes. "You know this can't be the same killer, right?"

I bit the inside of my cheek. In theory I knew it probably wasn't, but what if it was? How did he know? St. Martin had been in his thirties when he'd killed my mother. That made him only in his mid to late fifties now. So it wouldn't be impossible for him to be back.

"You know St. Martin drowned himself."

"That is what was assumed." I wasn't so sure I believed that.

"Can you handle this?" he reiterated.

"Yes, sir. I can handle it."

"Then get over there and oversee the scene. I'll let patrol know you're on your way. Coroner and crime scene should be en route soon." He stood up and opened the door. "Be careful."

"Yes, sir." I stood up and headed out of his office, hoping I wouldn't run into Jordan on my way out of the building.

3

DÉJÀ VU
MARCY

B
ack in the parking lot, I grabbed my siren from the floor and stuck it in the window, turning it on. I pulled out of the lot as cars got out of my way. Sure, the victim was already dead, but that didn't mean I should take my time getting there. She deserved my attention immediately, or as quickly as I could get there. I didn't want her suffering the indignity of whatever she went through for longer than she had to.

Thoughts of my mother's death played through my mind, but I shoved them away. I couldn't think about her right now. I needed to focus. I needed to be on my A game right now. I needed to catch the son of a bitch who'd murdered the victim. To do that, I needed a clear head.

Swerving, I took a corner too fast, and the tail end fishtailed. I let up on the gas. Getting into an accident was something I couldn't afford to happen at the moment, not just because of the expense, but also because I had a crime scene to get to. Ten minutes later, I pulled into the parking lot of the Windfair Apartments. I could see several news vans pulling in as well. LAPD patrol officers were already on scene, setting up a barrier.

"Detective Kendrick!"

I glanced over at a couple of the reporters, but kept my mouth shut as I headed straight for our guys in blue. I pulled out my badge and flashed it. "Keep them back. I don't want them getting a hold of any information. Clear?"

"Yes, ma'am." The uniformed officer nodded.

I entered the building and looked around. It was just a small foyer with a wall of post office boxes, a hallway that led to the lower apartments, and a set of stairs. There was a camera pointed at the mailboxes, but not at the door. Frowning, I turned back to the door and stepped outside. I scanned the building's exterior to see if there was a camera, but there wasn't.

I looked back at the officer by the door, debated asking if he could have someone get the security tapes, but decided to wait. There would be time for that. I went back in and up the stairs. Number twenty-five wasn't hard to find. There were two officers standing in the hallway outside the apartment. Once again, I flashed my badge.

"What have we got?" I asked, and then studied their faces. The two of them looked a little sick to their stomachs.

"Some sicko, if you ask me," one of them muttered. "The poor girl."

"It's not pretty, ma'am."

"Okay, how many inside?"

"Just one vic, ma'am. Officer Kim and Officer Desmond are inside, but they're in the living room, not in the actual crime scene."

"Great. When crime scene gets here, let them in, okay?"

"Yes, ma'am."

I moved through the door. I knew Officer Kim; he was a short man, with a wide, friendly, Korean face. "Hey, Kim. What can you tell me?"

Kim flipped open his notebook. "Not much, Detective. Victim, as far as we can tell, is twenty-four-year-old Michella Graves. This is her apartment. The door was unlocked, no signs of forced entry. The victim appears to have been strangled, and then... um... well, her face was removed. Damn, I hope that's the way it happened, at any rate."

"So she knew her killer?" I asked.

Kim shrugged.

"We don't know, ma'am," Desmond put in.

"Where is she?" I asked.

Kim tilted his head to a doorway on the right. "Through there."

I briefly closed my eyes to prepare myself for what was on the other side of the door. I knew I'd find a girl with her face gone, but what else was I going to find? Clenching my fist for a moment, I let it go, then pulled out a pair of crime scene gloves and headed into the room.

I stopped short at the sight, and my stomach rolled. The girl was seated on the bed; her left hand was behind her head, as though she were just relaxing back against the pillows; her right was tucked into a pair of lacy black panties. Her knees were open as though she were giving someone a show.

The girl's face had been completely removed. It was reminiscent of the photos I'd seen of Lemuel St. Martin's victims. I had a flash of déjà vu, but quickly pushed the vision away. That wasn't the only disturbing part. On her chest was a note. It wasn't just put there. It was stapled in place. No wonder Captain Robinson had a feeling this was going to be a long case. Regular murderers didn't leave notes and posed bodies. There was only a certain type of killer who did that. The serial type.

My fingers itched to remove the note, but I knew I couldn't. Not without crime scene there to take pictures. I wondered what was keeping them and shook my head. They'd get here when they got here. In the meantime, I needed to look over every detail of not only this room, but the entire apartment. And I needed to hear from the neighbors. There was no way this young woman hadn't made some sort of noise. Surely, she'd fought back, right? Nobody just lay there and allowed themselves to be strangled to death, which from the bruising on her neck was most likely how she died.

I was really hoping for DNA evidence beneath her nails. Maybe a chunk of her assailant's hair, or perhaps she'd bitten him. Could she have? I wouldn't know until crime scene checked her out. I walked around the bed, looking for something, anything. There were no marks on the carpet to show that something had been moved. None of the furniture was shifted even a centimeter. Nothing was broken.

I moved to the window and tested it. It was locked. So the killer hadn't come in or left that way, at least I didn't think they had. It was possible they had entered through the window and then locked it themselves though. I looked outside and took in the wide fire escape. Plenty of opportunity for someone to come in that way, since there was just an alleyway between this building and the next.

I headed back into the living room. "Hey, Kim, can you have a couple of officers start canvassing the building? See if anyone heard or saw anything?"

"Sure."

"Oh, and I saw a camera in the lobby area near the mailboxes; maybe there are a couple of other cameras in the building as well. See what we can find out about them, would you?"

"I'm on it," Desmond responded.

I went back to the entrance and stood there, scanning the room. The kitchen was to the left, the bedroom on the right, with the living room in the middle. "Did anyone find her apartment keys or the purse she used?"

"Kitchen counter." Kim nodded.

"Right, we'll need to bag those."

"I'll tell crime scene."

I nodded. "Any word on where they are?"

"Just pulled in, I think. Should be up any minute now," Kim replied.

He was right. A minute later, Dr. Damien Black, the coroner; Lindsey Stone, the head of crime scene investigations; and her photographer, Michael Portsmith, all came through the door.

"Hey, Marcy, what have we got?" Lindsey asked.

"Something ugly," I replied. "Damien, think you can give me a timeline?"

He nodded. "I'll do my best."

I led the way into the bedroom, and all three of them paused.

"Sweet mother of Pearl, the poor girl," Lindsey murmured.

"Took the words out of my mouth," Michael muttered, lifting his camera. "Any specific shots you all want?"

"Everything."

"Got it." He moved closer, focused his camera, and took a few photos. "Okay, Doc."

Damien moved toward the body and opened his bag. He grabbed hold of the arm that was propped behind the body's head and lowered it easily. "She's already been through rigor, from the looks of it."

I nodded as he pushed on the skin of the victim's thighs.

"She's been in this position for thirty-six to forty-eight or so hours, judging by the way the blood is pooling, and there's no foaming in the mouth cavity, so I'd say we haven't quite reached three days yet." Damien pulled out a thermometer and inserted it into the liver. "Sixty-eight point two." He frowned. "What's the temperature in here?"

"I'll go find out." I headed into the living room and found the thermostat. "Sixty-eight," I called back, then returned to the room.

"Liver temp isn't going to help us, then. Best I can do at the moment is say less than three days, but probably closer to two."

"Right. Maybe we'll catch something on the building cameras, and that will help. What can you tell me about that?" I gestured at the note. "And the cuts on her chest?"

"The cuts were made prior to death; see how they bled and then healed slightly? This, though, was done post-mortem." Using a pair of tweezers, Damien pulled out the staple and dropped it into a baggie Lindsey held out for him. He handed me the note.

I glanced at it and pressed my lips into a thin line. It read:

Let the Game Begin.

I allowed Michael to take a picture of it and Lindsey to bag it up.

"Do you need me in here?" I asked, hoping they didn't. I had a murderer to find, and I wanted him found yesterday.

"Nope, we got this. Go do your thing." Damien grinned.

"Right." I headed back out into the living room and checked in with Kim. "Anything from the neighbors?"

"Nothing. Nobody heard anything coming from this apartment for the last few days. The last time anyone in the building recalls seeing Ms. Graves was on Friday afternoon."

"So nearly three days ago?"

"Seems so."

"It fits with what Damien said," I murmured more to myself than to Kim. "What about the cameras?"

"We've got digital copies of everything for the last week."

"Great. Make sure crime scene takes them."

"Yes, ma'am."

"Who discovered the body?"

"That would be a"—Kim checked his notebook—"Ms. Lauren Halliday. She's outside with Officer Peters."

"Thanks." I headed back outside and found Officer Peters and a tearful blonde I assumed was Ms. Halliday. "Thank you, Officer Peters. Ms. Halliday, I'm Detective Marcy Kendrick; would you mind if I spoke to you?"

Lauren sniffled and shook her head.

"Can you tell me what brought you over to Ms. Graves apartment?"

"We're f-friends; she had-hadn't posted any-anything in two days," she sobbed.

"What do you mean she hadn't posted?"

"Michella always posts to Instagram, Twitter, and Facebook. She's like clockwork. I tried Snapchatting her, but she never answered. I started to get worried because she'd been at my place Friday night; we finished off a bottle of wine."

She hiccupped and wiped her eyes. "I thought... I thought something had happened to her."

"Why would you assume that?"

"I didn't... I mean I thought maybe a car accident... I didn't think... I never... oh my God, poor Michella! Who would do something like that to her?"

"I don't know, but I'm going to find out. What can you tell me about Michella? What did she do for a living?"

She sniffled again. "She was an Instagram model. People paid her to wear their things and post about it."

"Did she have any enemies?"

Lauren shook her head. "But there was something bothering her over the last couple of weeks, and she wasn't acting like herself."

"Do you know what it was?"

"No, she always said it was nothing and not to worry about it." She sobbed.

"I promise I'll find who did this to your friend." I rubbed her arm. "Do you have a way home?"

"I have my car, but—"

"That's okay, I'll have Officer Peters drive you home in your car. His partner can follow behind and pick him up. Is that all right with you, Officer Peters?"

"Yes, ma'am." He nodded.

I pulled him aside. "Make sure the press stays away from her. I don't want any details of this getting out to the public."

"Of course, ma'am."

Having done everything I could here, I headed back to the precinct to give a report to the captain and wait for the crime scene report.

4

SPENDING TIME WITH AN ANGEL
MARCY

Arriving at the precinct just before noon, I headed toward the captain's office, but Jason, his assistant, stopped me.

"He went to lunch," he commented.

"Did he say when he'd be back?" I asked. If I had time, maybe I'd run by the hospital and see if Angel was awake yet.

"No, but I know he's with the deputy chief of police. So probably going to be a while."

"Good to know. If he gets back before me, tell him I went over to the hospital, and I'll give him an update when I get back."

"Will do." He went back to his computer.

I turned around and went out to my car again. On my way to the hospital, I stopped at a convenience store and picked up a bag of cinnamon disks and a crossword puzzle book for Angel. The cinnamon disks were his favorite; he always ate them and would make me stop at the store for more if he ran out. And the crossword book was because I knew he was going to be bored out of his mind lying in that hospital bed for weeks on end. I also swung through a fast-food joint and ordered each of us a burger and fries, and myself a drink. Angel always drank water, so I didn't bother getting him a drink.

Ten minutes later, I pulled into the hospital parking lot and headed up to his room. I knocked on the door. I didn't want to interrupt if the doctor was in there.

"Yeah?" Angel called out, sounding just a little groggy.

I cracked the door open and poked my head in. "You decent?"

"Never, but come in anyway." He laughed.

"Good to see you still have your sense of humor." I smiled. "I come bearing gifts."

"You brought me fast food?" His eyes lit up like it was Christmas.

"No, don't be stupid; that's for me," I teased him. "I got you this." I held up the brown paper bag as I moved toward him and sat down in the seat next to the bed. "Here."

He opened the bag and grinned. "Aw, you brought me my favorite candy and crosswords; you do love me." He fluttered his lashes at me.

"You're a goof." I rolled my eyes and opened the bag of food.

"You really didn't buy me a sandwich too?" He looked so sad as he eyed the bag.

I gave him a devious grin and looked around surreptitiously, then handed over his burger and fries. "Don't get caught."

"Don't worry, this baby's gonna be gone before the nurse comes back. The food here sucks. I'm gonna die of starvation before they let me out."

I laughed. "Doubt it. The guys will make sure you have something good."

He grinned back and took a huge bite of the burger.

The two of us made quick work of the food, and by the time the nurse came to check on him, I'd put all the evidence in the garbage. "Oh, I didn't know you had a visitor. I can come back—"

"Don't mind her, Patty; she's just my partner. What do you need?" Angel said, making eyes at the cute nurse.

I shook my head. "I can step out."

Angel pouted. "You just got here."

"I'm not leaving, just stepping into the hall." I rolled my eyes. "Behave," I mouthed at him and grinned.

He winked as I headed for the door.

I stood in the hallway, my mind drifting back to the crime scene I'd been at earlier. The note had pretty much told us there would be more bodies coming. I had to wonder at the killer's choice of words... *Let the Game Begin*... Who was he playing with? The whole of the LAPD, or did he mean with his victims? I wasn't sure. I supposed we'd find out more soon, or with the next body.

God, I hoped there wouldn't be a next one.

Nobody deserved what had happened to Michella.

The killer was seriously disturbed. I wondered about the pose he'd put her in. Was it some sort of tribute to her being a model? I would need to do my research on her to know if it actually meant that or if it was just the killer fucking with us.

"Okay, he's all yours," Patty said as she joined me in the hallway a couple of minutes later.

"Oh, no, we aren't... I mean he's my work partner, not—" I felt my cheeks heat up.

Angel was a very attractive man, but given the fact that

he was my partner and had been friends with Jordan before he was friends with me... neither of us were ever going to act on any kind of attraction between us. And there was definitely something there, but again, I wasn't going to pursue it, and I was pretty sure Angel felt the same. We'd seen other female and male partners screw up by getting into relationships with each other, and neither of us wanted that.

"I just meant I was finished." Patty's eyes were wide, and she looked a bit startled at my stuttering.

"Oh. Right, of course," I replied, feeling completely embarrassed. "I'll just go in, then." I pushed the door open and went in quickly before she could reply, and I made an even bigger fool of myself.

"There you are. Thought the vending machine might have eaten you."

I laughed. "Nope, didn't even check it out. So, how's the leg?"

"I feel like I've got enough metal in me to make me Robocop now." He laughed, and I laughed with him.

"Hmmm, is this where I say, 'They'll fix you; they fix everything'?" I asked, smiling at him.

He nodded, looking thoughtful. "Could be..."

"Well, I don't think 'Tastes like baby food' or 'That's it, Buster! No more military aid!' works with this scenario."

"True, true." He laughed again, his eyes lighting up for a moment before turning serious. "So, you ready to talk about it?"

I tucked a strand of hair behind my ear. "You can read me that well?"

"We've been partners for two years. I can read your face like it's my own. You've caught a new case, and there's something disturbing about it. So spill it."

I told him what I'd walked into this morning. From the unlocked door to the way she was posed. How she'd been strangled, and her face removed. "It was so creepy, Angel."

Angel reached for my hand. "You're a good woman, that's why. I'd be worried if a scene like that didn't bother you. I have no doubt in my mind you'll catch him. None at all. You have always been good at puzzling things out."

I smiled. "Thanks. I hope you're right."

One thing about Angel, he was always positive. He could boost my mood with just a few words of praise. It was one of the things that I enjoyed most about him.

"Who did they put you with while I'm in here?" he asked. He sounded apprehensive, and there was a wrinkle in his forehead that told me he was worried.

"Nobody. I'm on my own."

"Wait, you've got no one watching your back?" He seemed almost angry about it and ready to leap out of the bed.

"Calm down, Robocop. Captain said they didn't have anybody. Besides, I wouldn't want a rookie even if there was one available." I smiled. "You're not so easily replaced, you know."

He smiled. "Still, you'll be careful, yeah?"

"You know I will." I grinned back at him.

"I mean it, Marcy; don't go chasing after this guy on your own. If he can do something like that... I don't even want to imagine him getting his hands on you."

I snorted. "As if he'd even come close."

Angel chuckled. "Yeah, what am I worried about? You're always prepared, aren't you?" Though he was attempting to keep his voice light, I could see he was still worried.

The investigation was just beginning, I didn't know who

the suspect was yet, but I'd be prepared for when I did. "You know it."

I was pretty sure that Jordan had told him at some point early in our marriage that I slept with my gun under my pillow at all times. It had freaked Jordan out and had continually been a bone of contention between us, but I always made sure to keep the safety on and kept the muzzle pointed away from his side of the bed and toward the wall. I was a very light sleeper, so the moment I heard a sound, I was wide awake, my gun in my hand and ready to fire.

Angel seemed to understand me better than Jordan ever had. He knew what I'd gone through. Jordan did too, but he'd never taken the time to understand the trauma that I'd experienced and how it had affected me. That should have been a red flag right there that told me not to marry him, but I'd been *in love*. Or I'd thought I was, anyway.

Looking back, there had been so many red flags. A whole platoon's worth of flags and I'd ignored every single one. I couldn't even blame it on the fact that I'd been young and stupid. I'd been over thirty. Plenty old enough to know better. So perhaps it had just been stupidity, but I knew I wasn't dumb. If I were, I wouldn't have been at the top of my classes in school. So maybe it was more naivety. I hadn't dated much prior to Jordan. Maybe if I had, I would have realized how controlling and misogynistic he actually was. How he'd attempted to gaslight me every chance he got. Honestly, I was pretty lucky that I'd caught him cheating when I did, and I was proud of myself for not bending to his will when he started to demand things.

"Hey, you okay?" Angel asked, squeezing my fingers.

"What?" I blinked and looked at him with confusion.

"You kind of disappeared for a minute there."

"Oh, right, sorry. Just thinking about things." I smiled, but I knew it didn't reach my eyes because thoughts of my failed marriage were still plaguing my mind.

"The case or something else?" he asked curiously.

"Oh, you know, just life..." I shrugged. "I'm glad you're okay, you know?"

"You and me both. I swear my life flashed before my eyes in the accident. It was... scary," he murmured. "Never pictured myself going out that way."

"I don't imagine anyone does," I replied.

"No, probably not. Still, makes me think about what I want in life."

"Oh?" I asked, wondering what it was he really wanted.

He yawned. "Nothing specific, just, you know, things," he said cryptically.

"I should let you rest." I smiled and then said, *"Excuse me, I have to go. Somewhere there is a crime happening."*

Angel narrowed his gaze at me. "Ha-ha, very funny. That's my line, or it will be once I'm out of here." He grinned, but I could see he needed to rest.

"Fine, don't share, then." I winked at him. "Seriously though, I need to get back. I've got to fill the captain in on the case and pick up the crime scene report if it's ready." I squeezed his hand and then stood up.

"Yeah, all right, leave me here to my candy and crosswords."

"Okay, Peggy Bundy. Don't let your ass get fat eating all those bonbons," I tossed over my shoulder as I headed out the door.

I could hear his laughter as I made my way down the hall.

5

CHILDREN SHOULDN'T BE VICTIMS
MARCY

I headed back to the station, my mind on everything but the case. I didn't want to think about what Michella might have gone through prior to her death. So I distracted myself with the car radio as I drove. I sang along to a Maroon 5 song, tapping my fingers against the steering wheel as I drove. It was after one, so I was hoping Captain Robinson was back from his lunch with the deputy chief of police.

As soon as I'd parked and headed in, my mind returned to the case. I started toward my desk, but nearly ran into Jordan's broad chest before I got there. I put my hand out as if to make him stop moving toward me, but pulled it back before I actually touched him. I didn't want to be anywhere near him, let alone touch the man ever again.

"What are you doing?" I asked, irritated.

"I want to know the details of the case. What did you find?" he demanded. His tone was almost accusatory. As if I'd done something wrong.

I gritted my teeth. Was he going to micromanage me

now? Since when was that his job? The previous lieutenant had always allowed us to just get on with our job, only asking for information if there was a problem. It was clear that Jordan wasn't going to emulate him. At least not where I was concerned.

"Look, the young woman was murdered. I'm waiting on the crime scene rep—"

"Where were you? You should have been here waiting for it. That's your job. Not galivanting about all of LA."

I glared at him. I wanted to tell him he was being an asshole, but that would get me into trouble. I had enough of that as it was because of him. "I went to lunch and swung by the hospital to check on Angel, not that it is any of your business."

Damn, was he going to act like this all the time? Maybe I was going to have to take up the captain's offer of moving to a different precinct. I didn't want to give Jordan the satisfaction, though, of having run me out of a job I loved.

"Well, where's the report?" he blustered, his face turning red.

Other officers nearby stared at him, and at me too. The way he was behaving, you would think I was being insubordinate.

"I just walked in the door," I replied. Clearly, I hadn't even made it to my desk yet, and he'd seen me come through the door.

"Kendrick! You're up!" Captain Robinson called from his office. "Head out to Hambly Hills, ASAP. We've got a child abduction. Patrol has the perp trapped in a house. Jason, get her the address."

Jason wrote something down on a piece of yellow notepaper and then handed it to me.

"We're not finished, Kendrick," Jordan blustered some more.

I ignored him and looked at the captain. "Leaving now, sir," I said. I took the paper and ran from the room as the captain yelled at Jordan to get in his office immediately. I wished I could have stuck around to hear what that was about.

Abductions were my least favorite cases. Children shouldn't be victims, ever. The fact that so many evildoers chose to perpetrate their crimes against innocent little children filled me with fury.

I jumped in my sedan, tossed the light on my dashboard, and sped off to Hambly Hills. Fifteen minutes later, I pulled up next to a line of patrol cars and parked. I found the officer in charge and asked, "What do we know, Carmichael?"

"Perp is an adult male, white, approximately thirty-five to forty years in age. Vic is a nine-year-old girl he took from a Walmart parking lot."

"Is he armed?"

"He has a large knife; we're not sure if there are other weapons in the home."

"Whose home is it?"

"Address is for a Clint Forrester; driver's license photo is a possible match for our suspect."

I nodded. "So we're thinking this is his house?"

"Yes, ma'am."

"Any reason you haven't gone in?"

"He's in the upstairs bedroom and is threatening to slit her throat if we enter, so Captain said to wait for you and hostage negotiation."

"They on their way?" I asked.

The officer nodded. "Anytime now."

"Anyone do a perimeter check?"

"No, ma'am."

I looked to his left at a nearby officer and said, "What's your name?"

"Officer Lloyd, ma'am."

"Great. Officer Lloyd, come with me." I pulled my weapon and headed for the neighboring house.

"Um, ma'am?"

I turned back to the officer in charge. "What?"

"Shouldn't we wait for hostage negotiation?"

I paused and tamped down my fury. "Officer Carmichael, he could be raping that little girl at this very moment. I'm not going to sit here and wait for that to happen." I turned around and headed toward the right side of the house.

"What are we looking for, ma'am?" Officer Lloyd asked as we crept across the backyard.

"A way in." I moved toward a window and tested it, but it appeared locked. I checked everything, the windows, and the back door, then spotted a smaller window near the ground. There was a basement. Moving to it, I noticed it was one of those windows that had just a turn lock on it. I could slide a piece of metal in between the upper and lower frame and easily open it. "Officer, go to my car and get the slim jim. It's under the passenger seat. Hurry." I handed him my keys.

"Yes, ma'am." He ran, following the same route we'd taken to get here.

I felt time was of the essence. Every second I wasted standing out here was a second that girl's life was closer to ending. The minutes seemed to tick by slowly as I waited for Lloyd to return.

"Finally," I murmured, taking the slim jim from him as he breathlessly handed it to me.

I slid the thin metal between the frames and pushed the lock open. I pulled it back out, then laid the metal down on the ground and pushed the window up. I holstered my weapon and started to position myself to go through the window, but Officer Lloyd stopped me.

"Let me go first, ma'am, make sure it's clear; then I can help you down."

I shrugged, but said, "Just hurry."

He sat down on the ground and went in feet first, dropping down to the basement floor, making very little sound. I followed behind, and he grabbed my waist, making sure I didn't fall as I entered, and immediately set me on my feet.

I pulled my weapon again and glanced around the dark room. It wasn't a finished basement. The walls and the floor were cement. There was a washer and dryer against one wall and a clothesline hanging from two poles in the center of the room. A freezer stood along another wall and hummed quietly. There was a set of wooden plank stairs that led up to the main part of the house. The two of us silently crept up the wooden staircase. Halfway up, a board creaked under Officer Lloyd's weight, not that he was overweight, but he was a larger, muscular man.

We both paused, listening to make sure our perpetrator hadn't been alerted by us before we finished our journey up the stairs.

When I reached the top, I turned the brass knob of the door slowly and pushed it open. As expected, we entered the kitchen, which had faux-wood kitchen tiles on the floor. It was a well-put-together kitchen and had all the modern stainless-steel appliances. There was a large wooden farm table with six chairs, and four bar stools stood in front of the long counter. A basket of fruit sat on the table. It appeared to be a friendly, welcoming kitchen, but knowing what this man was about to do, what he'd already done... I knew it was all just for appearances.

I could hear the girl screaming for him to let her go from somewhere above us. She was still alive, which filled me with a small amount of relief. I put a finger to my lips as we made our way through the kitchen and rounded the corner into the hallway. The floor and the stairs were both made of hardwood. It was going to be more difficult to keep our steps quiet.

When we finally reached the stairs, I mouthed, "Stay here," at the officer, not wanting his weight to make the steps creak again when we were so close to the perp.

He nodded, looking nervously up the stairs. I doubted he'd ever been in this sort of situation before.

I stayed on my toes as I made my way up the steps, keeping to the edge by the handrail. It was usually firmer at the edges since most people used the middle of the step when they walked up and down stairs. Once at the top, I was grateful to see the hall was carpeted.

I moved to the door at the end of the hall where I could hear that the man had the little girl trapped. I peeked through the partially opened door and saw the guy with his back to me. He had the girl backed into a corner. The little girl's tearstained face was pleading with him to stop. She had cuts on her hands where she'd attempted to push the knife away from her. I could see the blood dripping down her arms. She was sobbing. She was being so brave by fighting him, but I knew she wasn't going to last much longer.

"I've got nothing to lose, now," the man muttered. "She's already taken the kids away from me. She stole my girl. I had to find a new one... you look like her." The man continued to mutter as he handled her roughly, grabbing at her clothes, trying to get them off her while pushing the knife at her throat. "Shut up! Just shut up! They're gonna kill me anyway. I want this! Just once I want to do what I want!" he muttered, sounding like he'd completely lost his mind.

"LAPD! Drop the weapon!" I demanded, aiming my gun at him.

The little girl screamed as he grabbed her hair and spun around her small frame to face me, his knife poised at her throat. I could see that her top was torn, hanging half off her shoulder. She had cuts on her chest as well from the knife.

"I said drop the knife!" I shouted, staring into his half-crazed, bloodshot eyes. I wondered if he was on something.

The man snarled and moved the knife deeper against the little girl's tiny throat, nicking it badly. I was afraid that he was going to hit the artery. I could see the panic in her eyes. I wasn't going to allow this asshole to kill her.

"I will have what's mine!" he screamed as he pulled the child's head back by her hair, exposing more of her throat.

I could see the blood from the nick running down her pale skin to her chest in rivulets. I knew he wasn't going to let her go. I had to make a choice. I was running out of time.

"I said drop the fucking knife!" I gave him one more chance.

"What are you going to do?" he barked at me with a harsh laugh. "I'm gonna kill her before you even get a shot off!"

The little girl whimpered.

That was it. He'd made my decision an easy one.

6

A WORTHY SUSPENSION

MARCY

The man had no soul. I looked him dead in the eyes and pulled the trigger. I didn't miss. The bullet struck in his forehead, propelling him backward toward the corner. The hand holding the knife dropped from the girl's neck, and the weapon clattered to the floor. The little girl was pulled backward with him, as his fingers were tangled in her hair.

I rushed forward, dropped to my knees, and gathered her in my arms. "Shhhh, it's all right now, baby. I've got you. He can't hurt you anymore, I promise," I murmured into her hair.

She sobbed as she wrapped herself around me. "I want my mom," she cried.

"I know, baby, we'll get you to her as soon as we can," I answered as I heard the LAPD officers rushing up the stairs.

"Is he dead?" Officer Lloyd asked from the doorway.

"He'd damn well better be," I replied as I stood up with the girl in my arms. "Are the paramedics out there?" I asked, looking past him to Carmichael, who had led the charge behind Officer Lloyd, apparently. "She needs medical attention."

"Yeah, they're out there. Hostage just got here too, but from the looks of it, they aren't going to be needed."

"Nope." I brushed past them and down the hall toward the stairs. "Carmichael, get crime scene here ASAP."

"Yes, ma'am."

I walked out of the house through the front door with the girl in my arms. I could see the ambulance waiting just past our line of patrol cars and headed for it. I tried to hand the child off to the paramedics who ran toward us, but she clung to me.

"Baby, you're gonna have to let me go. These nice paramedics need to take care of your wounds," I said, looking in her face. "You're going to be okay now. I'm going to make sure your mother gets here to you."

She sniffled. "Thank you," she whispered.

"An officer will come and talk to you about what happened, okay? I'm going to need you to be brave and tell them everything," I said, realizing she was the only witness to me killing her captor. I didn't have Angel to back me up, and Officer Lloyd hadn't come up the stairs with me either because I'd stupidly thought the perp might hear us if he did. "Are you going to be able to do that?"

She nodded.

"Good. If you need me, I'll be right over there." I pointed to where Carmichael was standing in the front yard.

"We need to get her looked at now," the medic said as he took her from me.

I turned and headed toward Carmichael and stopped next to him. He was speaking with a man in a dark brown suit who looked about ten years older than me. I assumed it was the hostage negotiator, and I was ready for an onslaught of questions.

"Why did you go in, Officer?" the man asked rudely.

"It's Detective."

The man sneered. "Fine, why did you go in, Detective? You knew we were on our way."

"You're right, I did know you were on your way. However, that little girl would have been raped or dead by now if I hadn't gone in."

"You don't know that."

"I do know that. I saw him. I spoke to him. You weren't there."

"Because you interfered when you shouldn't have!" he bellowed.

"Look, I made the right call. You were taking too long."

"I'm putting in a complaint with IA," he tossed over his shoulder as he marched away.

I shook my head. Of course he would. "Who is he, anyway?" I murmured to Carmichael.

"Sergeant Bell, one of the lead negotiators for SWAT."

"Is he any good?" I asked, wondering for a moment if I should have allowed things to play out and not gone in.

Carmichael shrugged. "He's got a good record, if that's what you mean. Can usually talk the perps out."

I frowned. It wasn't what I wanted to hear. "Think he would have talked this guy out?"

"Not before he harmed the girl. I saw those cuts; looks like you got to her just in time."

I nodded. I thought so too. "Crime scene's here." I walked toward Lindsey and Michael.

"Busy day today," Lindsey commented. "What's the scene look like? Anything we should be prepared for?"

I held out my service weapon. "You'll need this. Guy is dead in the upstairs corner bedroom facing the street." I pointed to the window of the room. "Girl is going to be okay; she's with the paramedics now."

"Got it." Lindsey bagged my weapon and handed it to one of her techs.

I turned back to Carmichael. "Has the girl's mom shown up?"

"Mrs. Goodwin is on her way. We had an officer staying with her until we had her daughter, Cara, out of the house."

"Good. Make sure the ambulance waits for her before they take Cara to the hospital."

"Will do."

I went back inside the house and up the stairs to speak to Lindsey. Damien had shown up while I was talking to Carmichael, and I wanted to tell them what they needed about the crime scene so it could all be handed off to another officer to finish the investigation, since I was now a potential witness.

"So, what happened up here?" Lindsey asked as I stopped outside the doorway of the active crime scene because I didn't want to contaminate any evidence they might collect.

"Officer Lloyd and I entered the house through the basement; then we made our way to the entrance stairs. I asked him to stay downstairs because I didn't want him tipping off the perp that we were in the house. With the stairs being wood, I was afraid they might creak."

"Gotcha. They do, by the way."

"So when I got here, the guy had Cara backed into that corner." I pointed to the one his body now lay in. "He had a knife at her throat and was trying to rip her clothes off. I could see that she'd been fighting back; there were knife wounds on her hands and arms, as well as on her chest."

"So where were you when you took the shot?" she asked.

I pointed toward the spot I'd been standing in, about a foot into the room. "There. He and Cara were standing about where his feet are now."

Lindsey nodded. "Michael, mark the spots and get pictures, please."

"Yes, ma'am."

"Have you IDed him?" I asked.

"Yes, his name is Clint Forrester," Damien answered from next to the body.

"So this was his house," I said, more to myself. "Need me for anything else?"

"Nope, I think we're good. You'll need to give a full statement back at the precinct." She turned back to Damien. "Do you have any questions for Marcy?"

"How was Mr. Forrester acting before you killed him?" Damien glanced up from the body. "I mean, did he seem like he was high?"

"I did think he might have been on something, I don't know what, but he seemed strung out. His eyes were bloodshot, and he was muttering a lot."

"I'll check for the usuals, see what we find. I can see a few track marks in between his fingers, so I suspect he was on heroin, but I'll know more soon."

"I'm heading back to the station, unless you need me for anything else?"

"No, I think we've got it all covered now. See you." Damien gave me a nod.

Back in my car, I sank into the driver's seat. I saw Cara's

mom arrive and rush to the ambulance. I was glad the little girl was okay.

I drove the speed limit back to the precinct, wondering how it was only three thirty. This day seemed to be going on forever. At the station, I was stopped by Jordan again on the way to my desk.

I could tell by the look on his face he was about to spit nails. "It was a justified shoot," I said preemptively as I held up my hand to ward off his tirade.

"You killed another suspect!" Spittle flew from his mouth, and his face was cherry red. "You're a trigger-happy vigilante cop. And hostage negotiation has already put in a complaint. I'm adding my own. You're making us look bad by shooting suspects!"

"I'm doing my job! That little girl's life was on the line!" I yelled back at him. "He was going to rape and murder her. She's nine, Lieutenant. She'll have scars for life from what he did to her, and I'm not just talking mental scars. I mean literal scars. No child deserves that." If I could wring his neck, I would. I was so done with his attitude. I shouldn't have to put up with him anymore. We were no longer married.

"I don't fucking care. You've shot your last suspect, Kendrick! That's it! I am personally going to make sure that IA throws the book at you! You need to be made an example of!"

"Captain, you know this was a clean shoot," I said, seeing him coming out of his office.

Robinson didn't look happy. His forehead was creased, and his lips were pressed into a thin line as he made his way over to us.

"She needs to be suspended and brought up on charges," Jordan demanded.

"Kendrick," Robinson started, he sounded even less happy than he looked, "I don't have a choice. You're suspended pending an IA investigation."

"But, sir, what about my other case? The Instagram model. I was just getting started on it. I've got the crime scene report to go over—"

Captain Robinson shook his head. "I'll have to hand the case off to Hummel, at least until IA clears you."

Jordan smirked and pulled smartly on his suit jacket. "They won't, not this time."

I flexed my fingers, really wishing I could punch his gloating face. However, I held myself back. That would only make things worse. "Sir, please."

"I'm sorry, Kendrick. My hands are tied."

"I understand, sir," I replied, but I really didn't. I was pissed off. It was a clean shoot, and he knew it. I was pretty sure Jordan knew it too, but he was going to make sure IA scrutinized everything, and if he could, he'd make them throw the book at me.

My ex-husband was a complete dick.

7

BROTHERLY LOVE
MARCY

I was too angry to drive, but I needed to get away from the station. Normally, I would have tossed the keys to Angel or made him drive his car for us, but I couldn't do that this time. Instead, I called my brother as I paced the walkway in front of the building.

"Hey, sis, what's up?" Stephen sounded mellow over the phone, seemingly in a good mood.

I hated to spoil his disposition, but I really needed him right then.

"Can you come pick me up from the station?" I asked. I could feel the adrenaline wearing off from my argument with Jordan and the tears beginning to well up in my eyes. It had been a shit day, and I really needed someone normal to talk to. I needed family. My brother.

"Sure, I'll be there in five. Just finished a job for Clinebecks, right around the corner."

"That's great," I replied, trying to hold myself together.

Stephen had gone into computer tech at UCLA after graduating high school. I'd worried about him doing that, but he'd proven himself and made me proud. I was sure Mom was probably proud of him too, up in heaven. He'd gotten his degree after four years and now worked as an IT consultant around the city.

He never really understood my desire to go into law enforcement after what we went through. He wanted nothing to do with the law and thought most cops were worthless. He'd never liked Jordan, he'd made that clear from day one, but I hadn't listened when Stephen had tried to tell me what a jackass Jordan was. I'd just thought he was jealous because I wouldn't have as much time for him as I'd had in the past.

I should have known better, but again, hindsight. I couldn't change what had happened. If I could, I'd go back to the night that Mom—

I stopped myself there. The last thing I needed was to think about the night Mom was murdered. My thoughts were already a mess.

"You sound funny; everything okay?" he asked.

"No." Everything was a blur in my head, and my emotions were all over the place.

"Bad case?"

"Yes, but it's not the case." My throat was tight as I struggled to hold off the tears. I glanced up and saw his black truck. "I can see you pulling into the lot. I'll tell you in the truck."

"Okay." He hung up right as he pulled up next to me.

I opened the door of his Ford F-150 and climbed in. Leaning across the seat, I hugged him, then promptly burst into tears. I wasn't normally a crier, but today had been extremely stressful.

"Shit, what the hell happened?" Stephen asked, rubbing my back.

I couldn't speak for a couple of minutes. I just needed to get it all out. Once I'd calmed down and wiped my cheeks, he handed me a couple of tissues from his glove box. I dabbed at my eyes and then blew my nose. "Sorry. It's been a crap day."

"How about I take you out to eat, and you can tell me about it?" he offered.

"Sure, okay."

He drove us to Gracias Madre in West Hollywood. He knew it was my favorite. I loved their wet burritos, and they made fantastic cocktails, not that I wanted anything with alcohol. I didn't want to deal with the hangover tomorrow.

As we walked in, a man called out, "Hey, Stephen, long time, dude." He had dark hair that was slightly balding, and a beer gut that his suit jacket wouldn't quite cover.

"Hey, Mike. You remember my sister, Marcy?"

"Of course, how are you? Still taking down bad guys?" His blue eyes brightened as he held a hand out for me to shake.

I tried to smile as I shook his hand. "Hi, yeah, I'm good. Still with the LAPD. How've you been?" I didn't really care; I was just being polite.

"Pretty good. Started my own place, Shepard Insurance, we do it all, commercial and residential, as well as car, motorcycle—sorry, force of habit, but you get the idea." He smiled just as his phone began to ring. "Oops, better take this." He pulled out a silver phone from his pocket. "It was really good to see you both. Stephen, give me a call sometime, and we'll go for a beer."

"I will," Stephen replied.

I glanced over my shoulder and watched him walk out the door we'd entered moments before. Mike Shepard was an old friend of Stephen's from high school, I remembered him hanging around, trying to chat me up, but I'd never been interested. I was glad he seemed to have lost interest over the years.

Once we were seated, Stephen said, "Talk to me. Tell me what had you an emotional wreck in my truck."

I first told him that I'd caught a pretty nasty murder; I didn't give him details because we were in public and could be overheard. I just told him it was bad. After the waitress took our orders—Stephen ordered a Paloma and a West Coast IPA as well as the Tacos Del Mar, and I ordered the wet burrito and an agua fresca—I explained about Jordan and the run-in I'd had with him this morning before the Instagram case and then again after I'd saved Cara's life.

As we ate, I could see Stephen getting more and more irritated with what I was saying.

"The guy is such an asshole. I can't believe you were married to that fucker."

"Yeah, I know. He's just trying to look out for the department. But I don't understand what he's got against me. At least as far as the job goes. Sure, I've killed a few bad guys, but they've all been justified shoots, and Internal Affairs cleared me every time. For some reason, he's determined to get me kicked off the force though."

"Can he do that?" Stephen guzzled his IPA and waved the bottle at the waitress for another. The tequila was long gone, and I was glad he hadn't ordered any more of it. He'd get drunk faster on it than the IPA, and I didn't want him driving if he'd had too much.

"He's going to do his best, I think. It doesn't help that the hostage negotiator put in a complaint too because I took his glory." I snorted as I finished off my burrito.

"You're the best detective they've got. They are lucky to have you," Stephen ranted as he nodded his thanks to the waitress for the bottle of beer.

I was a little concerned with how quickly he downed it and realized I needed to calm him down. "I appreciate you thinking so, I just wish I didn't have to go through suspension every time, but I suppose this one is worth it. I saved that little girl's life before the guy had a chance to harm her. Jordan can bluster all he wants. I'll be cleared."

"Still, I can't believe that asshole has the nerve to do this to you after all the shit he put you through."

"It'll be okay. The captain is fair, and IA is thorough. I don't think they're out to get me. Not really. They're just doing their jobs," I said, still trying to calm him down.

Once we finished our meal, Stephen paid the bill, and we got back in his truck. He pulled out of the lot in front of another car, swerving into the next lane, barely missing being hit. Cars all around us honked angrily as he raced down the road.

"I can't believe they gave him the promotion over you. Those bastards are nothing but a good-old-boy club. I knew you shouldn't have gone into law enforcement; look at the shit you have to put up with. They're a bunch of assholes with guns who do nothing to protect the people of Los Angeles. You're out there busting your ass for them, and they treat you like shit. It's not fair."

"Slow down!" I said, holding on to the "oh shit" handle above the window. "You're going to get us killed!" I watched in terror as he swerved around a car, coming close to hitting their rear bumper.

Stephen was breathing harshly, but finally pulled the truck over to the shoulder of the road and turned the engine off a minute later.

"What the hell, Stephen?" I muttered once my heart had stopped racing.

"Sorry. Sorry, I just—" He stopped, gripping the steering wheel tightly, and then he banged his head against it. He took a deep breath and added, "I'm just so fucking angry at him—"

"Who?" I questioned as I leaned back against the seat.

"Your fucking ex. He's a fucking tool, and it makes me so angry that you were with him at all, and that he's still treating you like shit."

I sighed. In a way, I knew where Jordan was coming from. I'd shot several suspects in a short period of time. All my shoots were justified, but I could see how it looked to the press. They didn't see my day-to-day work. They only saw that I had once again killed a suspect. Never mind the fact that I had been shot at by them, or that I was trying to save a little girl's life. They didn't care about those facts. All they cared about was selling the story. And they could sensationalize the story because I had killed several suspects now.

"Look, he's just looking out for the department. I get that. And I'm not really worried about IA. They're going to clear me. I might not have had another cop with me when I took the shot, but the little girl can attest that I saved her life. She was pretty damn brave, and I doubt she'll have a problem answering IA's questions when they talk to her and her parents. Hell, the paramedics can back up what I said because they were the ones to bandage all her wounds."

Stephen took a deep breath and looked up from the steering wheel. "I'm sorry I nearly got us killed."

"You don't need to get so angry over my shitty ex." I smiled at him. "Come on, take me back to the precinct so I can get my car."

He started the engine, put on his turn signal, and then pulled onto the road. "I'm always going to be here to protect you. You're my little sister," he murmured, almost as if he were talking to himself.

I reached over and rubbed his arm. "Are you okay?" I questioned, feeling a strange sense of concern for him.

"Yeah, I'm fine," he answered as he glanced over at me.

Something in his eyes had me wondering if he was telling the truth, but I didn't push him. Stephen had always been one to bottle things up. If something was bothering him, he just avoided it or ignored it. He never spoke about it. I don't think I'd ever even heard him talk about what happened to Mom. Any time I brought her up, he quickly changed the subject, saying we shouldn't dwell on it.

Ten minutes later, he pulled into the station's parking lot and drove over to my car, stopping behind it. "You okay to drive home?"

"Yeah, thanks for dinner. I'm sorry I cried all over your shirt." I smiled, trying to lighten the mood.

He chuckled, but it wasn't a happy sound, and his parting smile didn't quite reach his eyes. "Any time, little sister. We're family. I love you. Call me if you need anything."

"I will." I opened the door and jumped down. "Drive safely, okay? I don't want to hear on the news how you wrecked your truck."

"I'll be fine."

I watched him drive away, wondering again if that was true, because in my heart I knew that there was something going on with Stephen that I wasn't privy to and that I should worry about him.

8

LAID UP
ANGEL

My mind played back over the accident in slow motion. I saw the light turn green, didn't even think to check the street as I started across the intersection. I heard the squeal of tires again as the driver of the other car tried to slam on their brakes before T-boning me. I felt the crunch of the cars before mine spun out of control and slammed into the light pole on the passenger side.

I supposed I was lucky to be alive, but I didn't really feel it at the moment. Right now, I was feeling pretty damn sorry for myself, laid up in the hospital with my leg shattered in several places. I hated being in the hospital. I hated how uncomfortable I was. I couldn't move with my leg elevated and held in traction. I had to stay in one position and, damn, my ass hurt. It had only been a few days, and I was already going stir-crazy.

The nurses tried to alleviate some of my boredom, but they could only do so much. Besides, while they were all adorable, there was only one woman I really wanted to have paying attention to me. The problem was that she was my partner. Not only that, but she had also been married to a friend of mine up until six months ago.

The door opened, and Nurse Patty entered the room with a big smile. "You're awake early, Mr. Reyes," she commented.

I sighed, but smiled back. "Yeah, couldn't sleep. This position isn't really all that comfortable, you know."

"Yeah, I can imagine. I'm a total side sleeper, so I would be going crazy," she replied. "Can I get you anything? The kitchen doesn't open for breakfast for another hour or so, but we've got a few snacks stashed at the nurses' station."

"No, I can wait. I'll probably just watch the news; it should be on in a few minutes."

"I just need to check your vitals really quick; then I'll let you do that, okay?"

I nodded and held my arm up for her to put the blood pressure cuff on. She was finished within two minutes and was gone. I half wished she'd come back and flirt with me, but ever since the day she'd walked in and saw Marcy here, she'd been more reserved and had stopped flirting. I wasn't sure what she'd seen that day; perhaps it was my admiration for the woman.

Still, it probably wasn't wise for me to get involved with the woman who was my caregiver. Didn't they look down on that at hospitals? I didn't want her to get into trouble. Besides, I wasn't really interested in Patty, though she was very pretty.

I decided I needed a distraction from my thoughts, so I turned on the local news. I stared at the screen as the image of my partner flashed on the display, and pressed the volume button to hear what was going on. Panic made my heartbeat pick up, as I feared something had happened to Marcy.

"—*was on scene yesterday when LAPD Detective III Marcy Kendrick rescued the abducted child from alleged child abuser and kidnapper Clint Forrester. Mr. Forrester had been accused of sexually assaulting his eight-year-old daughter by his now widow, Mrs. Kendra Forrester. Mrs. Forrester had filed for divorce six months ago after her daughter reported the assault to a teacher. Mr. Forrester had been fighting the charge, claiming it was all his daughter's imagination; however, given the circumstances that played out yesterday, with the kidnapping and attempted rape of the little girl—who will remain anonymous—from the Walmart parking lot, his account of the events, in this reporter's opinion seems to be doubtful.*"

"You think?" I muttered.

"*Mr. Forrester was allegedly holding the child at knifepoint when Detective Kendrick and another LAPD officer entered the home via a window in the basement, though it was only Detective Kendrick who confronted Mr. Forrester. When he would not release the child or drop his weapon, Detective Kendrick shot him, making this her fourth deadly shooting in the last year. It is our understanding that Detective Kendrick is now on suspension, pending a review by internal affairs.*"

I muted the TV. I didn't need to hear any more. I should have been there. I should have had her back. It bugged the hell out of me that I wasn't. I couldn't help but think that if I'd been there, Marcy wouldn't have been suspended. I had to wonder what the captain was playing at, suspending her when she'd clearly made the right call. The man was holding a child at knifepoint; was she supposed to wait until he killed her?

I reached for my phone, which thankfully I was allowed

to have, to call her but saw that it was really early, barely past six a.m. Knowing Marcy, she was probably still asleep because she'd stayed up late, no doubt pissed off about her suspension. I figured she'd come by here at some point today to let me know what was going on.

It took her longer than I expected.

The door opened just after one p.m., and Marcy's head popped through the crack she'd made. "You're not having a sponge bath with Nurse Hottie, are you?" she asked, looking about the room with a smile.

"Nope, you're safe to come in." I grinned. "You don't seem as pissed off as I imagined you'd be."

"So, you heard? Who called you? Did Jordan come over here to gloat?" Her visage changed, and I knew her ire was up.

"No, haven't seen Jordan. It was on the news this morning."

"Oh." She seemed to instantly deflate as she sank into the chair next to my bed.

"Want to talk about it?" I asked.

"What? The shooting or the suspension?" she replied dryly.

"How about both?"

She pursed her lips and then nodded. She went over what had led up to her shooting the suspect, and then how she'd gotten into it with the hostage negotiator.

"Well, shit. That's not good. What took the guy so long to get there?"

"Don't know, didn't ask. The guy was a tool. Anyway, he filed a complaint with IA, and when I got back to the station, Jordan was on a rampage. Screaming and carrying on— you'd think he thought *I* was a serial killer the way he was acting. He got his way though. Captain Robinson suspended me, and now I can't work the actual possible serial killer case."

"Who's he giving it to?"

Marcy rolled her eyes. "Hummel."

"What? Hummel couldn't find his ass if you handed it to him." I snorted.

"I know." She sighed. "Hopefully, IA will be quick this time. I know Jordan was bugging them the last time I was suspended, trying to keep me from coming back. Hell, I haven't—*hadn't* even been back a day when this happened."

"I should have been there." Even I could hear the regret in my voice.

"No, it wouldn't have mattered. I'd have asked you to stay at the bottom of the stairs for fear of us tipping him off."

"It might have. I might have gone up the stairs once you told him to drop his weapon. Then I could have been there to witness the shoot."

"I'm sure Cara has told them what happened. She might be young, but she witnessed everything, and her life was the one being threatened. That has to count for something, right?"

"Hopefully."

"I just—" She stopped as her phone started ringing. "Hang on, it says it's a call from the county jail," she murmured as she pressed the button. "Hello?"

Marcy's face lost all of its color, and she seemed to grow smaller as her shoulders hunched and curled inward. "Yeah, okay, I'm heading over now. What time is your bail hearing? Do you need a lawyer? ... Okay, I'll call one for you. Just hang tight. I'll be there as soon as I can."

"What happened?" I asked as she hung up the call.

"It's Stephen." She shook her head and looked at me with disbelief. "This is all my fault."

"What is?"

"He's in jail because he assaulted a police officer. Namely Jordan, which I would have loved to have seen. But of course, Jordan is being an absolute asshole and is pressing charges."

"How is that your fault?" I didn't understand her leap of logic.

"Because last night, after I was suspended, I called Stephen, and I was complaining about Jordan and how he was behind both this suspension and my last. I guess Stephen was more drunk than I'd thought, because he must have gone after Jordan when he dropped me off." She pressed her fingers to her eyes, as if trying to keep herself from crying.

"He's your brother, and he cares about you. There was already some bad shit between the two of them after what Jordan did when the two of you were married, so I can see where Stephen's coming from. Did he assault Jordan while he was on duty?"

"No, but you know Jordan, he's going to press every advantage he's got."

I did know Jordan, and he'd been acting the fool for a good while now. Cheating on Marcy with a twenty-two-year-old college girl was just the tip of the iceberg. I'd told him he was stupid at the time, and I'd hated keeping it from Marcy. She didn't know it, but I had manipulated things so that she would find out about the affair. It wasn't that I wanted their marriage to break up. I hadn't. But I didn't think she deserved what Jordan had been doing to her. Since then, I'd pulled back from my friendship with Jordan. I'd kept things amicable, but I didn't ask him over for a beer or to go shoot hoops after work anymore.

Still, I knew I could do some good here, maybe. "Want me to talk to him? I can probably get him to drop the charges."

Her face lifted, and a look of hope grew in her eyes. "Could you?"

"Of course. I can't promise anything, but I'll see what I can do."

The smile that lit her face could have powered a million suns. "Thank you." She stood up, leaned over my bed, and hugged me. "I should go. I told him I was on my way."

"Come back and see me soon, yeah?" I said lightly, trying not to show how much I had enjoyed that hug.

"You know I will. I'll even bring your favorite burger and fries next time."

I grinned. "Then you'd better make that real soon."

She winked. "I will." Waving, she left the room.

As soon as she was gone, I picked up my phone, scrolled through my contacts, and hit Jordan's number.

"Brasswell," he answered.

"Hey, Jordan, it's Angel."

"Angel, hey, how's the leg? I've been meaning to get over there to see you, but you know how it is. New job and all. I've been pretty busy trying to put out fires. Mainly fires started by my ex-wife. You wouldn't believe the amount of paperwork that I have had to deal with because of her penchant for shooting suspects. I hope IA actually throws the book at her this time."

"Do you really hope for that?"

"What?"

"I mean, Marcy's a great cop. She takes her job seriously,

and she saves lives. She saved that little girl's life just yesterday."

Jordan blustered. "That's entirely beside the point. She didn't have to be the one to go in there. She could have waited for the hostage negotiator; there was no indication the guy was going to kill the girl—"

"Except that he'd already escalated to kidnapping a random child, and was continuing to hold the girl while LAPD surrounded his house, and was actually threatening her life the entire time."

"Is this why you called? To talk about my wife?" Jordan sounded peeved.

"Not exactly. I called because Marcy was here just a few minutes ago when she got a call from her brother, who's in county lockup because of you."

"He punched me in the face. I'm an officer of the law. He can't just—"

"Were you on duty when he punched you?"

"What does that matter?"

"Because if you weren't, then you can't claim he punched an officer of the law. He was merely punching his former brother-in-law who cheated on his little sister, who was also the reason she was suspended from her job. He was just being a protective big brother. Something I'd think you'd understand."

"I—"

"Come on, Jordan, you know you're overreacting. You're pissed off that Marcy left you. Your ego was damaged because she nearly beat you out of that job. The only reason you got it is because she was under investigation for shooting that perp. Which she wouldn't have been if you hadn't made such a stink about it."

"It's the fourth suspect she's fatally shot."

"You're right, but it was a justified shoot, and you know it. You were the one that made them drag things out by going back over the previous shoots and nit-picking over everything she's ever done, all so you could gain points over her."

"They chose the better candidate."

"Maybe so, but I think you're punishing her because she left you."

"Fuck you, Angel."

"No thanks." I chuckled. "You're not my type."

"Funny, man." He sighed. "He busted my lip and gave me a black eye."

"And he spent the night in lockup. Don't you think that's enough?"

"No."

"Come on, he's not a bad guy," I pressed. "He had good reasons for punching you."

"Maybe."

"You'll drop the charges?" I asked.

"I'll think about it," he answered.

I knew he'd probably draw it out as long as he could, but in the end, he'd drop the case. "Good. So, when are you coming by to see me?"

Jordan laughed. "Soon. Want me to bring you anything?"

"Nah, I'm good. Just bored out of my mind lying in this bed twenty-four seven."

"I don't envy you at all—unless you got a hot nurse there taking care of you..."

"They're not bad." I laughed. "Definitely not complaining about them."

"Glad to hear it. Maybe you'll end up marrying one of

those hotties; 'bout time you found someone to put a ring on."

"Nah, that's your department. I don't do matrimony." I laughed again, but the image of Marcy's face floated through my mind, and I had to quickly shove the vision away. I definitely couldn't be thinking of her in that way.

Not with her ex-husband on the phone.

9

AND THINGS GET VERY STRANGE
MARCY

It took hours for me to get Stephen out of jail. He'd used his one phone call to call me, once they had finally allowed him to have it. I had called a lawyer, which cost me several hundred dollars, who then went with Stephen to his bail hearing. Once bail was set, I had to take out a damn loan to pay for it because it was more than what I had in my savings account. The judge wanted to make an example of him for assaulting a police officer. If I could punch Jordan in the face and get away with it, I would. After finally getting Stephen out of jail, I'd taken him home and gotten him to agree to come for dinner at my place tonight.

I hadn't slept much after dealing with Stephen's shit, and when I woke up around ten this morning, I started cleaning. I didn't have anything better to do. It wasn't like I could go to work since I was suspended, and I really wished I could. I was itching to get my hands on the case report of the Instagram model killing. I turned the news on this morning, but there still wasn't a mention of who she was or the manner of her death. I was glad about that. It meant that we'd been successful in keeping that information out of their hands. I just didn't know for how long.

As I vacuumed the living room, I noticed my phone vibrating on the coffee table. I switched off the machine and picked it up.

Irritated, I said, "What do you need, Jordan?"

"Don't take that tone with me. Do you know what your brother did?"

"Seeing as I spent hours yesterday trying to bail him out of jail, yes, I am aware."

"Well? What do you have to say for yourself?"

"Me?" I was completely outraged. "Stephen had every reason to come after you after everything you've done. Don't you dare turn this around on me."

"The two of you are loose cannons. You shouldn't even be a cop!"

"Are you kidding me?" I growled into the phone. So much for Angel getting him to drop the charges. I should have known that Jordan would be a stubborn asshole. Angel probably tried, but when Jordan wanted something, he was tenacious about it.

"You both need anger management!"

"What the ever-loving fuck are you—" I stopped and took a breath. "Did you call just to harass me?"

"No, I called to tell you that you and your brother need therapy. You're both fucked up. He drinks to excess and takes his anger out on me for your asinine actions—"

"Excuse me?"

"You heard me. His anger at me was misplaced. He should be angry at you for killing a suspect and being suspended. He had no reason to attack me like that."

"You know what? I don't have to do this with you anymore. We're not married."

"But I am your superior."

"Not at the moment you aren't! I'm on suspension, remember?" I snarked. "So unless you want to make this a work thing, I'm done speaking to you. You want me to take this to the union? Air all of our dirty laundry out before them? Because I can tell you there is quite a lot of it. And I will bring up every single bit of it. Do you hear me?"

Jordan huffed into the phone.

"That's not an answer."

A moment later all I heard was a click. He'd hung up on me.

Sighing, I set the phone down on the table again and dropped onto the sofa. The man was exhausting. I didn't know what I ever saw in him. Love wasn't just blind, it was deaf and stupid too.

I rubbed my temples, trying to ward off a headache. That was the last thing I needed. I got up and headed to the kitchen for some Tylenol, then got back to work cleaning my apartment. Once it was done, I started dinner. I was making lasagna from scratch, well, not totally, I'd bought the pasta at the store. Still, it took a while.

Stephen arrived at six.

"Hey, the food is nearly ready; just have to pull the lasagna out and put the garlic bread in."

Stephen hugged me. "Smells great." He looked around the apartment. "You cleaned?"

I shrugged. "Didn't have much else to do."

"Oh. Right."

I looked at him; something seemed off. His eyes were

bloodshot, and he seemed pensive. He also looked as though he'd lost weight. I wondered if he'd looked this way for a while, and I just hadn't noticed because I was too preoccupied with all my own stuff going on and then trying to get him out of jail. "Everything okay with you?"

"Huh? Oh, yeah. Sure. I'm okay, I guess."

I frowned. "Have a seat. I'll just get the bread in the oven; be a minute, tops."

Stephen sank down on the couch. "Got any beer?"

"Yeah, one sec," I called back. I pulled the lasagna out and put the bread in the oven to warm up. Moving to the fridge, I pulled out a couple of beers and brought him one. "Here you go."

"Thanks." He popped the tab and immediately guzzled the drink, then wiped his mouth with the back of his hand.

I took a sip of my own beer. "How's work?"

"Fine, I guess. Not too busy."

"Good." I sat there wondering how to bring up the whole Jordan thing. I didn't want to piss him off and make him go after Jordan again. "So... I don't think Jordan is going to drop the charges."

Stephen shrugged and finished off his beer. "Figured he wouldn't. Guy's a tool." He got up and headed into the kitchen.

I followed him and glanced at the oven. The bread still had another couple of minutes, but I could get our plates ready and pulled two out of the cabinet. "He called this morning to see if I knew about you hitting him."

"Of course he did." Stephen popped the top of another beer.

I sliced the lasagna and then put a heaped square on a

plate for him and another on a plate for me. "Will you get the salad from the fridge?"

Stephen opened the door and pulled out the large salad bowl.

I got two bowls from the cabinet and served salad in each bowl, then carried them to the table, which I'd set earlier. By the time I returned to the counter, the oven was beeping. I turned it off and removed the bread. I put two slices on each plate and then carried the plates to the table. "Come sit; everything's ready."

Stephen grabbed a third beer from the fridge and joined me. He'd finished off the second when I wasn't looking. "This looks great."

"Thanks. I used the recipe from Mom's file." It was one of the few things I'd been able to keep when we were taken into foster care after Mom's murder. Nearly everything else, which wasn't much, had been sold off. I'd gotten just a few small knickknacks and Mom's small card file of recipes.

"Didn't she say it was her mom's?" Stephen asked, his fork halfway to his mouth.

"Yeah, they were all recipes she'd gotten from Grandma."

He nodded and took a bite. After a moment, he said, "It's good. Grandma would be proud of you."

The thought made me smile. I didn't really remember her; Mom had only taken me to see her once that I could recall. They hadn't gotten along. Grandma hadn't approved of what Mom did for a living, and she'd died shortly after that visit. I think I'd been about four or five at the time. Looking back now, I wondered why Grandma hadn't tried to take me and Stephen from Mom, considering Mom was hooking to keep a roof over our heads and food on the table.

"You ever wonder why Grandma didn't help Mom?" I asked, looking at him across the table.

"Mom wouldn't let her," Stephen answered without looking at me.

"What do you mean?"

"Grandma tried to take us. Mom said no. Said we belonged to her, and Grandma couldn't have us." He snorted, but he had a look in his eyes that I couldn't decipher.

"I suppose Mom couldn't stand to have us so far away from her." I missed her despite the fact that we'd had so little time with her when she was alive. She was nearly always with one of her men and had often left Stephen in charge of me when we weren't in school.

"Yeah, that's what she was thinking." Stephen guzzled his beer and got up to grab another.

"You okay?" I was worried about how much he was consuming, but hoped the lasagna would balance things out.

He sat back down and drank half the beer he now held. "You ever wonder how far you'd go to repay someone who got you out of a hellish circumstance?"

I blinked, wondering where the abrupt change of subject had come from. It took me a moment to consider his question. "I don't know. I guess I'd go pretty far to repay them if my circumstances were as awful as all that."

He nodded and took another drink, then set the can on the table. He picked up his fork, took a bite, and then said, "Would you kill for them?"

Again, his question had me confused. I wondered what had brought on this philosophical conversation. It was all very strange, especially coming from him. Stephen wasn't known for being philosophical. "I don't think so. Not unless it was a life-or-death situation, like with that little girl. I mean, I've killed before, but only because I didn't really have any other choice. I was either being shot at, or someone else's life was in danger, and I needed to act. So, no. I don't think I'd kill just to repay someone who got me out of a terrible situation. It wouldn't be right."

"Hmmm." Stephen took another forkful of his food, but he wouldn't meet my eyes.

"Are you okay?" I asked again because he really hadn't answered me. His questions had me really concerned, and that, along with his drinking, him spending time in jail for punching Jordan, and everything... was starting to really concern me. It was like he was spiraling out of control for no reason that I could understand.

"Uh... yeah, I guess." He shrugged. "I'm just not sleeping real well."

"Why not? What's going on? Is everything really okay at work?" I knew I was tossing too many questions his way, but he was making me anxious.

"Don't know, just not. Nothin's really going on, everything's fine. Work's good. Like I said, we're not too busy." He finished off his plate and carried it to the kitchen.

I heard him rinse it off in the sink and put it in the dishwasher before he returned to the table with yet another beer.

"I've got dessert," I commented as I stood up and headed back to the kitchen.

"You haven't finished your dinner yet," he called after me.

"It's fine," I replied and returned to the table with the chocolate pie I'd bought at the store, a knife, fork, and a plate. I cut him a nice big slice and set the plate in front of him. "I'll have some in a minute, after I finish my lasagna." I smiled.

"I could have waited." He took another sip.

I was just glad he wasn't slurring his words. "I only have another bite left; go ahead." I finished off my dinner, then cut a piece of pie and put it on my dinner plate. There was no sense in getting another plate dirty.

As we ate our dessert, Stephen pulled his phone out and looked at it.

"What's up?"

"Text from Mike. He wants to grab a beer tomorrow after work." He sent a reply and then shoved the phone back in his pocket.

"You gonna meet up with him?"

"Sure, I guess. He asked how you were doing. I'm guessing that crush he had on you back in high school hasn't gone away."

"Don't even think about it. You aren't setting us up. I wasn't interested then, and I'm certainly not interested now." I shook a finger at him.

Stephen snorted. "Duly noted. Mike's not your type anyway."

"Oh yeah? So what do you think my type is?" I challenged.

"Hmmm, going by your track record, I'd say asshole with an emphasis on ass," he teased with a twinkle in his eyes.

"Very funny." I glared at him. "Seriously though, don't set me up with him."

"I wouldn't. He went through a messy divorce not too long ago."

"Oh? What happened?"

Stephen shrugged. "From what I heard, she accused him of verbally and mentally abusing her, but there were no records of the cops being called or anything like that, so it was all her word against his. Still, she was awarded a big chunk of his money and the house."

"Wow," I murmured as I recalled everything I knew about Mike. Back in the day, he'd been pretty full of himself. Cocky, I supposed, maybe a little bit of a bully toward others. It was why I'd never flirted back when he'd tried it with me. I'd seen the aftermath of some of his breakups and hadn't wanted that for myself.

When we were finished with dinner, he helped me clean up as he drank the last beer from the fridge. I decided to broach the subject of a visit to Mom's grave. I usually went alone, but this week was important, and I wanted Stephen to go too. I wasn't sure why, but Stephen didn't like visiting Mom's grave. I supposed it was because we'd both witnessed her being murdered, and it was hard.

"So, you know the anniversary of Mom's death is this week."

He sighed. "Yeah?"

"Will you come with me to the gravesite?"

"I guess."

"Do you ever wonder what things might have been like if Mom hadn't been murdered?" I asked as we put the last of the dishes in the dishwasher.

"I don't like to think about it. You can't change how things happened, Marcy. Believe me, I've tried."

"What do you mean? You tried to go back in time?" I teased, trying to lighten the mood a little.

"No. I just mean... Mom was... she wasn't the best mom,

you know? When she died... when that man broke into the apartment... all I wanted to do was protect you. I was afraid he was there for you. I didn't know it was the Face Flayer they'd been talking about on the news. I was terrified he would see us, discover us under that bed." Stephen's whole body shook.

This was the most I'd ever heard him talk about that night. Usually, anytime I brought it up, he'd change the subject. I wondered if he had the same nightmares about that night that I did, but I didn't want to ask.

"Mom fought him so hard," I said softly. "I wanted to help her."

"I know you did. I couldn't let you though. He'd have killed you too. I couldn't lose you," Stephen replied.

I reached a hand out to him, and he gripped it. "Thank you for keeping me alive that night," I murmured. "I just wish we could have helped Mom."

"I know."

"I can't help but think he's still out there somewhere," I whispered. "I don't believe he's just stopped killing. I think he just stopped killing here."

"You don't think he's dead?"

"They never found his body in the river. I know he jumped, and he supposedly never resurfaced, but what if he did? What if he could hold his breath for a really long time and swam far enough that they didn't see him?"

Stephen arched a brow as if this was something he hadn't considered. "I'm pretty sure he's dead. I mean, they shot him right before he jumped. And that river is deep. I'm gonna bet they didn't try real hard to recover him."

"But it's possible that he lived, right?"

"Okay, yeah, maybe, but I doubt it."

I sighed. "Either way, it pisses me off that he escaped justice." I bit my lip. "Can I tell you something?"

"Always."

"I think that might be why I always take the head shot. I don't want them escaping justice." I had never admitted that out loud before. Every shoot had been justified, but I knew that in at least two of the cases, I probably could have downed them with a shot to the chest, and they might have lived. A tiny part of me felt a little guilty over that, but they were serial killers or had the potential to be serial killers. There was definitive proof of their crimes, and in every case, my life and others' were on the line. I knew I'd made the right call.

"You know, we can only count on each other for justice, sis. I know you're a cop, but you're the only one I trust."

The way he said it had me slightly worried. I knew he had a problem with Jordan, he always had, but I didn't understand why it seemed like he didn't trust any cop but me. I was about to say something to figure out what he meant, but he stood up suddenly.

"I should go."

I decided to let the matter drop. It wasn't that important anyway. I was more concerned with him driving after having so many beers. "Maybe you should stay the night? You've had a lot to drink..."

He shook his head. "I'm okay. Barely even buzzed; the food took care of it."

"Are you sure?" I bit my cheek out of worry.

"Yeah, I'll be fine. It's not like I have to go far. Less than thirty minutes if traffic isn't bad."

"Text me when you get home?"

"Sure." He leaned down and kissed my cheek. "See ya later," he said as he walked out the door.

"Bye, please drive careful."

"I will."

I worried about him for the next twenty minutes until I got the text saying he was home. Feeling relieved, I headed to bed.

10

NIGHTMARES AND MEMORIES
MARCY

"Marcy, come with me," Stephen whispered, shaking my shoulder.

Groggily, I blinked myself awake. "Why?"

Stephen tugged my hand, pulling me from the bed. "Stay quiet."

I could hear something going on in the living room of our apartment. "What's going on?"

"Shhh, he'll hear us." Stephen held my hand tight as he led me toward my open bedroom door. He put a finger to his lips as we crept out of the room and across the hall to Mom's room. I heard a man's voice, but I couldn't understand what he was saying. I wondered why we were going to Mom's room if one of her men friends were here. She wouldn't want us in there. I started to protest, but Stephen put his hand over my mouth and pointed underneath Mom's bed.

I shook my head. I didn't want to go under the bed, especially if Mom was going to be in here with her friend.

"Hurry, we have to hide, and this is the only place." He sounded urgent, and the look on his face said he was scared.

I didn't understand why, but I finally agreed and crawled under the bed. Stephen was right behind me, sliding under on his belly. He wrapped his arm around my back and brought his hand up to cover my mouth. I wanted to lick his hand to get him to let go, but Mom screamed then and sounded terrified. I started to move. I needed to go help her.

Stephen shook his head and held me tight. He wasn't letting me go. We were as far under the bed as we could get. Mom's bed was set in the corner of her room, so the underside was blocked on two sides, but from where we were, we could see out into the room. Mom continued to scream, and she was getting closer to the room. A moment later, she passed through the doorway and attempted to shut the door, but a man was there, blocking the door from being shut.

His hair was curly and looked greasy. He forced the door open, and Mom flew back, landing on her butt. The man strode into the room and grabbed her by the hair, pulling her up.

I wanted to yell at him to let her go, but Stephen's hand on my mouth kept me quiet.

"Shut the fuck up, bitch!" he growled at Mom.

Mom struggled, clawing at his hand in her hair. "Leave me alone! Get out of here!"

He shook her and tried to drag her from the room, but Mom wasn't letting him. I watched his face and saw it. The moment he decided taking her out of here wasn't worth it. He'd have to settle for doing whatever it was he was going to do right here. My eyes widened as his large hand closed around Mom's throat.

Stephen held me even tighter, as if he knew I was going to thrust myself out from under the bed to get to Mom.

Mom made choking sounds, and her face was turning redder in the moonlight coming in through the window. She clawed at the hands around her neck, but her attempts were getting weaker. Her movements were slowing. She couldn't breathe.

"Mom!" I screamed in my head. "Don't die, Mom, please!" I could feel tears falling down my cheeks, pooling against Stephen's hand across my face.

Within a few seconds, her lifeless body dropped to the floor.

"No!" I wanted to lash out, but couldn't move.

The man straddled Mom's body; he had some kind of knife in his hand. He cut away her shirt and underwear, which was all she'd been wearing. I closed my eyes because I couldn't watch him, but I could hear him violating her. He was grunting and groaning three feet from me and Stephen on the floor.

When I dared to open my eyes after the sounds stopped, I was even more horrified to see him slicing the skin from Mom's face. It was then that I knew who he was. They'd been talking about him on the news.

The Face Flayer.

I felt sick to my stomach.

The Face Flayer was in our apartment, had murdered Mom, and there was nothing I could do. Mom was gone. Taken from us by this evil man. I stared at him, wanting to memorize his face so that I could tell the police every single thing about him. I wanted them to catch him and make him pay for what he'd done to Mom.

I knew from the news that he'd killed at least seven women, eight now counting Mom. She would be his last. I promised myself and Mom. I'd make sure they got him if it was the last thing I ever did.

After he finished stealing Mom's face, he got up, kicked her body, then strode from the room. A few minutes later, we heard the front door slam.

Stephen and I didn't move. I don't know what we were

waiting for as we lay under the bed, staring at Mom's broken and dead body.

Eventually, Stephen moved his hand from my mouth. "I think it's safe now," he whispered, but he didn't move.

My brain yelled at me to get out from under the bed, to run to Mom, but it was like I was frozen. My body wouldn't work. I choked on a sob as I stared at Mom.

"Marcy, are you okay?" Stephen whispered.

"No," I answered; my voice was barely there. I don't even know if he heard me.

He started to move, sliding out from the side of the bed. His hand grasped mine, and he pulled me out behind him. I didn't fight him. I couldn't. My arms and legs were like jelly, all wobbly, and I had no control over them. Stephen pulled me to my feet, then wrapped his arm under my knees and picked me up, carrying me from the room. Past Mom's body on the floor. He set me on the couch in the living room.

The room was a mess; everything looked busted.

"I'm calling the cops," he said, leaving me alone.

I started to shake. I couldn't make it stop, couldn't control it. It seemed like only a minute passed before an officer was patting my cheek, trying to pull me out of it.

"I saw him. I saw him..." I murmured over and over again.

I WOKE IN A COLD SWEAT, still shivering from the memories of that night. My heart was racing as if I'd just lived through that whole experience again. I tried to block the rest of that night from my thoughts, but my mind was having none of it. I remembered telling the officer everything I could recall about the man who'd murdered Mom. He'd had curly brown hair that looked greasy and unkept. It had fallen past his shoulders. His nose had been large and prominent on his face. I couldn't tell the exact color of his eyes in the moonlight, but they were light in color, somewhere between blue and light gray. He'd been thin, and I hadn't thought he'd be as strong as he had been.

I ran a hand down my face as I tried once again to push away the memories of what followed that night. How the officers had made us each pack a bag with as much of our belongings as we could. I had run into the kitchen and grabbed Mom's box of recipes that had been Grandma's originally. I somehow knew we weren't ever coming back here, and I'd wanted it. I'd also grabbed a couple of pictures and Mom's favorite angel decorations from the shelf, and stuffed them in my bag with my clothes and a doll Mom had given me one Christmas.

From there, Stephen and I had ended up in a group home. They'd tried to find us a foster family, but nobody had wanted to touch a pair of kids who'd witnessed what we had. I'd been ten and Stephen fourteen. The group home had been difficult, but at least we were together until Stephen went away to college at eighteen. The state had covered his tuition as long as he made decent grades. I'd had four more years there, and they hadn't been all that great with him gone. Still, I kept my head down and studied. All the while I'd been determined to find the man who killed Mom.

I knew who he was by then. Lemuel St. Martin. The police had tracked him down from my description of him. He'd led them on a chase, and they cornered him on a bridge, where he wouldn't give up. They shot him as he jumped into the water, but never recovered his body.

Everyone thought he was dead and gone, everyone except me. Logic said that they were right. That St. Martin had died on that bridge from the gunshots, or he'd drowned in the river, but my heart couldn't accept that. Without seeing his body, I couldn't believe it. I wouldn't. So I'd gone into law enforcement and pored over the case files every chance I got.

I knew the Face Flayer case backward and forward. And I knew it was entirely possible that after twenty-six years, the man was back. Not only that, but I'd been taken off the case because my stupid ex-husband and that jackass negotiator were determined to get me kicked off the force.

My fists clenched in the damp sheets. I couldn't let that happen. I needed IA to clear me so I could finally catch the son of a bitch who'd murdered my mother. Visions of her lifeless body filled my mind again as if it had just happened. I pressed the heels of my hands to my eyes, as if that would make the vision go away. It didn't.

I dropped my hands to the mattress and glanced over at the alarm clock. It was almost five a.m. I didn't have to go to work, but I didn't think I could go back to sleep. Instead, I got up. I took a long hot shower and finally managed to push the memories back into the box I kept them in, in my head. I dressed and then set about making breakfast as I turned on the news.

The lead story was about Michella Graves. They'd finally discovered who she was and that she'd been murdered, but thankfully, they'd kept the part about her face silent. That was one piece of good news. As I took a bite of toast, the conversation with my brother floated through my head. It had been kind of weird for him to be asking the questions he'd asked. I wondered again what had brought them on.

After I cleaned up my breakfast mess, I made a list of things I needed at the store and went out to get them and run some other errands. I usually saved all this for Sundays, which was generally my day off, but since I was currently suspended, I figured I'd get things done early. I filled up my gas tank, went through the car wash, then picked up the groceries I had on my list and headed back home.

When I reached my apartment door, I stopped. My door was slightly ajar. Concern filled me as I set my bags down on the floor in the hallway and drew my private weapon. I'd had to turn my service weapon in, but I always had a spare and never went anywhere without it.

I put my shoulder to the door and nudged it open a bit as I made my way inside. I started past the door and then felt a sharp pain in my head as something hit me.

I stumbled forward as a person in a black hoodie shoved past me and out of my apartment. I shook my head and rubbed the back of it as I looked around. I saw one of my favorite bookends on the floor. That must have been what the intruder hit me with.

I turned back toward the door, and as I made the hallway, I heard the elevator doors closing. "Shit," I muttered.

I ran farther down the hall toward the stairs. I might be able to catch the bastard if I hurried. I stumbled down the stairs, holding on to the rail with one hand, my gun in the other. I flew out of the stairwell to the lobby and turned for the elevator, but when the doors opened, there was no one inside. "Fuck!"

I didn't know where to look now. The guy could still be in the building, or maybe he'd gotten off on a different floor and taken the stairs the rest of the way. It was five floors down from my apartment, so it was possible.

I ran to the parking lot but didn't notice anything

unusual. The cars all seemed to belong to the people in my building, as far as I could tell. Nothing looked out of place.

I shook my head, put my weapon back in its holster under my shirt on my hip, and pulled out my phone. I dialed dispatch as I headed back upstairs and explained what happened. They said they'd send a patrol unit over.

I picked up the bag of groceries once I was back upstairs and headed for the kitchen with them. I put them away as I waited for patrol to show up. Once that was done, I went back to the hallway to wait. I probably should have just stayed out here, but I didn't want my ice cream melting any more than it already had, and figured my fridge and freezer were probably not high on an intruder's list of places to look for things to steal.

Officers Kim and Desmond stepped out of the elevator a few minutes later.

"Detective, we got a call about an intruder?" Kim said as they approached.

"Yeah, got home from grocery shopping, found my door ajar. When I went in, I got hit from behind, and the guy took off. I tried to chase after him, but lost him."

"Anything taken?" Desmond asked, notebook in hand.

"I'm not sure. I haven't really looked."

"Have you been inside other than when you encountered the intruder?" Kim questioned.

I nodded. "I went to the kitchen and put my groceries away so they wouldn't spoil. I didn't go anywhere else, though, and came right back out here."

"Okay, we'll dust for prints, check the door and all that. Why don't you look around, see if anything's missing."

I followed them into the apartment and started to look around. My TV and DVDs were exactly where they always were. So were my stereo and CDs. I headed back to my bedroom and looked through my closet and dresser and then through my jewelry box. Everything seemed to be there.

"I don't know. I'm not seeing anything missing," I commented as I came back into the living room.

"Maybe he'd only just gotten in when you got home," Kim suggested.

"Looks like he used a lockpick on the door. There's some scratch marks."

"What about prints?" I asked.

"We'll grab yours from the system to rule you out, but we've got a few from the door and off the bookend."

"Great." I was angry that my place had been violated.

"You might think about adding a deadbolt; your current locks are all too easy to pick." Desmond indicated my front door.

"I'll do that," I agreed and decided I'd head to the hardware store as soon as they were gone.

11

NO RECOGNITION

KILLER

K illing Michella had been the highlight of my week. I relived that shit in my dreams every night, and I couldn't wait to do it again. Unfortunately, her death had barely made a blip on the news radar. She'd gotten a mention, but there was nothing about the manner of her death or the note I'd left behind. I'd gotten no recognition from the media at all.

Of course, I hadn't expected the LAPD to share much about her death, they were always tight-lipped when it came to murder, but I had thought there'd be a bit more hoopla over how she died and the way I'd posed her. So it irked me when there wasn't. It pissed me off even more when there was massive coverage of the dickhead who'd kidnapped a child and had been in a standoff with the cops while he'd held the little girl at knifepoint.

I had to admit I was glad to hear that my beloved had taken the dirtbag out. What kind of cretin diddled and hurt kids? Let alone their own kids. That was just sick. He deserved to die, and I was pleased that Marcy had gotten another kill.

I bet she really enjoyed that one. Taking out a guy like that had to give her immense pleasure. I wondered if she fingered herself while she thought about making that particular kill. Thinking about her pleasuring herself got my dick hard, and I had to shift in my seat.

I read in the newspaper that she'd been suspended again for shooting the bastard, so it put my game on hold for a moment, which was fine. I'd had things to plan before stepping up my game.

I'd decided on my next move. The woman's name was Leanne Williams. Lovely Leanne, as I thought of her. She wasn't as beautiful as my beloved, but she would do nicely.

Leanne had long, honey blonde hair, big blue eyes and a sweet smile. She worked at Juggs, which was a restaurant here in LA, as a waitress. The girls there all wore low-cut white tops that tied under their boobs to show off their flat bellies, with short black skirts that barely covered their asses and three-inch heels.

My lovely Leanne wasn't just a waitress. She was also an aspiring actress.

She had gotten a few bit parts in a couple of TV shows, playing sluts and prostitutes, so she fit in with my agenda, even though she was a wannabe actress, not a prostitute like Lemuel liked them. However, I knew she'd sleep with a director to get a part she wanted; she'd done it before and had bragged about it in one of her Twitter posts. So she slept with men for both money and fame, which technically made her just as bad as a real prostitute.

I followed Leanne around town. She spent her days going to auditions, and her evenings taking food and drink orders from drunk, horny men who came to stare at the girls' tits at Juggs. She had no problem letting them feel her up for a higher tip. I'd watched her do it, so I didn't feel bad at all for what I was planning to do to her. She, like Michella, led men on. All she really wanted was their money or, if they were part of the acting world, a chance at fame.

That was where I came in. I had created a new persona, complete with business cards and a fake website, so if she looked me up, she'd think I was legit. The name I had chosen even belonged to an actual director, though I knew for a fact he wasn't in LA. He was directing a play in New York City. His online presence, though, was nil, which worked out well for me.

Now, I sat in her section at the restaurant and waited. I watched her flirt with every other man in her section. Even though it was a restaurant, ninety percent of the clientele were men. It wasn't really a family kind of place. More a place for guys to come check out the girls and pretend to watch sports on the big-screen TVs.

I glanced over at the guy at the table next to mine and noticed that he had his hand on her ass under her skirt. I wanted to break his fingers, but I held back. She'd be all mine soon enough.

"Hey, darlin', what can I get for you?" she asked a few minutes later as she approached me.

"I'll have a burger and fries, with a gin and tonic," I answered, smiling up at her. I'd worn a suit so I'd look the part I was playing.

"You got it," she replied with a wink and sauntered away.

I watched her give my order to the bartender. As she leaned over the bar, her tight little ass was exposed to me. I couldn't wait to be buried deep in that ass.

She returned a few minutes later with my drink and set it down. "Can I get you anything else while you wait for your food, sugar?"

"I'm good, but..." I hesitated, looking at her as though I was trying to place her face. "I was wondering... you look really familiar... you're an actress, right?"

Her smile lit up her face. She really was beautiful. I'd enjoy having that face as part of my collection. "I am. I've had a few small parts now in some TV shows; maybe that's where you saw me? I'm hoping to get more of a lead role soon."

I nodded, putting a thoughtful look on my face. "You know, I've got a role I think you might be perfect for."

"Oh?" she said, sounding wary, as though she'd heard that line one too many times.

"Let me give you my card. It's got my website on it and my phone number. If you're interested, give me a call, and we'll set up an audition." I pulled the card from my wallet and handed it to her.

She glanced at it, then turned to me. "What kind of role is it?"

"It's for a play that's headed to Broadway, which I know is all the way in New York, but if you get the role, we'll put you up in a hotel for the duration of the play."

Her eyes widened. "Really? Why are you here in LA looking for actresses? Aren't there a ton of them in New York?"

I frowned. "There are, but none of them have what I'm looking for. They're missing the kind of charm that you have in spades. That, paired with your looks, you'd suit my lead heroine role perfectly."

She bit her lip and simpered. "What kind of character would I be playing?"

I had prepared for this. "She's a strong woman, knows what she wants from life and what she's willing to do to get it. She's a take-life-by-the-horns kind of girl. Every guy wants her, but she's got big plans, and nothing is going to stop her from achieving her dream."

"Wow, that sounds like the kind of woman I want to be," she murmured, fingering my card.

"Leanne! Order up!" the bartender called.

She looked over her shoulder and then back at me. "I have to get back to work, but... I'll... I'll call you. Oh, and I'll be right back with your order."

"I'm looking forward to it, but don't wait too long to call. I'm only in town for a week or so." I gave her my best fake smile and lifted my drink, downing the contents.

She brought my food over, and I ate it without really tasting it. The food honestly wasn't all that great, but then nobody really came here for the food. I stayed for a little while, enjoying how she flitted from one table to the next, earning big tips. She returned with another gin and tonic for me, and I asked for my bill. I paid in cash and even left her a nice tip, hoping it would encourage her to use the card.

Even if she didn't, I would have her.

I knew where she lived.

I knew every aspect of her life.

She wasn't going to get away.

12

DESECRATION OF THE DEAD
MARCY

I was still rocking my suspension when I woke up Monday morning. Stephen and I had gone to Mom's grave on Saturday afternoon. I'd brought a vase of flowers to set in front of her headstone. Weeds had grown around her gravestone, which was just a gray slab with her name and date of birth and death on it. I spent about thirty minutes pulling all the weeds and making her grave look nice again. The caretaker always made sure the grass around the graves was trimmed, but he didn't always get a chance to weed.

I'd said a few words of prayer for Mom while Stephen bowed his head. He'd hardly said anything the entire time, but he'd come, and that was what counted.

I hated that I always had to drag him to the graveyard to see her. He never wanted to go, but I guessed it was because it was hard to be reminded about what had happened to her. She'd been our whole world when we were younger. Mom had doted on him, and I was pretty sure he was her favorite. It wasn't that she was unkind to me, far from it; I had been her princess. But Stephen was her "little man." She'd always paid him special attention. Letting him stay up later than me, giving him extra treats. She made sure I had everything I wanted too, so I didn't complain. I don't think she knew that I knew about it, and Stephen never brought it up either. I supposed he'd thought it was his right as my older brother to get extras.

Still, despite him being stoic and quiet, it had been a nice afternoon, and when we'd finished at the gravesite, we'd gone out to eat. Nothing fancy, just to a fast-food place, where I'd had some chicken tenders and fries. Afterwards, I dropped him at his apartment and then drove to the hospital to visit Angel.

I spent about two hours there, playing a few rounds of gin rummy with him, which I lost, before heading home. He'd been in high spirits during our game, and it made me smile. I was glad to see him improving, even though he was stuck in that bed for a while longer.

On Sunday, I'd taken the time to go to a church service, something I did only occasionally because most of the time I slept in and missed it. After that, I spent the day watching movies and eating junk food, then going to bed way too late.

Now, I was wide awake, and I didn't know what had woken me so suddenly. Then I heard it again. My phone was ringing, vibrating itself toward the edge of the nightstand. I grabbed it and stared at the screen in confusion.

Hitting the answer call button, I said, "Hello?"

"Good morning, Detective Kendrick, it's Mark Dawson. I hate to be calling you so early in the morning, but we have a situation here."

Mark Dawson was the caretaker at Chadwick Cemetery

where my mother's grave was located, and I couldn't help the panic that rose in my chest at his words.

"A situation?" I questioned as I rubbed the sleep from my eyes.

"Yes, I'm afraid we had a vandal enter the cemetery sometime last night, and... well, there was quite a bit of damage to your mother's grave."

"Oh my God. How many graves were damaged? Have you called the police to report it?" I scooted to the edge of the bed, putting my feet on the floor.

"Er... well, no... that's the thing. Only one grave was damaged."

That gave me pause. "What are you saying?"

"The only grave damaged was your mother's."

"That can't be right; who would do that?"

"I don't know. I thought perhaps you might have an idea."

"What? No, why would I know? I was just there on Saturday with my brother; we cleaned up the gravesite and put out new flowers. I can't think of anyone who would do something like that." I stood up and ran my hand through my hair.

"What would you like for me to do?"

"I'll be there soon. I want to see the damage and take pictures before I make any kind of decision, so don't do anything yet, okay?"

"No problem. I'll be here working on the property." He hung up.

I hurried to get dressed and then called Stephen, but he didn't answer. He was probably still asleep, so I didn't worry too much about him. I was too upset anyway that someone had vandalized our mother's grave.

I got in my car and drove the twenty minutes to the cemetery. After parking, I speed-walked toward her grave. Before I even reached the site, I could see the damage the vandals had done to it, and gasped with shock.

Whoever had done this had been extremely angry. That was the only thing I could think of upon seeing the shattered tombstone, the torn-up grass, the smashed vase and the stomped-upon flowers. A crowbar lay among the rubble of the busted stone.

I pulled my phone out and took pictures of the damage as Mark walked over. "I can't believe someone would do something like this." Tears filled my eyes, and I brushed them away.

Mark shook his head. "I've never seen the like. We don't have any cameras around here, so I can't even tell you when it happened. I was here all day yesterday, left about six, so it had to be some time after that. The cemetery gates aren't locked at night, but after this, I might have to have a word with the property manager to see about changing that policy. Damage like this can get pretty pricey to fix."

I sighed. I was going to have to fork out a large sum to repair the tombstone, but I doubted it could be repaired. I'd probably have to buy a whole new one. "Do you have a wheelbarrow I can use to get rid of this mess?"

"Sure, we've got one. What do you want to do for a grave marker after we haul all this away?"

"I don't think this one can be fixed."

"No, probably not." He frowned as he looked over the damage.

"I guess I should order a new one; do you have a catalog?"

He nodded. "Back at the office. Don't usually work with

that end of things myself, but they always leave one there for people who might be looking to buy something new for their loved one's grave."

"I'll take a look once we're done." I stared at the mess. "I should file a police report." With that in mind, I called the station to talk to the captain while Mark went to get the wheelbarrow.

"Hey, Jason, it's Marcy; can you patch me in to the captain?"

"Sure thing, give me one second."

A moment later Captain Robinson's gruff voice sounded over the line. "Kendrick, you're still on suspension, so I hope you're not calling to talk about the case—"

"No, sir. I'm at my mother's grave, and someone vandalized it."

"Oh. I'm sorry to hear that; do you need me to send patrol?"

"I'm not sure there's much they can do, but there is a crowbar that might have some prints on it."

"Can you bag it and bring it in? I don't want to send patrol out there if I don't have to."

"I can do that. I took pictures of the damage as well."

"Good. It will help if we find out who did it. Think it's tied to your break-in the other day?"

"I don't know. Maybe? But who would be targeting me and have the audacity to desecrate my mother's grave?"

"You've pissed off a number of people lately; can't rule anyone out."

"I doubt Jordan or that hotshot negotiator would break into my apartment or vandalize a grave to get back at me, sir."

"I wasn't talking about them, Kendrick. You know there

are some real wackadoos out there who think you're some kind of vigilante cop and that you like killing suspects."

That was a stretch, wasn't it? The two things were probably not related. However, I said, "Maybe. It's a theory, anyway. Look, I'll be there in a little while to file the report. I've gotta clean this mess up first and order a new headstone."

"See you later, then." He hung up.

It took the better part of an hour for Mark and me to get the area looking halfway decent. When we finished, he—thankfully—took care of the debris, and then I joined him in the office to choose a new headstone. They were all expensive, and I hated having to dip into my savings to pay for it, but it was for Mom, so it was worth it. I chose a black granite headstone that stood about thirty inches high. It had angels engraved on the sides, with Mom's name, date of birth and date of death centered on it in the middle. Above that, it read *In loving memory*.

Once that was done, I headed to the station with the crowbar wrapped in a plastic garbage bag that Mark had given me. As I drove, I called Stephen again.

"Hey, sis, what's up?" he asked, sounding groggy.

"Someone vandalized Mom's grave," I seethed. I was still angry about it, and I supposed I wanted him to be as upset as I was.

"Um... what?" He sounded confused.

"What do you mean 'what'?" I asked, feeling exasperated by his question. "Someone took a crowbar and demolished her headstone, smashed the flowers we brought, and tore up all the grass around her gravesite. It was an absolute disaster."

"Oh... that's not good; do you need me to come help clean up?"

"I already took care of it," I growled into the phone, wondering why he seemed so nonchalant about it. "I'm pissed off at whoever did this, Stephen. Aren't you?"

"Right, I mean, yeah, I am too... of course I am. Who would do something like that?" Stephen sounded more upset now.

"I don't know, but I took pictures, and they left a crowbar behind, so I'm heading to the station with it to file a police report."

"Oh, good idea, make sure the captain knows what's going on. I mean between this and the break-in at your place, maybe somebody's targeting you?"

"Yeah, I've already talked to the captain, and he suggested the same, but I don't know who that could be."

"What about Jordan? He's got it in for you. I could see him doing something like this."

"Jordan may be a dick, but I don't think he'd go so far as to vandalize a grave."

"You're probably right. He wouldn't do something that would make him look bad. At least not that kind of thing, I guess. I suppose Jordan cares way too much about his reputation to do something like that, and he probably wouldn't be stupid enough to leave a crowbar behind."

"Exactly. So yeah, probably not him."

"Right, but there are a lot of crazy people out there in the world, and you've got to be careful. You have your weapon on you, right?"

"Of course, I always do."

"Good. It scares me that you put yourself in these kinds

of situations, sis. Promise me you'll keep an eye out for anyone being suspicious around you, okay?"

"Yeah, I will," I agreed. "I ordered a new headstone for the grave. It cost a fortune, but it'll look nice."

"Oh. That's good." He paused, then added, "Um... do you need some money to go toward the cost?"

"No, I got it. Took a chunk of my savings, but as long as I still have my job, I'm good. If that changes, I'll let you know." I smiled as I pulled into the station and parked. "Hey, I gotta go. I'm at the station."

"Okay, be careful, Marce."

I ended the call and headed into the precinct, bagged crowbar in hand.

13

AMBUSHED BY A WANNABE REPORTER

MARCY

As I entered the station, I looked around, praying that I wouldn't run into Jordan. Luckily, he was nowhere around as I headed to Captain Robinson's office. I stopped in front of Jason's desk.

"Hey, Jason, is he in?"

Jason looked up from his computer and then smiled. "Let me see if he's available, one sec." He picked up the phone and hit a button. "Sir? Detective Kendrick is here... yes, okay, I'll send her right in." He returned the phone to its cradle and flipped a hand up toward the door. "You can go on in."

"Great, thanks." I passed his desk and opened the captain's door. "Good afternoon, sir." I closed the door behind me.

"Have a seat, Kendrick. Is that the crowbar?"

"Yeah." I handed it over. "Who do you want me to send the photos to?"

"Send them over to crime scene. I'll have one of the techs come pick this up." He slid a paper over to me. "Fill this out, and we'll see what we can do to find whoever did this."

"Any prints come back from the bookend?" I asked.

"No, just yours."

"Damn."

"My thoughts exactly. Whoever did this knew what they were doing and wore gloves. I want to send crime scene over to sweep your place for listening devices," he added.

"Wait, you think they bugged my apartment?" The idea that someone had broken in was bad enough, but now I had to worry about someone listening to me inside my home? I sank back against my chair, feeling like my life was coming apart at the seams.

"I just want to cover all the bases. If they broke in and didn't take anything, and only hit you so they could escape, it makes me think there is something else going on."

"Okay, send someone over to check. This has me all kinds of weirded out."

"It might be a little while, depends on what's going on."

"Thank you, sir. Any word on when IA is going to want to talk to me?"

"No, they're dragging their feet. I know they talked to the victim—Cara Goodwin, and to the perp's ex-wife about his behavior prior to this event. I think they're saving you for last."

"Great. I wish they'd hurry things along. How's the Instagram model case going? Hummel making any progress?"

The captain gave me a look.

"I know I can't work on it, sir, but I saw what he did to that girl, and I really want justice for her."

"I know you do. Hummel and Vance are recanvassing the building. Hummel thinks it's probably one of her ex-boyfriends or a deranged fan. We'll see what they come up with."

I didn't think it was anyone with an actual connection to her. That felt off to me because my gut was telling me there was more going on than what we were seeing with her murder. Still, I didn't voice my opinion. It didn't matter at the moment because it wasn't my case anymore, and Hummel had his own way of doing things.

"Once IA clears you, I'll put you back on it if Hummel and Vance don't solve it. For now, go ahead and fill this report out, and we'll see if we can't figure out who's harassing you."

"Yes, sir." I took the clipboard with the report paperwork. It didn't take me long to fill it out with all the pertinent information. I handed him the report. "I should go."

"I'll text you when they're on their way."

"Thank you, sir." I stood up and headed for the door.

"Kendrick, I am sorry about your mother's grave."

I nodded, but didn't say anything more as I headed out.

I stopped at a hardware store on my way home and picked up a new deadbolt lock for my front door and everything I'd need to install it. It wasn't cheap, but I was able to rent a hole saw and a drill for the project, so at least I didn't have to purchase those.

As I stepped off the elevator into the hallway, I saw the second-to-last person I wanted to see standing outside my door. Nicholas Pound considered himself an intrepid reporter, boldly and courageously calling out all the things he considered "crimes" committed by law enforcement. Mostly he liked to focus on me, because I was just that lucky. I took a deep breath and steeled myself for his barrage of offensive questions as he jogged over to meet me.

"Detective, a minute of your time," he began, holding his silver phone up like he was recording me.

I noticed the stickers on the back of his phone as I glared at him. "Go away."

"I just want to know why you once again murdered a man in cold blood and think you can get away with it because you carry a badge."

"That's not what happened." I pushed past him, but he stayed on my heels.

"I heard you took the law into your own hands and didn't wait for hostage negotiations to talk the guy down, isn't that true?"

"I'm not speaking to you; I'm not giving you anything." I hated that he lived in the same apartment building and thought that gave him the right to come badger me anytime he wanted. I couldn't even have him removed from the property since he lived here.

"You're just as bad as a serial killer. What's this make, four murders you've committed now?"

I rounded on him, my eyes blazing. If looks could kill, he'd certainly be a dead man. "I haven't murdered anyone. I have been cleared by Internal Affairs every time, and I will be cleared once again."

"Is that because you're bribing them? What, are you sleeping with the guys doing the investigation? Is that how you're getting off?"

"How dare you! If you don't leave me alone, I'll file a restraining order."

"You can't stop the press, Detective Kendrick. I am the press! The world needs to know what kind of monster you are. I'm going to make sure that everyone knows."

He seemed manic and obsessed, and I just wanted to get away from him. I quickly shoved the key into the lock on my door and pushed my way inside. Nick tried to wedge his foot in the door so he could keep pestering me, but I wasn't having it. "Back off, or I will have patrol here in five minutes flat to arrest you for trespassing," I roared as I closed my door on him.

He pulled his foot back, but shouted through the closed door, "Don't think I'm not going to write about this! I'm going to tell everyone what a demented cop you are!"

I set everything down, then yanked the door open again and got right in his face. "That bastard kidnapped a nine-year-old little girl and had a knife dug into her throat! I did what I had to do to save her life, and I'd do it again. IA is going to find me innocent, and the shoot justified. Now get the fuck away from my door." I stepped backwards into my apartment and slammed the door in his dumbfounded face and felt an overwhelming feeling of regret.

I shouldn't have done that.

Everything I'd said was true, but engaging with Nick was a pointless exercise. He was going to spin my tirade to suit whatever agenda he was pushing. And usually that agenda was *Cops are bad, and Detective Marcy Kendrick is the worst cop on the planet.*

Sighing, I locked the door, then picked up my bag and took it to the kitchen. I wouldn't be opening the door any time soon to install the deadbolt. Not with Nick right outside waiting to hound me some more.

As I rummaged in the fridge to find something to eat, my phone buzzed in my pocket. I pulled it out to see that the captain had texted.

Crime scene techs are on their way.

I hoped Nick would be gone once they got here, and I could install the new lock while the tech searched my apartment for listening devices. It wasn't how I had envisioned spending the rest of my Monday, but I'd feel better once both tasks were finished.

14

IMPRESSING MARCY
KILLER

The room was bright when I woke up. Somehow, I'd missed my alarm. I normally tried to be up with the sun, but it seemed I'd slept in until well after noon. As I stretched, I realized I'd fallen asleep in front of the computer, hadn't even made it to bed. No wonder I hadn't heard my alarm.

I clicked out of the blog I'd been reading last night before I'd fallen asleep. It hadn't made me happy to read what my favorite blogger had written about my beloved. He'd been overly harsh and called her a stuck-up bitch. I knew that wasn't true. She probably didn't like the questions he'd asked. She was sensitive about children, and I couldn't blame her for that. The asshole she'd killed had it coming for what he'd done. I didn't know why Nick couldn't see that. I'd have to leave him a nasty comment later about his attitude. Still, he remained the only blogger I knew who kept me up to date on what the LAPD, and Marcy especially, were up to.

I decided to check on my next game piece to see if she'd

taken my bait. I pulled the burner phone from my desk drawer and looked at it. I had a voicemail. There was only one person it could be. Lovely Leanne. I called in to listen to her message.

"Hi, um... my name's Leanne Williams? We spoke the other day at Juggs? You said you might have a role for me? I... well, I was interested in setting up an audition, if you could call me back?"

Hearing her voice, so hesitant, made me grin. I'd hooked her. After a glance at the clock to check the time, I returned her call.

"Ms. Williams? It's Hunter Malone. I'm returning your call."

"Mr. Malone, it's good to hear from you. As I said in my call, I was hoping to set up an audition?"

"I'm leaving tomorrow to return to New York, and my time is not only limited, but valuable," I told her.

"I understand, and I will make myself available whenever you want. Just give me a time and a place, and I promise I'll be there. I'd really love this part, sir."

"I imagine you would." I paused as if thinking about it. "I have the use of the Variety Theatre this evening. Meet me there at nine p.m."

"Isn't that kind of late?" she hesitated.

"Not in my world. I have an entire day booked with things, and that is the only time I have available. If you aren't interested—"

"I am interested. Sorry, yes, I'll be there."

"Great." I hung up, pulled the SIM card from the phone, broke it into two pieces, and then tossed it in the garbage. I'd pitch the phone as well on my way to meet Leanne. I had several hours before I was to meet her, and I had things to get ready.

At eight I walked out of my apartment building with a black bag. I'd packed everything I'd need to handle Leanne. All I needed now was a car. I didn't want to use mine; I didn't want traces of Leanne in my personal vehicle. So I walked a few blocks, entered the parking lot of another apartment complex where there were a number of cars. I found an older model and tested the handle. It was locked, but that didn't stop me. I pulled out a slim piece of metal and slid it between the glass and the car frame, tripping the lock on the door.

Opening the door, I tossed my bag onto the passenger seat, pulled the area below the steering wheel out, and hot-wired the car. It took me less than three minutes, and I was on my way to the theater. I'd chosen it because it was located in a run-down part of town, mostly empty buildings stood around it, and the theater itself had been closed for some time due to needing renovations.

I parked the car at the side of the building, where I knew there were no security cameras. In fact, there were no security cameras anywhere in the area, though there was a traffic cam two blocks over that I'd had to pass through to get over here. I didn't break any traffic laws, so I knew I'd be fine.

I stayed in the dark, next to the building and out of sight as I waited for her. I was wearing rubber-soled shoes so she wouldn't hear me coming, and I had my rag of chloroform ready to go. She arrived just before nine, parking directly in front of the building. That wasn't a problem. It didn't matter that she'd driven herself here, I had never been in her car, nor would I be.

She got out and walked toward the door of the theater. I

watched her pull on the door, trying to enter, but found it locked. She frowned and looked around, then dug into her purse.

While she was distracted, I made my move. She had her back to me, making it easy for me to wrap my arm around her and cover her mouth and nose with the rag.

I held her around the waist as she struggled, trying to claw my hand away from her face, but I was stronger. A moment later, she went limp in my arms. Picking her up, along with her purse and everything she'd brought with her, I carried her to the car I'd driven here in, put her in the backseat, and got to work tying her up. I didn't want her to wake up before we got to the abandoned warehouse where I'd prepared everything for her.

Like with Michella, I used a ball gag to keep her quiet. I didn't want anyone hearing her if she woke up before we got there. It took twenty minutes, and she remained out of it the entire time, which worked well for me. I pulled the car right up to the warehouse door and then dragged her out of the backseat, tossed her over my shoulder, and carried her in.

I laid her on the dirty queen-sized mattress on the floor. There had been a group of vagrants squatting here, but I'd paid them to leave for the night, so I had this place all to myself.

I tied a rope around Leanne's cuffed wrists and attached it to one of the metal poles that stood a few feet from where I'd moved the mattress. Once she was secured, I went back out for my bag of toys. I set it down next to the mattress and pulled out a pair of sharp scissors. I cut off the top she was wearing, pulled off her shoes and pants and tossed them into a pile. I wouldn't be leaving them here, so I wanted to be sure I kept them close by.

Since I knew no one would hear her here, I decided to remove her gag. I wanted to enjoy her screams. I didn't have to wait much longer for her to wake. When she did, she stared at me and said, "Hunter? What the fuck? Why am I tied up? What did you do to me?"

"Nothing yet, but as promised, I'm going to make you famous."

She paled. "What do you mean?"

I pulled out my large hunting knife and straddled her hips. "I have plans for you, my lovely Leanne. So many plans, but first, I want to see you bleed for me."

"What? No! Oh my God!"

I drew the blade of the knife along her tender flesh, and she screamed so prettily for me. "Oh, that's perfect; let's recreate that, shall we?" I could feel her heart pounding beneath my hand on her chest as I cut her.

She tried to buck her hips to get me off her, but I was having none of it. I put the tip of my knife on her stomach, and her eyes widened. "Please..." she begged, tears falling from her pretty blue eyes. "Please stop."

"Behave, or our time is going to be over before I'm ready." I glared down at her.

She whimpered, but nodded, indicating that she understood. Of course, I was sure she thought I meant I planned to let her live, but that wouldn't be the case.

"Now, let's see what I have to work with..."

"Stop..." she cried out.

"You don't tell the director what to do. I tell you!" I growled in her face.

She cried out, and that made me smile.

"Yes, that is what I want from you."

Leanne tried to shrink away from me again.

I gripped her chin hard and stared into her eyes. "Did I tell you to move?" I moved the knife over her body.

She squeaked, and her eyes widened as she realized I was serious. "Please don't!"

"Then you don't fucking move unless I tell you to."

She nodded, the tears flowing faster.

I played with her, enjoyed everything I could take from her.

She kept begging me to stop, but I ignored her pleas. They meant nothing to me; she was merely a plaything in my game with my beloved. I expected the pleading as well as the screaming, which was why we were here in this deserted part of town.

When I'd taken everything I wanted, I wrapped my hands around her neck and cut her off mid-scream. Her eyes bulged, and she bucked under me, her face turning red, then slightly purple. I squeezed tighter. When I looked down a few minutes later, Lovely Leanne was gone.

She'd been adequate.

Not as good as my first game piece, but decent.

I cleaned myself up and then set about taking my trophy. Leanne was a little more messy than Michella had been, since I'd made her bleed more, but that was all right. I used her clothes to clean up most of the mess.

I slid the flesh of her face into a baggie and gently put it away in my bag. When that was done, I undid her bindings, dressed her in the lingerie I'd brought for her, then carried her out to the car, where I set her down on the garbage bags I'd spread out over the backseat. I didn't want to get blood in the car since I intended to return it. I wasn't an actual thief; I had merely borrowed it without their knowledge for the night.

I checked the warehouse to make sure I wasn't leaving anything behind. The mattress had a couple of small blood-stains on it, but I flipped it over so none of the vagrants would notice it when they returned. Happy with how things looked, I went out to the car and drove to Juggs. It was nearly three in the morning, so they were closed, which was how I'd planned everything. I drove around the back of the restaurant into the alleyway, where there were two large dumpsters. There were no cameras or lights back here, which wasn't very smart of them considering how dark it was.

I pulled Leanne from the car, then settled her on the ground in front of one of the dumpsters. Like Michella, I posed her, then attached the note. I tossed her clothes into the dumpster behind her along with her purse, shoes, and the garbage bags from the backseat of the car.

Feeling successful, I drove the car back to the parking lot I'd gotten it from and parked it as close to its original spot as I could, put the steering wheel section back together, got out with my bag, and locked the doors.

Whistling, I headed home with my trophy. I'd found the perfect place to display them where no one ever went, but I'd wait to go there tomorrow night. For now, I was exhausted, but elated. I couldn't wait for my beloved to hear of my latest move. I hoped it would be enough for LAPD to bring her back on the case. If not, that was all right. I had planned for that as well.

All in all, it had been a great night, I thought as I passed through the door of my apartment building.

15

AN UNEXPECTED CALL
MARCY

I knew I was dreaming again, but I couldn't make myself wake up. I was frozen under Mom's bed with Stephen's arm wrapped tight around me, holding me in place. I struggled against him. I wanted to break free and save Mom, but he wouldn't let me go. In my head, I knew I wasn't a child anymore and that Stephen was just trying to keep me safe, but my heart was crying out for the only parent I knew.

Mom had never known who my dad was. Hadn't known who Stephen's dad was either, from what she'd said. Both had been "clients," as she'd called them. I'd asked her why she'd decided to keep us, and she'd said because some of her clients liked doing it with pregnant women and paid more for the luxury. That had icked me out, so I'd stopped asking questions after that.

Eventually, the nightmare played out, and I was able to break free from it, sitting up in bed with my blankets wrapped around me like a vise. I was breathing hard as I glanced at the clock. It was just past five in the morning. Way too early for me to be up considering I was on suspension still. It had been over a week, and IA still hadn't talked to me. I was starting to get worried. Thankfully, though, they hadn't found any listening devices in my apartment, so that was one less worry at least.

I got up and headed for the bathroom. I figured a hot shower might help loosen up my muscles, which were wound tight from the nightmare. I shook my head, trying to clear remnants of it from my mind. I hated dreaming about that night, but I was pretty sure it was brought on by the case that I was no longer allowed to work.

I wanted to solve Michella's murder. I wanted to know for sure if Lemuel St. Martin was behind it.

I pictured the scene in my head. There had been no indication that the door had been forced or the lock picked. So, did she know her murderer? Did she let him in?

Nothing in the apartment indicated there had been a struggle. Could the murderer have cleaned things up? Maybe, but I didn't think so. It looked normal; nothing was broken or seemed out of place.

I doubted Michella had just lain there and allowed the murderer to cut and then strangle her, so what did that mean? Could she have been drugged? That was a very real possibility. One I actually hoped for. If she were drugged, then maybe she wouldn't have known what was happening to her. That was probably the best-case scenario.

I hadn't seen any indication that she'd been restrained, but that too could have been possible and would be in the crime scene files. At least it should be. If only I had access to them.

I wondered what Hummel and Vance had been able to accomplish. Had they found a former boyfriend who would be good for it? My gut said they wouldn't, but I could be wrong. She was an Instagram model, so maybe it was a crazed fan. But that seemed like a stretch, especially given the note the murderer had left that implied there were more to come.

Who was he playing this game with? I wondered. He hadn't indicated any specific person. Was that on purpose? Was it part of the game?

I didn't regret shooting Mr. Forrester, but I did regret the timing. If only I'd gotten to look at the crime scene files prior to being sent out for that abduction, I'd have a much better hold on Michella's case.

I paused. There was nothing to say I couldn't dig into her life to see if I could find some connection between her and her killer. Maybe I'd discover a name in her followers that I recognized.

Lemuel St. Martin's name passed through my head, but I dismissed it. Even if he were alive, he wouldn't be dumb enough to use his own name to follow a girl he planned to kill. Everything I'd read about him and the original case said he was an educated man.

I let the water sluice over me as I continued to think about the case that was no longer mine until the water started to cool; then I quickly washed up and got out. After dressing, I headed to the kitchen to make an omelet. I pulled the eggs, milk, cheese and butter from the fridge and got out the cast-iron skillet. As I was about to crack my first egg in the bowl, my phone rang. Sighing, I set the egg down and pulled my phone out to look at the caller ID.

"Damn it, what is he calling for?" I muttered as I stared at the screen. I debated letting it go to voicemail, but knew he'd just call back. "What now, Jordan? You know it's not even six a.m., and I'm on suspension, remember?"

"Not that I agree with it, but your suspension has been put on hold. Captain wants you back at work ASAP."

I put the egg back in the carton and shoved the box back in the fridge along with the milk, cheese and butter. "I'm on my way in, just need to change—"

"No, there's been another murder, same guy. He wants you at the scene."

"Oh, shit. Okay, what's the address?" I scrambled to my bedroom to change into work attire.

"Know where Juggs is?"

"Yeah, I know the place." It was a restaurant where the waitresses dressed pretty skimpily without being obscene.

"Right behind there. They think the victim was one of the waitstaff."

"Wait, they recognized her?" If that was true, then maybe it wasn't the same guy, because he would have taken her face.

"Not exactly. Someone found her purse and some bloody clothing in the dumpster she was posed next to."

"They tampered with the scene?" I was going to bust some heads when I got there.

"I don't know who found it, Kendrick; just get over there before I regret calling you."

"How come I'm off suspension?" I asked, keeping him on the line, more to annoy him than anything else. I had put my phone on speaker so I could change while I talked.

"IA spoke to the girl and her mom, as well as Carmichael and Lloyd. They determined that you made the right call by going in. I still don't agree that shooting him was the right thing to do, but it's not my call. They haven't closed the investigation, but it looks like you'll be fully cleared, and the captain didn't want to wait around for them to dot the i's and cross the t's."

"What about Hummel and Vance? Have they found anything?"

"No, with you out, and us being short on detectives, they didn't have a lot of time to dig into the case. I know they canvassed the first vic's apartment building again and spoke to her friends, looked for an ex-boyfriend, but didn't come up with anything."

"I knew they wouldn't," I mumbled as I slid on my blazer.

"What was that?"

"Nothing. Just talking to myself. I'm heading out now."

"Good, and try not to shoot anyone, okay?"

"Ha. Ha. You're so funny." I rolled my eyes as I hung up.

I grabbed my badge from my dresser and attached it to my belt, then slid my private weapon into its holster on my hip. I wasn't going to be without a weapon, and since I didn't have time to stop by the precinct to pick up a new service weapon, my own would have to do. Making sure I had everything, I picked up my keys from the table in the living room and rushed out the door, only stopping to lock my new deadbolt on the way out.

16

ORIGINAL OR COPYCAT?

MARCY

I parked my car in Juggs' parking lot, where several other police cruisers were parked, as well as a news van for Channel 37. I got out of my car and headed for the crime scene tape that was blocking the side of the building to the back alley. A patrolman I didn't know was there guarding the area so no unauthorized people gained access to the scene.

I pulled my blazer aside and showed him my badge. Without a word, he gave me a nod and lifted the tape for me. I ducked under it, not even breaking my stride as I headed back to the scene. Damien and Lindsey were already there, and Michael was taking pictures.

"What have we got?" I asked as I joined them.

"Same as the first girl," Damien replied. "Only this one looks like she's been sliced up a bit more."

"Peri- or postmortem?" I asked, taking in the girl's posed body. I had yet to look at where her face should have been.

"Arms and breasts are perimortem; face is post, same as victim number one."

"Michella," I murmured. I hated calling them "victim number whatever." They were women, previously living, breathing people who hadn't deserved what happened to them. I didn't want to take their personhood from them in death.

"Right. So everything indicates we're dealing with the same perpetrator."

"Did he leave a note this time?" I asked.

Lindsey handed over the note, which was now in a plastic evidence bag.

Such a pretty and fragile pawn, she'll never be famous now.

"Do we know who she is?" I questioned as I read the note again.

"Leanne Williams according to the driver's license in the purse that was found in the dumpster." Damien was still hovering over her body, trying to shift her.

"Is she still in rigor?"

"Yes, she's only been dead about seven hours, I'd guess. I'll be able to tell more once I get her back to the lab," Damien replied.

"Was she killed here or elsewhere?"

"We think she was killed somewhere else and placed here," Lindsey said over her shoulder as she bagged up some of the things from the dumpster. "I think the only thing that pertains to the vic is this bag and these scraps of clothing, but we're bagging everything to go through it all."

I nodded. "So what do we know about her? Anything?"

"Just that she worked here." Lindsey gestured toward the restaurant. "You look perplexed; what's up?"

"It's what the killer wrote on the note," I answered. "I'm thinking she might have been an actress. Or at least trying to be one."

"Maybe, yeah," Lindsey agreed.

"Anything else you can tell me?" I asked.

"Not at the moment," Damien commented as he motioned to a couple of his assistants, who helped him get Leanne onto a gurney for transport to the coroner's office for autopsy. "I'll let you know more when I know more."

"Great." I stood there for a moment longer, thinking things over. Everything about Michella and Leanne reminded me of the Face Flayer. I couldn't decide if it was actually him, or if I was dealing with a copycat.

It was too much of a coincidence for this killer to know how to remove the face without damaging the muscle and sinew beneath. They'd practiced it, but on who? Or what, maybe? I wondered if there'd been any reports of mutilated animals in the area. I'd have to check on that. I was pretty sure that no person would allow someone to practice this skill on them, so that left animals. Unless I was dealing with some kind of psycho surgeon? I supposed I couldn't rule that out.

That was all if the original killer, Lemuel St. Martin, wasn't our current killer. And I had to wonder if that might be the case. The women weren't his usual fare. They weren't prostitutes. And the notes were different. St. Martin had never left notes like this. His had always said the same thing: *Who's pretty now?* Because of that, I was fairly certain that I was dealing with a copycat.

"Detective? Everything okay?"

I felt a hand on my arm and looked toward it, then up to Michael's face. He held his camera in one hand and was studying me with concern. "Oh, yeah, just thinking about our killer, trying to get a handle on him."

He nodded and dropped his hand. "I'm going to take more shots of the area."

"Since you've all got this handled, I'm going back to the precinct to read the report on Michella Graves. I haven't gotten to see it yet."

"Just a heads-up, I know you probably suspected it, but she was sexually assaulted before she was murdered," Damien said. "I suspect the same for this vic as well."

I had assumed as much, considering the provocative clothing. "Thanks for the warning. Any semen?"

"No, no DNA on her or in her that wasn't hers."

"Well, that's unhelpful." I sighed. "This guy isn't going to make it easy for us."

"Nope." Damien stood and glanced toward the gurney that was being loaded into the back of his van. "And I don't think he's finished."

"You're probably right. Find me something, Damien."

"I'll give it my best shot."

I paused and looked back. "I'm right about cause of death for both of them, aren't I? Strangulation?"

Damian nodded. "Yep."

As I left the scene, several reporters called out questions, but I ignored them. I wasn't going to give them anything, and I hoped that the rest of the LAPD wouldn't either.

Twenty minutes later, I headed for the captain's office. "Is he in, Jason?"

He glanced over his shoulder, then back to me. "Let me see if he's busy." He took his job as gatekeeper to the captain seriously—probably because Captain Robinson would rip him a new ass if he didn't. A minute later, he put the phone back on the receiver and said, "He says you can go on in."

"Thanks," I murmured and headed for the office. I knocked and went right in.

"Detective, glad you're back. Have you gotten with Hummel and Vance for the case files?"

"No, sir, not yet. I came to update you on the scene." I took the chair opposite him and explained what we'd discovered behind Juggs.

"So we are looking at a serial."

"It looks like it, sir. And—"

"Go ahead. I know what you're going to say." He folded his arms.

"I know everyone believes St. Martin is dead. That he was shot and fell off the bridge into the river. But what if he's not? What if he somehow survived?"

"Kendrick, that's not possible. It's been twenty-six years."

"I know, sir." I stared down at my hands. "It's just... the scenes are eerily familiar. So what if who we're dealing with is a copycat? Someone who's studied the St. Martin case and—"

"Is picking up where he left off?" he finished for me.

"Maybe?"

"All right, I tell you what. I want you to get the case file from Hummel on Graves, and then you can go down to the cold-case room and see if there are any outstanding similar murders. If there's nothing there..." He let his words trail off as if that should be the end of it.

"May I also do a database search, sir? See if there are similar cases anywhere in the US?"

He frowned. "I'll give you time to chase down a connection via the past, but I still want you staying on top of the current murders. And I'm not sending you out on any other jobs for the time being. I want your attention focused on this guy."

"Yes, sir. Thank you." I stood up and returned to the main office. Instead of going to my desk, I passed it and strode over to Hummel's.

"You're back, thank God." Hummel handed over a hefty file. "This is everything on Graves."

I opened the folder and started leafing through it. "What, if anything, did you and Vance discover?"

"Not much. Autopsy report is in there. We recanvassed the building; none of the neighbors could give us anything about the night she died. They did say she lived alone, they rarely saw her with anyone over, and only a few women came to visit her. We spoke to a couple of her contacts, and it turns out that she had two older gentlemen in her life in the past year."

"She was dating older men?"

Hummel shrugged. "I wouldn't call it dating so much as... they provided her with money, and she made them feel young again, if you know what I mean."

"So she was hooking?"

"No, not exactly. More like they were her sugar daddies. We spoke to both and cleared them. Dan Proctor was in Hawaii with his wife and kids. William Franks was teaching a night class and was seen after midnight on campus security cameras."

I frowned. "What was he doing there so late?"

"His class ended at ten, and then he said he was 'tutoring' a student. He gave me her name, and she corroborated his story."

"Did you learn anything else?"

"Her girlfriends said that Graves wasn't really attracted to men. She dated them for what they could give her, but she preferred women."

"Really?" I drew back in surprise. "That could open up a whole other pool of candidates."

"What do you mean?" Hummel asked.

"Some men don't take rejection well."

"Right, but how are you going to find those guys?"

"I'll go through her social media. She's bound to have unsolicited direct messages, unless she's deleted them. If she has, I'll have to contact the companies and see if we can get back copies of anything sent to her."

"Better you than me."

I didn't mind the slog work; sometimes that was where you found the right pieces to a puzzle. "Anything else I should know?"

"Everything we know is in there, but I think I've told you most of it."

"Okay, thanks." I turned and went back to my desk. I took a few minutes to look through the file. Damien had been extremely thorough in the autopsy. He'd discovered a fiber in her nose, tested it, and found it held chloroform. So that had to be the way he'd subdued her, but had he kept her subdued? Toxicology didn't show any in her system, according to the rest of the report.

I picked up the phone and called the coroner's office. "May I speak to Dr. Black, please? This is Detective Kendrick." I waited for them to put him on the line.

"Detective, I don't have the autopsy even started yet—"

"No, I know. I just got the report on Michella Graves. You found a fiber with chloroform on it, but none in her system, how is that possible?"

"It doesn't last. Dissipates after about eight hours."

"And she had been dead much longer than that by the time we got to her." I sighed. "Did you pick up anything else unusual?"

"There was slight bruising on her wrists and ankles, very faint. I think she was restrained, but with something fairly soft, so it didn't show up until later."

"Okay, thanks, good to know."

"Anything else, Detective?"

"Not right now. Let me know when you've got that autopsy done."

"You'll be my first call," Damien replied before hanging up.

I set the file aside, went to the break room to grab a cup of coffee, and then headed down to the cold-case room. I spent a couple of hours there going through possible cases that might match, dating back as far as twenty-six years ago, but none of them felt right, since all the victims still had their faces intact.

After grabbing a quick lunch from a food truck near the precinct, I started going through the computer crime database, looking for similar murders.

By the end of the day, I had nothing. There were no similar cases. It looked like either Lemuel St. Martin had died, or he'd stopped killing for twenty-six years, which was probably far-fetched.

And that meant that we were dealing with a copycat.

17

INSTA FAME AFTER DEATH
MARCY

My head hurt by the time I had gone through all the old possible cases and all the computer data. As I got in my car, I called Stephen to see if he wanted to meet for dinner. I didn't want to be on my own after viewing photos of so many dead bodies today, not to mention seeing one up close and personal early this morning.

"You've reached Stephen; you know what to do," his voice-mail chimed.

"Hey, it's me; are you screening your calls? I just wondered if you wanted to go to dinner. Call me back."

I sat and waited for a few minutes, but my phone stubbornly stayed quiet. I tried twice more to reach him, but he never answered. I hated to admit how worried I was about him, especially since he'd gotten into it with Jordan. I thought about going by his apartment, but I didn't want to bug him if he was busy. I just wished he'd call me back.

Still, I didn't want to eat alone, so I decided to pick up some fast food and then visit Angel at the hospital.

With a large brown bag of deliciousness in hand, I knocked on his hospital room door. "I come bearing gifts," I said as I pushed the door open.

"Hey, you. Wasn't expecting you." His eyes widened. "Is that what I hope it is?"

"If you were hoping for a double bacon cheeseburger with everything, and a large order of fries, absolutely." I sank down next to him in the chair by his bed.

"Give me now. I had a rubbery piece of meat they called a pork chop earlier; I'm starving." He reached for the bag.

I laughed, but it sounded hollow to my ears. I was still worried about Stephen; plus the case was stressing me out too. We ate in silence, both enjoying the food as we inhaled it. I sipped my soda and leaned back in my chair with a sigh.

"Okay, spill it. What's troubling you, partner? Is it the case?"

"Not really. More my brother's been acting strange lately. Getting overly angry and lashing out, and I've noticed he's drinking a lot more. I tried calling him earlier, and he's not answering."

"Is he working?" Angel looked at me with concern and understanding.

"I don't think so. He's usually home by now."

"Maybe he's on a date."

"That could be it." Stephen hadn't told me he had a date, but maybe it was a last-minute thing. "Thanks. I was ready to go over to his place and check on him."

"Hell, I can just see you now, busting in on him with some girl. He'd love that." Angel chuckled.

I gave him a mock shudder. "No, thank you. I'll wait till tomorrow and see if he calls."

"Good idea." He grinned. "So how's the suspension going?"

"I'm back at work. We got another body."

"Damn. Not even two weeks between kills? So what are you thinking?"

"Definitely a serial killer. I'm thinking copycat at the moment, unless St. Martin's MO has evolved over the years, which is still a possibility." I went on to explain my deep dive into cold-case files and national crime data.

"So this guy has studied the original case and has decided to emulate him?"

"Yeah, but with his own sick twist of cutting them up. He's even leaving notes on the bodies, but they're different than St. Martin's were. And these women aren't traditional prostitutes, like St. Martin killed."

"But they're selling their bodies?"

I shrugged. "Michella might have been with men for what they could give her, but she wasn't a hooker. She was an Instagram model and had some wealthy benefactors."

"Ah, so not your average girl on the street corner."

"No, definitely not."

"What about the second one?" Angel asked.

"As far as I can tell, Leanne was a waitress with aspirations of being an actress. I haven't confirmed that particular part yet, but I'm waiting for crime scene to finish up their report for me, and the autopsy."

"Black working on it?"

"Yeah, said he'd call as soon as he had something for me."

"Hopefully he or crime scene will find you a connection between the two women."

"That's the hope, but this guy is thorough. There was no

extraneous DNA on Michella. My bet is Leanne is the same. I'm not sure how we're going to catch this guy if he doesn't start making some mistakes."

"They always do. You'll puzzle this out well before he thinks you will. I have no doubts. Just wish I could back you up."

"Me too. How much longer are you stuck here?" I asked.

His expression turned sour, and he glared at the door. "At minimum, two more weeks."

"Seriously? Why?"

"They said if I don't want to lose functionality of my leg, I need to stay in traction. Then I'll move to a rehabilitation facility, where I'll have to do physical therapy. I could go home if I had someone there to help, or hired in a nurse, but I'm not doing that. Besides, the company of the guy who T-boned me is paying for all this, since he was on the clock at the time."

"You don't want twenty-four seven personal care from some hot girl in a nurse's uniform? I thought that was every guy's dream," I teased.

He rolled his eyes. "I'm sure that would be fun for about five minutes if she really was a hot girl; more likely though, she'd be in her late fifties and have the personality of a drill sergeant."

I laughed. "Probably." I looked around the room and noticed he had a couple of bouquets of flowers, and there was a teddy bear holding a get-well-soon balloon. "I see you've had a few visitors?"

Angel glanced to the window ledge where they were all perched. "Yeah, a few. The bear is from my ma. She had it sent up from the gift shop, but she hasn't flown in for a visit."

"Why not?" I was kind of shocked. Angel's mother was

one of those women who liked to spoil him. I had assumed she'd be here as much as possible considering he was nearly killed.

"I might have downplayed the accident for her. I didn't want her to worry."

"If she ever finds out, you're toast."

He narrowed his eyes at me. "You'd better not tell her."

I grinned slowly, like I now had something good to use against him if he ever pissed me off. "Or what?" I challenged.

"Oh Lord. Please don't; she'll come up here and smother the shit out of me. Don't do that to me."

I laughed. "You know I won't. I'm not that mean."

"Thank you." He leaned back against his pillows, relaxed again.

"Since your mom's not around, is there anything you need from your place? Need me to pick up your mail or anything?"

"No, I'm good. My neighbor is taking care of getting my mail and watering my plants."

"I had no idea you had a green thumb." I smiled at the thought of him talking to his plants to make them grow and stay healthy.

"Well, they're safer than having a pet, meaning I can forget to water or feed them, and they won't die on me immediately." He chuckled.

"There is that." I glanced at the time. "I should probably go. I'm heading to the station early tomorrow so I can dive into the case files. I'm hoping Damien will have the autopsy report ready by then."

"Thanks for the burger and fries. Keep me updated on the case, all right?"

"Of course. See you," I said as I headed out of his room.

By the time I reached my apartment, I was exhausted. All I wanted was to fall into a deep dreamless sleep. That didn't happen. Instead, I spent the entire night reliving my mother's murder again, only this time it was mixed with my fears about Stephen and this copycat killer.

One minute Stephen was under the bed with me, and the next he was in a drunken stupor, angrily striking out at Mom and the copycat killer, who had no face. Strangely enough, St. Martin's distinct visage didn't enter the nightmare. I woke up at four a.m. covered in a sheen of sweat, my sheet drenched from my fevered dream.

I couldn't go back to sleep, so I pulled the sheets from the bed and tossed them in the laundry. I remade the bed with clean sheets, then headed to the bathroom for a shower. I organized my thoughts as the water cascaded over me. I had a number of things I wanted to accomplish today, first and foremost combing through Michella's case file again. I really wanted to know if there was a connection between Michella and Leanne. Something nobody had thought of.

After my shower, I dressed for work and then made breakfast. I switched on the news for some noise, but had to stop as the newscaster mentioned the name of our latest victim. I set down the butter knife and turned the TV up.

"—was found murdered behind Juggs, where she worked as a waitress in the evenings. Ms. Williams was an up-and-coming actress, having played minor characters in several popular television programs. Donations for her funeral can be made—"

I turned the TV off. I was right, she'd been an actress; however, I was a bit angry that they'd released her name before I'd had a chance to see the crime scene report on her. Hell, had anyone even notified her family before this press release? If not, I was going to make some heads roll. Nobody deserved to find out their loved one was murdered on the morning news.

Speaking of loved ones, I decided I should call Stephen again since I'd not heard back from him. If he didn't answer, I was going to stop by his place and check on him. After the nightmares I'd had about him, I was even more worried.

Thankfully, after ringing four times, he picked up. "Yeah?" he said, sounding like I'd woken him from a deep sleep.

"Hey, it's me; are you okay?"

"Wha—I... it's, like, six twenty in the morning, sis; what's going on?" he grumbled.

"I know it's early, but—" I stopped as I realized he should be up, dressed, and about to walk out the door. "Shouldn't you be awake and getting ready for work?"

"Uh... oh, yeah, guess so. Must have overslept and missed my alarm. Thanks for calling," he muttered, but he sounded far away, like he was getting ready to hang up.

"Wait! I called because I was worried about you. I tried calling you last night, but you didn't answer."

"Oh, yeah? Sorry, got busy, then fell asleep. Didn't even check my phone."

"Are you sure you're okay?" I frowned. He'd never acted like this before, never ignored my phone calls, never lied to me. And I *knew* he was lying.

"I'm fine. Damn, I'm a grown-ass man! I don't have to answer to you. Fuck, I'm gonna be late. I'll talk to you later." He hung up.

I stared at my phone, feeling frustrated. Did he think I was trying to mother him or something? I hadn't meant to, but he was acting shady, and that set off warning bells in my head. Something was very wrong with him. The problem was I had no idea how to help him. He always acted like the tough older brother, and I knew he wouldn't talk to me.

I shoved my phone in my pocket and drove to work. I'd give him a little while to calm down, and then I would send him a text. Maybe by then he'd be back to his normal self, having worked through whatever was bothering him.

I knew it was going to be a bad day even before I walked into the precinct. That was confirmed when Jordan confronted me as I walked to my desk. Seeing his still fading black eye and slightly busted lip from his run-in with Stephen made me smile inwardly, though I did my best not to show it.

"Kendrick! You're late!" he said by way of greeting.

I rolled my eyes and didn't care that he saw me do it. "No, I'm not. I walked into the room right at seven." I moved past him to my desk.

"There's been a shooting at the Gas and Go on—" he started.

"Send Davidson or Nylon."

"I'm in charge here. I'm the one who makes the call on who goes—"

"Take it up with Captain Robinson. He told me yesterday he's not sending me out on any other cases; he wants me working the Graves and Williams cases."

He sputtered some more.

I sat down and picked up the phone but paused as I looked up at him. "Anything else?"

He turned on his heel and stormed into the captain's office, probably to complain about me, but I didn't care.

I dialed the coroner's office and waited.

After a brief conversation with one of his assistants,

Damien got on the phone. "Did you not get the report I sent over?"

"No, are you sure it made it to me?" I asked, going through everything in my inbox.

"I swear—" he muttered; then I heard him shouting for one of his assistants, followed by a muted conversation with them before he returned. "Seems Bates gave the file to your lieutenant per his request. You'll have to take it up with him."

I gritted my teeth. That fucker. "Thanks." I hung up, jumped up from my desk, and marched toward the captain's office, where Jordan was talking to Robinson. I knocked on the door, which was open, and they both paused. "Did you insist that the coroner's assistant give you the autopsy report on Leanne Williams instead of leaving it for me on my desk?"

Jordan puffed up his chest. "As your lieutenant—"

"Give her the report and send Davidson out to the Gas and Go shooting," the captain said, cutting him off. "Kendrick is not going out on calls until further notice. She's got her hands full trying to catch this son of a bitch. Am I clear?"

Jordan huffed, but didn't answer. He just glared at me.

"Lieutenant?" Captain Robinson warned. "Are we going to have a problem?"

"No, sir," he finally gritted out. "The file is on my desk."

"Thanks." I turned and started to leave, but then asked, "Hey, did someone notify Ms. Williams' family prior to the news releasing her name?"

"I sent Hummel over yesterday after we had confirmation of her ID. I think you were neck deep in the national crime database at the time. Figured you'd rather continue that than go break the news to her parents," Robinson answered.

"I didn't know and was concerned when I saw the broadcast this morning. Did the parents give Hummel anything?"

Robinson shook his head. "I don't think he stayed to ask questions. Just broke the news."

"I'll have to do a follow-up with them," I muttered, then headed straight to Jordan's enclosed office, opened the door, and found the file sitting open on his desk. I grabbed it and went back to my desk. I didn't know what kind of game Jordan was playing, but I was tired of butting heads with him.

Lindsey wove her way over to my desk, a thick file folder in her hand. "Hey, brought you the crime scene report on Williams."

"Thanks, I appreciate it. Did you find anything interesting?"

"Not sure. She had an appointment for nine p.m. the night she died with some director."

"Oh? Got a name for this guy?"

Lindsey nodded. "Hunter Malone. She had his business card."

"Great. I'll give him a call and see if he met with her." I flipped through the file until I came to the photograph of the card. "Anything else?"

"Nothing that stood out. Want to get lunch later?" she asked.

"I'll have to play it by ear; can I call you?"

"Sure, let me know." Lindsey smiled and then wound her way back through the detective pool and out of the office.

I picked up the phone and dialed the number on the card, but found it was disconnected. "Strange," I murmured.

I turned to the computer and plugged in the website listed, but it came up with an error code, so I did a little digging. It took me a while to find the guy; his social media was just about nil. Finally, after a few calls to some casting agents in town, I got a proper number and called him.

"This is Hunter Malone; how may I help you?"

"Mr. Malone, you're a hard man to reach. My name is Detective Marcy Kendrick with the LAPD."

"Detective? What's going on? Has something happened?" He sounded panicked.

"That depends, sir. Do you know a young lady by the name of Leanne Williams?"

He stayed quiet for a moment, then answered, "I can't say that I recognize the name. Why do you ask?"

"The young lady in question was murdered, sir, and she had your business card, along with a scheduled appointment with you for nine p.m. on the night she died. I was hoping you could tell me about that?"

"I didn't have an appointment with her. I didn't even know her!" He sounded genuinely confused. "How did she have my card?"

"So you're denying the fact that you had an appointment with her?"

"Of course I'm denying it. I'm not even in California right now. I've been in New York for the past six months, directing a play on Broadway. You can check. When did she die? I am sure there are people here who can verify that I was with them here in New York."

I sighed. I was sure he was telling the truth. Still, I took down his information and called to verify his alibi. He hadn't been lying. Which left me to wonder exactly how Leanne had come to be in possession of his card.

Was it even his actual card? The number on it was wrong, so what if it wasn't his real card? I should have asked for a description of it while I had him on the phone. Since I had Hunter's real number now, I sent him a text to ask.

A moment later he replied with a picture of his business card. It was completely different than the one we had in evidence. That made me wonder if the killer met her at the restaurant and gave her a fake card. Was it possible I could discover him that way?

I crossed my fingers for a bit of luck, then called the restaurant. "Hi, who am I speaking with?"

"This is Cassandra; may I help you?"

"Yes, hi, Cassandra, my name is Detective Kendrick with the LAPD. Are you the manager?"

"No, ma'am, I'm just a hostess. Is this about Leanne? I just hate that that happened to her. Do you know who did it?"

"We're working on it. Might I speak to your manager, please?"

"Of course, one sec..."

"This is Sam." A new voice came on the line a moment later.

"Good morning. My name is Detective Kendrick of the LAPD, and I'm working on Ms. Williams' case. Do you have cameras in the restaurant?"

"Sure, yeah."

"Excellent. Would it be possible for me to come check the video footage?"

"Yes. We keep video footage for about a week before it's deleted, unless we have an unruly customer that we have to prosecute."

I sighed. That was a pretty short window. "Did Ms. Williams ever have to deal with an unruly customer?"

"Sure, all the girls have. Nothing recently though."

"Please save the surveillance tapes for me. I'll come by to see them as soon as I can."

"Of course, Detective."

I thanked him and disconnected.

I spent a little more time going over both case files and made a few calls pertaining to Michella. There was a name with no follow-up, and I wanted to check it out. "Hello, Mr. Warren? My name is Detective Marcy Kendrick with the LAPD. I wanted to ask you about a woman you may have... dated? Michella Graves?"

"Yes, I was sorry to hear about her death; she was a sweet girl. What can I tell you about her?" the man asked.

"Can you tell me how you met Ms. Graves?"

"My friend Dan Proctor introduced us. I won't beat about the bush. Ms. Graves was a lovely girl with a penchant for nice things, and both Dan and I were willing to give her those things. I believe one of your other detectives has already spoken to Dan?"

"Yes, sir. It looks as though he was unable to reach you though?"

"I was in the hospital when he attempted to contact me. I just returned home this morning. I have a spinal injury, you see. I'm paralyzed from the waist down."

"I'm sorry to hear that, sir." That being the case, there was no way this guy was my killer.

"I've been this way for more than ten years, ma'am, fell off a horse. Back to Ms. Graves, she had no problem being my date for certain charity functions, and spending time with me for... shall we say a healthy paycheck?"

"Thank you for your time, sir. I appreciate your candor."

"No problem, Detective. Have a pleasant rest of your day."

"Thanks," I murmured before hanging up.

I spent the next hour pulling up the social media accounts of Michella and Leanne. It seemed they had both gained instant fame upon their deaths. They both had huge followings, and their accounts were full of messages of sorrow at their demise. The only good news was that so far, nobody knew they had been murdered by the same killer, nor that he'd stolen their faces.

If you could call that good news.

18

MISOGYNY AT ITS FINEST

MARCY

After closing down my computer, I called Lindsey, and we decided to meet for lunch at a small Italian bistro not too far from Juggs. We waited for a table in the bar, but neither of us ordered alcohol.

"How's the case going?" she asked as she sipped a clear soda with a maraschino cherry in it.

"It's not." I sighed. "I checked out the social media on both women, and it doesn't look as though they knew each other or even had cross-over fans. The first woman"—since we were in public, I wouldn't use anyone's names, and Lindsey knew that—"had a few benefactors, but they all have alibis. I haven't found anything much on the second woman, but I'm heading to her place of employment after lunch to take a look at some surveillance video."

"So what did the director have to say?" she questioned.

"It wasn't him. He's been in NYC, and his alibi checks out. The card was fake. I'm hoping whoever gave her the card is on camera."

"Ladies, your table is ready," one of the waitresses said.

I hopped off my stool, carrying my cola. I already knew what I wanted, and so did Lindsey. We'd eaten here numerous times and generally ordered the same thing. "I'll have the chicken fettuccine, salad and breadsticks with Alfredo sauce."

"I'll have the same," Lindsey added.

"I'll get that order in for you."

When she left, we returned to the conversation about the case.

"I really hope you catch this sick bastard."

"I'm doing my best. Doesn't help that I was suspended right after the first one. I feel like I'm playing catch-up."

"And doing it without a partner. How is Angel, by the way?"

"Hanging in there. Bored out of his mind, I suspect."

"When's he back?"

"He's in traction for a while longer, then has to go to rehab, so he's out for a while."

"That sucks. They going to put you with another partner?"

I shook my head. "Captain said there isn't anyone. Honestly, I don't want a new partner."

Lindsey grinned. "Well, not when your partner is such a hotty like Reyes is, hmmm?"

I felt my cheeks heat. "It's not like that, and you know it. He and Jordan are friends; I could never; he would never."

Laughing, Lindsey said, "Uh-huh, keep telling yourself that. That man would bend over backwards for you."

"No, that's just because he's a good partner," I denied. "I'd do the same for him."

"I'd probably believe you more if you didn't go all pink in the face when you talk about him."

I knew Lindsey was teasing me, but it made me anxious. "Can we change the subject, please?"

"If you don't want to talk about your love life, how about mine?" she commented as the waitress brought our food.

"You have a love life?" I arched a brow at her teasingly.

"Ha-ha. Yes, I do. And it's absolutely in the toilet right now."

"Why is that?" I asked as I took a bite of my pasta.

"It's great for about the first two dates, then work calls, and I have to leave, and they get all squeamish." She rolled her eyes.

"What do you mean?"

"About what I do. They think it's weird that I'm around the dead, and they head for the hills. I don't think I've had a guy last more than three dates. I need a better pool of men to date from."

Not having thought about dating in such a long time, I hadn't even considered what kind of men were available to me now that I was divorced. "That's seriously depressing."

"You're telling me. Why do you think I want to live vicariously through you and Detective Reyes?"

"He's my partner."

"And?" She drew the word out, making it sound much longer than it should have been.

"And I'm not dating him, end of." I stabbed my fork into a piece of chicken as if to drive home my point.

"Hmmm, if you're not, then maybe I should."

I flashed my eyes at her, suddenly filled with jealousy, but I didn't say anything, just angrily took a bite of bread.

She smirked at me. "That's what I thought."

I rolled my eyes and ate some of my pasta.

From there the conversation turned to lighter topics, and

soon we were paying our bill and heading out. I drove the short distance to Juggs and parked. My mind flashed to the scene behind the restaurant for a moment before I shook it away. I'd probably never be able to drive by here without seeing Leanne posed up against the dumpster in my head.

Sighing, I got out and went inside.

The manager, Sam, had been expecting me and led me to the office, where he had everything set up for me to look at the tapes. "These are the tapes we have for the past week, and the unruly customers from the past month. Leanne only worked three of the days we have tapes for, so those are here. And then there was only one unruly customer that was hers, so that's this tape. I've got the first one cued up for you."

"Thank you." I pressed play on the first one, but had to fast-forward until Leanne came into view. I watched men flirting with her, putting their hands on her, heard them making lewd comments to her, and eventually had to pause the screen to look at the manager with narrowed eyes. "Are they all like this?"

"Like what?"

"Handsy and rude and just basically assholes?"

He shrugged. "It's that kind of place, and the girls know if the customer gets to be too much, we'll back them and throw the guy out, but for the most part, the girls make great tips and will put up with a lot before that happens."

I shook my head. It was misogyny at its finest. "It's sexist and disgusting how these men behave."

"What do you expect in a restaurant called Juggs?" he replied. "We cater to men. The girls know how these guys act before signing on. The more they allow, the higher their tips. Some of these girls go home with over a thousand in tips a night."

"It's just wrong," I murmured as I returned to the tapes. Despite there being a few really handsy men, not one of them handed her a card or was recorded saying anything to her about being a director and asking her to audition for anything. The tapes were a dead end. Even the unruly customer tape was a bust. The guy had stuck his hand up her skirt, and Leanne had immediately had him thrown out.

"Did you find anything?" Sam asked, coming back into the room an hour later.

"Other than a bunch of sexist assholes, there was one possible guy, the one you're prosecuting; do you have his information?"

"Sure, I'll get that for you." He pulled a file from the cabinet next to the desk and then wrote the info down for me. "I still can't believe somebody killed her like that. I've made sure the girls don't leave alone, and I or one of the other guys walks them out to their cars."

I took the note from him and glanced at it. The pervert's name was Gary Lawrence. "I'm glad you're making sure they're safe, but I don't think Leanne was killed behind the restaurant. I think she was only put there because she worked here."

"That doesn't make it better, Detective."

"No, it doesn't." I stood up. "Well, thank you for letting me look these over. Can you make a copy of the unruly guy for me? And if you do come across anyone who seems suspicious, please contact me." I handed him my card.

"I will. Where do I send the copy?" he asked as he pocketed my card.

"You can send it by courier to the precinct. Just put my name on it; it'll get to me."

"Okay, I can do that." He glanced toward the computer

screen, which was frozen on the guy I was interested in. "I hope you catch whoever did this."

"I promise you that I will." There was no doubt in my mind I would catch him.

After leaving Juggs, I drove to the coroner's office. I wanted to view the two bodies. I walked down the hallway to Damien's office and knocked.

"Come in," he called, his back to the door.

"Hey."

Damien turned and smiled. "Detective, what brings you by?"

"I was hoping to get a look at the bodies and ask a few questions."

"Of course, come on back." He led the way into the lab area, then pulled open two of the body cabinets. "Victim number one, Ms. Graves, and this one is our latest, Ms. Williams." He pulled back the sheets on both.

I looked from one woman to the other. "Were there any hesitation cuts?"

"None. The guy is as skilled as a surgeon."

I nodded. I had thought as much. "The other cuts, they weren't fatal?"

"No, they both definitely died from asphyxiation due to being strangled, I believe during coitus."

"Any defensive wounds on either of them?"

"Again, no. I believe both women were restrained." He lifted Michella's wrist. "You see this mark?"

I looked at her wrist; it was a very faint line of a bruise.

"I think whatever kind of restraints he used did this. It had to be something basically soft, but had a thicker edge to it, so that when she tugged, it put enough pressure on this spot to bruise it just slightly."

"So what are you thinking?"

"Modified fetish cuffs so they don't break apart with enough force."

"So maybe our killer is into the BDSM scene?"

"Possibly, or he's just using those tools to restrain them while he abuses them. Anyone can order them online without having to be part of a club."

"Well, great." I gave him a sour look.

"Sorry I can't be more help."

"It's not you. Just spent two hours watching men being complete perverts and assholes."

"Were you at a strip club?"

"No, watching surveillance tapes at Juggs."

"Ah. So just as bad, then."

"Yeah." My shoulders dropped as I gave the young women one last look. "Thanks for showing them to me and answering my questions."

"Anytime, Detective."

"I'll see you later," I commented as I left.

As soon as I walked into the precinct twenty minutes later, Jordan ambushed me. I wished he would go to hell and stay there. "What do you want?" I set my purse down on my desk.

"I want to know where you are with the case."

I hated having to report to him. I knew he was a senior officer, and if he were anyone else, I probably wouldn't be feeling this way, but because it was Jordan, all I wanted to do was tell him to fuck right off and leave me alone. Of course, I couldn't do that and still have a job tomorrow.

"I'm working the case. There are a lot of similarities between these two murders and the murders from the Face Flayer twenty-six—"

"These murders have nothing to do with that old case of your mom's. Her murderer is dead and gone. What is with your obsession with that case? Not everything is connected to it!"

My cheeks heated at his ranting. I clenched my fingers into fists, wishing I could deck him. I took a deep breath and counted to twenty as he screamed in my face. I was so close to saying "fuck it" and punching him anyway. The only thing that stopped me was the fact that if I did, I might never solve these murders.

"Are you finished?" I murmured, keeping my voice even and my anger tightly tamped down.

"Just work these two fucking murders and find me the killer without bringing your mom's shit into it." He turned and left.

I stood there staring after him.

"Hey, you okay?" Hummel asked as he approached me.

"Yeah. Just—"

"I get it." He looked over his shoulder toward Jordan's office. "He's under a lot of pressure."

I arched a brow at him. "You are not excusing his behavior, are you?"

"No, I mean, he's new to the job, and he's wanting to make a good impression on the higher-ups."

"Well, he missed." I smirked.

"Yeah, this killer is really messing with him."

"Well, he can stop taking his anger out on me. I'm the only one he yells at like that."

"Probably because you two have history." He shrugged.

"And because he thinks he's better than me and that I'm some vigilante cop who's out to make him look bad." I rolled my eyes.

"Everyone knows that's not true."

I shrugged.

"Hummel and Vance, you're up! DV in Hambly Hills," Jordan said from his office door.

"Gotta go," Hummel murmured.

"Kendrick, get back to work!" Jordan shouted.

I didn't bother to reply, but in my head, I flipped him off.

The copy of the surveillance tape arrived, and I did a little digging into Gary Lawrence. Turned out to be a dead end; he had an alibi for the times of both killings. Home in bed with his wife during Michella's murder, which I verified with his wife, and on a cruise ship headed for Hawaii during Leanne's. There was no way Gary was our perp. Unfortunately.

I spent the remainder of the afternoon going over the details from Michella's and Leanne's cases. I hoped to find a connection between the two, but aside from being murdered by the same killer, there didn't seem to be any intersectionality. They didn't share hair or eye color, they weren't in the same profession, nor were they the same age. The only thing that seemed the same was the connection to the original Face Flayer.

Despite what Jordan had demanded, I pulled out the old files. The first woman who had died twenty-six years earlier had somewhat resembled Michella. Both were redheads; both had green eyes. Leanne, too, also matched his second victim in looks. So was I wrong about this being a copycat? Was this Lemuel St. Martin, reliving his past but with a new twist? Had he spent the last twenty-six years planning to recreate the chaos he'd caused back then? Had he gotten smarter about his kills?

Before, he'd chosen women society didn't much care

about; it had taken four murders before the cops back then even started warning women about the serial killer or for it to even make the news. I recalled Mom being worried at the time, considering she was in the same profession as those women being killed, and she had tried to screen her johns, obviously not well enough, considering Lemuel had found his way into our home and murdered her.

I remembered her warning me and Stephen to make sure we locked the door with both locks. She had also been returning home earlier in the day, not wanting to be out on the street after dark. The night of her death, she'd come home at about five. She'd told us she had a client coming at six and for us to stay in our rooms and not come out or show ourselves, since he didn't know about us. I'd thought it was one of her regulars; she didn't normally invite clients to our home unless they were.

Looking back now, I wondered if Lemuel had somehow made Mom think he was somebody else when he'd set up the meet with her. The facts seemed to support my reasoning. And if that was the case, I wondered if he was doing the same now. He'd obviously pretended to be Hunter Malone for Leanne. That was how he'd gained access to her. It made sense that if it had worked in the past, it would work today.

However, if it was Lemuel St. Martin committing these murders today, then where had he been for the past twenty-six years? He hadn't been incarcerated anywhere; I'd checked that to be sure. A killer like him didn't generally quit killing. Normally they escalated, the need to kill driving them to find new victims. So why hadn't he escalated? Sure, the cops were onto him, at least here in LA, but that didn't mean he couldn't have gone elsewhere and continued his killing spree. The problem was that I'd checked for that too, and there just weren't any murders that matched his modus operandi.

He could have changed his MO and then reverted back. My mind played devil's advocate, but my gut was telling me that that wasn't what was going on.

At the end of the day, I hadn't really come to any conclusions or gotten anywhere close to catching this guy. With a heavy heart, I headed home, hoping I'd catch a break tomorrow.

I slid a frozen dinner into the microwave and then poured myself a glass of wine. I decided I was going to spend the evening relaxing with a book on my tablet, but while I waited for my meal to heat up, I logged into my personal email. I wasn't expecting anything. I usually only logged in and cleared it out about once a week, but it had been longer than that since I'd checked it.

I started deleting all the stupid spam mail, then paused as one caught my eye. It wasn't spam.

It was from someone calling themselves Face Flayer.

A chill went down my spine. I hesitated, my finger hovering over the email as I read the subject line.

Do you like my work?

19

KILLER TALKS
MARCY

My heart started to race. Was this some kind of sick joke? Some asshole who knew about my past tormenting me? Or... was this the actual killer making contact?
My frozen dinner was forgotten, and my hand shook as I opened the email.

My dearest Marcy,

I am so happy you have been reinstated at work. I have been looking forward to engaging with you, as I know you are the only one who can truly appreciate my work and will play this game as it is meant to be played. Did you like my first move? Michella was such a delight to kill. Her brilliant green eyes shone with pleasure and bulged so nicely as I strangled her. I should have taken them as a trophy as well as her face.

Leanne was almost as lovely as Michella, and she

screamed so prettily as I had my way with her. It was
such a shame it ended too soon. I do like to draw it out,
extend the pleasure of their death. It seems only fair.

I was upset to find that they didn't rate but a mere
mention on the news. I think they'd be disappointed as
well, as I know they both wanted fame and fortune.
Perhaps in time they will get that, as our game continues.

I look forward to your response. We have much to discuss,
don't you think?

Ever yours,
FF

I had to read through it multiple times, and each time
the horror of what those women went through played
through my mind. I wanted to respond, but I couldn't orga-
nize my thoughts. I wasn't even sure if I should reply. The
idea of talking to him, even via email, was terrifying. It took
me right back to being a kid and watching him—if this really
was him—murder my mother.

In the end, I had to know. I began to type.

FF,

Are you really Lemuel St. Martin? The original Face
Flayer? Where have you been for the last twenty-six
years? Why are you back? Why do you target women?
Why these women?

Detective Marcy Kendrick

I hit send and then began to panic. What if it was him? Did he know where I lived? Did he know I watched him murder my mother? Would he come after me? I set my tablet on the table and stood up. I couldn't sit still while I waited for a response. It could take hours before—

Ding.

I spun around to stare at my tablet on the table. It had just chimed with an incoming email. I grabbed it and saw it was his response. Pressing my lips firmly together, I opened the email.

> *To clarify, I don't target women, I target whores. Whores who use men for money and fame.*
>
> *FF*

He'd ignored my question about whether he was St. Martin, and where he'd been for the past twenty-six years, so I decided to ask a more personal question.

> *Does that include my mother? Was she a whore who used men for money and fame?*
>
> *Detective Marcy Kendrick*

I didn't get up this time; his reply came back within seconds.

> *Yes, that would include your mother. In fact, she might have been the worst whore of all, bringing men into her home with children there to see. Her death did you a favor. It made you into the woman you are today.*

*Tell me, my dearest Marcy, do you plan to kill me if you
catch me?*

FF

I gasped reading his words, and rage filled me. Oh, I
wanted to kill him all right, but death was too good for this
bastard. He needed to rot in prison for the rest of his life
before the devil got his soul, if he even had one. I hoped he
did and that he'd suffer for eternity for the murders he'd
committed. Still, I needed to answer him.

*I will catch you, and I can't wait to watch you go through
the humiliation of a trial and spend the rest of your life in
a cage like the violent animal you are.*

Detective Marcy Kendrick

I probably didn't have to sign it every time, but I wanted
to keep reminding him that I was a law enforcement officer. I
wasn't some random woman or someone for him to call "his
dearest." The idea that he thought I was anything of the sort
to him made me want to puke.

*You disappoint me, my sweet. You see, we have much in
common, and I so greatly admire you. Your strength and
beauty and the fact that you have found a way to be
successful in murder. You target those who prey on
defenseless women and children, and I find that
fascinating.*

*I must go now, but I will contact you again soon, my
dearest.*

Ever Yours,
FF

I read through the message several times. It was almost
as if he'd been here in this room with me, and that was
terrifying.

Completely freaked out, I jumped up and ran for the
front door, checking to make sure it was locked. Then I
moved about the apartment, checking every window to
make sure they were all locked too. I kept my hand on my
weapon, which I hadn't removed since coming home. It was
my service weapon, which had been returned to me, finally,
shortly before leaving the station earlier. My private weapon
was still in my purse, which I went and retrieved. I wanted as
many weapons around me as possible.

Laying my personal weapon on the counter within reach,
I grabbed my phone and dialed Angel.

"Hey, partner, what's up?" he answered.

"I—" I barely even got that much out before I burst into
tears.

"Marcy? What's wrong? What's happening?"

I couldn't even cough out the words I wanted to say. I was
too choked up with a flood of emotions.

"Fuck! Why am I stuck in this fucking bed when you
need me?" he muttered. "Look, I'm calling the station on the
hospital phone. I don't know what's going on, but I'll get
patrol over there in five minutes flat. Just give me a sec—"

"No!" I managed to get out through my sobs. "No,
don't..."

"I don't understand... what's going on?"

I still couldn't get my thoughts together enough to speak through my tears.

"Okay... okay, just calm down. Take a deep breath, Detective. Breathe with me... ready? Inhale... exhale... Inhale... exhale... okay... that's it... now, Detective, tell me what's going on."

His soothing voice and the way he called me detective reminded me I wasn't that weak little girl watching my mom get murdered. I was an officer of the law, and I needed to act like it. I followed his instructions, and it helped to calm me down.

"Sorry," I murmured after a moment. "Overwhelmed, I think."

"What happened?"

I took another calming breath and wiped my cheeks. "He contacted me."

Angel paused, then asked, "Who?"

"The killer. The one who murdered Michella and Leanne, and maybe my mom." That last part I whispered.

"Fuck, how the hell?"

"I don't know."

"Tell me everything. Did he call you?"

"No, it was email. Let me read you the conversation." I moved to my living room and grabbed my tablet, bringing it back to the kitchen counter. I read him the entire email thread.

"So he doesn't come out and say he murdered your mom, just that she qualified... could be this guy is the current murderer and is playing games with you. Trying to mess with your head. You need to tell Jordan."

"What? No the fuck not! I'm not telling Jordan that this

guy is messaging me; he'd pull me from the case immediately."

"Marcy, he's our superior officer—"

"He is not superior."

"Semantics. If you won't tell him, then take it to the captain. Robinson isn't going to pull you from the case. He wouldn't let Jordan pull you from the case either."

Angel was right, but I still didn't like the idea of telling Jordan. "Yeah, okay, I'll talk to Robinson."

"It's the right thing to do, the safest thing. You know what this guy is capable of, and I don't want him coming after you. It's creepy that he's being affectionate with you. You need to be careful."

"I will. I just wish he'd answered my question about if he was St. Martin or not."

"I think he wants you to believe that he is."

"Maybe." I thought about it, and Angel was probably right. "I should call the captain now."

"Damn, I wish I were out of this hospital bed. I really hate that my being here has left you on your own." His voice held remorse and a little bit of anger.

"It wasn't like you chose to be in that accident. You didn't cause it. I'm just glad you survived it." I smiled. Even though he couldn't see me, I hoped he could tell by my voice that I was happy he was still around.

"I know, it just sucks that I can't help you."

"You can help me by doing everything the doctor tells you so you can get back to the job."

"Yes, ma'am." He chuckled.

"I'll talk to you later."

"Keep me updated."

"I will." I hung up and then dialed Robinson's cell.

"Robinson."

"Captain, it's Kendrick. I have a situation." I explained about the emails between myself and the killer. "What do you want me to do?"

"I want our techs all over it, but I want you to keep this guy talking. He has a rapport with you, and we can use that. Maybe he'll slip up and give us something to work with. Give me your email log-in and password, and I'll pass it on to IT."

I did as he asked, but hated giving up my log-in information. I was one of those lazy people who used the same password for nearly everything; now I felt like I needed to go through and change all my others. The problem was I'd probably forget what the new one was five minutes after I created it. I did it anyway, just because I didn't want to run the risk of someone getting into my accounts. It took me the next few hours to get everything changed, and then I crashed.

20

TOO MUCH CRIME, TOO FEW DETECTIVES

MARCY

After a quick shower, I headed to the kitchen to make some coffee and discovered that I'd left my now soggy frozen dinner in the microwave last night. I pitched it in the trash and made myself a bagel and cream cheese while my coffee brewed.

I poured the coffee into a to-go mug, stuck my bagel between my teeth, grabbed my purse and keys, and left. I made sure to lock my door before hurrying out to the parking lot. I wanted to check in with the tech guys before I got started on anything, to see if they'd been able to trace the email address the killer had used.

At the station, I set my purse and mug on my desk, then strode down the hall to the IT department. These were the guys who handled all things cyber connected. I knocked on the door and went in.

Several of the techs looked up as I entered.

"What can I help you with?" Marshall, the tech closest to the door, asked.

"I'm Detective Kendrick. Captain Robinson gave

someone here my email and stuff last night—it's about a case."

"Right, that was me. I was going to come find you later. I have questions."

"Oh?"

"Yeah, how'd this guy get your email? Do you have it posted somewhere?"

"Yeah, it's on my Facebook page."

"Okay, that explains that. Have you accepted any new friend requests? Is your page public or private?"

"No, I don't think so. And I have no idea if it's public or private. I just use the account to talk to some friends from high school and to keep up with what's going on in their lives."

He shook his head like I was doing it wrong. I probably was, but I didn't get on there all that often, and I rarely posted anything except the occasional funny meme or maybe a picture of food that I found delicious.

"So, were you able to find him?" I asked.

"No. He's used a generic email address, you don't have to verify anything with them, and the IP address is for a coffee shop in the heart of LA. You could stake it out, but my guess is you won't be able to find him that way."

I sighed. "Great."

"The good news is we'll continue to monitor your email, and when he messages you again, maybe we can pinpoint his direction in that moment."

"Okay, thanks." I headed back to the detective pool and found it deserted. That wasn't unusual, we were short-staffed, and crime didn't stop just because we were missing detectives. I sat down at my desk and pulled out the case files again.

Jordan interrupted me. "We've got a DV. I need you to head over to Crestview and get it sorted out."

"Captain said I wasn't to go out on calls—" I started to remind him.

"I don't care. We're swamped here, and you're an able body that can go handle this. Now go," Jordan demanded.

"Fine, but it's on you if he asks why I'm not one hundred percent focused on catching this killer before he strikes again." I grabbed my purse, checked my weapon on my hip, and left.

This was the downside to being understaffed. Everyone had to multitask, even if there was a serial killer on the loose. A domestic violence call could go multiple ways, and I hoped this one would be easily dealt with.

Patrol was already there when I got to the scene. It was a team I didn't know, so I walked over to introduce myself and find out what we were dealing with.

I read his name tag. "Officer Banks, I'm Detective Kendrick; what have we got?"

"Two victims, husband came home to find his wife and her boyfriend getting friendly. Wife was stabbed in the chest, boyfriend ran, got lucky and was only stabbed in his shoulder before he barricaded himself in another room."

"Where's the husband?" I asked as I looked around the scene.

"Still inside, refusing to put down the knife. We were able to get the boyfriend out through a window, we can see the wife on the floor in the bedroom, pretty sure she's dead, but the husband is in there with her."

"Right." I pulled my weapon and turned toward the house. "What's the guy's name?"

"Oliver Meaders."

"Wife's name?"

"Susan."

I nodded and headed in. "Mr. Meaders?" I called as I worked my way to the bedroom at the back of the house.

He didn't answer, but I could hear him ranting.

"Mr. Meaders, I need you to put the knife down so I can check on your wife, Susan," I said as I entered the room.

"She's a fucking lying bitch!" His face was red, and he had tears pouring down his chubby cheeks. His hair was light brown threaded with gray.

"I understand you're angry at her, sir, but she needs medical attention. Please put down the knife. I really don't want to have to shoot you."

"God, Susan, why?" he cried as he dropped the knife and fell to his knees next to her. He put his face down in her neck. "Why would you do this to me?"

I moved toward him, kicked the knife away, and grabbed his arm. "Come with me, Mr. Meaders; then we can get someone in to help your wife." I could tell she was already gone, but he didn't seem to realize that.

"Why won't she answer me?" he sobbed. "She won't even say she was sorry."

I led him from the room and out of the house. Paramedics raced in as soon as we were out, and Officer Banks joined me, locking cuffs on Mr. Meaders' wrists.

"Officer Banks is going to read you your rights and put you into his patrol car now, Mr. Meaders."

"What about Susan? And that guy? Will they be okay?" he asked.

I shook my head. "I don't know, sir, but I doubt it."

A few minutes later crime scene showed up. "Hey, Jack, who do you have with you?" I asked upon seeing them.

"Bryce. What are we walking into?"

"Deceased woman, the homeowner's wife," I explained. "He came home, found her with another guy, and stabbed her in the chest; pretty sure she's dead. Paramedics are with her now. I'm going to go take a statement from the boyfriend."

"We'll take it from here."

I spent the next hour wrapping up the scene, then returned to the precinct just before lunch. I wasn't all that hungry, so I just grabbed a glazed donut from the break room and got busy going over the case files again.

My mind kept going back to the email conversation though, and I kept wondering if I was missing some connection. By the end of the day, I hadn't accomplished anything that I'd wanted to. I still had no leads. I put everything away and went out to my car. I decided to call Stephen and see how he was doing.

"Hey, sis," he answered.

"Hey, I've been worried about you."

"I'm fine. Sorry I was out of it the other day. How about I bring a pizza by, and we can catch up?"

"Sounds better than the frozen dinner that's waiting for me."

"I'll see you at your place in half an hour." He hung up.

I tossed my phone on the passenger seat and drove home. As I got off the elevator, I wasn't paying attention and ran right into Nicholas Pound. I really didn't want to deal with his bullshit tonight.

"Detective, how does it feel to live a charmed life? Getting away with murder like you have on multiple occasions?"

"I'm not talking to you." I shouldered my way past him to my door, stuck my key in the lock, and hurried inside.

"I can't believe they let you off the hook again. Are you sleeping with someone in IA?" he screamed as I slammed the door in his face.

I twisted the deadbolt lock as well as the handle lock just for good measure. As I moved deeper into my apartment, Nicholas started to bang on my door.

"Go away!" I shouted at him, coming back into the living room.

He didn't listen, just continued to hurl accusations at me as he hit my door. I was five seconds from calling it in to the station and getting patrol to do a swing-by, but then he'd probably use it to write even worse stuff about me. Luckily, that was when Stephen and Mike showed up.

"If you don't back away from my sister's door right now, Nicholas, you're going to find yourself with my fist planted in your face!" Stephen growled.

"I'd do what he says if I were you," Mike threatened.

I turned the locks and yanked open the door to see Stephen, two boxes of pizza in one hand and his other clenched in a tight fist ready to bust into Nicholas. Mike looked just as angry; his face red as he pointed toward the elevator. I wondered why he was there, but I had more important things to worry about at that moment.

"Leave," I demanded, looking at Nicholas.

"This isn't over! You can't stop the press! I will find out the truth!" He backed away, looking half-crazed.

I rolled my eyes as Stephen and Mike came in, and I slammed the door. "Thanks, I was afraid I was going to have to call patrol."

"No problem."

"Hi, Mike, didn't know you were coming." I gave him a tight smile.

"Hey, yeah, sorry, didn't mean to crash your sibling time, but Stephen said you wouldn't mind. You don't, do you?" He gave me a smile, and I supposed he thought he looked charming.

"Of course she doesn't." Stephen set the pizzas down on the kitchen counter and then pulled a bottle of gin from his jacket pocket. He got three glasses out of the cabinet.

"None for me. I'll have a soda."

"Suit yourself." He poured himself a full glass of gin. "Mike?"

"Sure, I'll have a glass. You should have let me pick up some wine for Marcy." His hand went to my lower back, and I shifted away a little.

"No, it's fine. I'd rather have a soda." I turned to look at him. "So, were you with Stephen when I called?"

"Nah, ran into him at the pizza shop. We didn't get to grab that beer the other day, so I figured I'd invite him over, and we could all catch up," Stephen answered for him.

"Yeah, I haven't gotten to hang with you guys in years. I've really missed this."

I gave him another tight smile before opening the cabinet to grab three plates. "How do you know that guy in the hall?" I asked, curious. Stephen had used Nick's name, but I couldn't recall ever mentioning it to him.

"The asshole called me at work for a quote about you when you were suspended. I told him to fuck off and leave you alone." He glared at the door. "Looks like he didn't get the message."

I sighed. "He's always like that. He thinks I'm some vigilante at best, or a murderer at worst."

"The guy is a parasite who brings nothing but misery to the world," Stephen muttered as he downed his glass of gin and poured himself another.

"Who is he?" Mike asked.

"Just some online blogger who thinks I'm a vigilante cop."

"Don't forget trigger-happy." Stephen tossed me a look, then took another swallow of his gin.

"Right." I sighed. "Let's grab some pizza and take our plates into the living room; then we can talk about something other than that jerk." I handed them each a plate, and we chose our slices before heading to the sofa and chairs. "How have you been? Did the charges get dropped?"

Stephen rolled his shoulders as he sat down on the sofa. "Yeah. Jordan dropped the charges, but warned me to stay away from him, or he'd have me charged again." He shrugged and took a bite of his pizza.

"He can't unless you hit him again, and don't get me wrong, I'd love for you to hit him again, theoretically, but I don't want you getting into trouble, especially over me."

"The guy's a douchebag."

He was getting angry again, and I didn't want that. "Yeah, but I have to work with him, so I'd rather not have you antagonizing him, if you can help it."

"Then he needs to lay off you. Let you do your job."

"Who are we talking about?" Mike asked, looking from me to Stephen. He sounded curious, but there was a look of anger in his eyes that had me shifting in my seat.

"My ex-husband. He's now a lieutenant, which puts him above me in rank." I'd never say he was my superior, even if technically he was.

"And you hit him?" Mike directed his question at Stephen.

"Because he got Marcy suspended. Didn't last though; she's already back at work." Stephen grinned. "How's it going, by the way? Got a new case?"

I nodded and set my pizza back on the plate as I prepared myself to talk about the case. Mike was already aware of St. Martin and what happened to our mom, so I wasn't worried about bringing it up. "Yeah, and... I think he's back, Stephen."

Stephen paused, his slice of pizza halfway to his mouth. "Who?"

"The Face Flayer," I whispered as if St. Martin might actually hear me talking about him.

"Marce, he's dead. He can't be back."

Mike just stared from me to Stephen as he finished off a slice of pizza.

"We don't know that he's dead. They never found his body. It's just... listen..." I told them about the case, though I knew I shouldn't. Neither of them were cops. I didn't share major details of the current case with them, but Stephen had been there twenty-six years ago. He'd seen Lemuel St. Martin murder our mother. He'd kept me safe from him. He could help me sort through my thoughts between those cases and my current ones. And Mike knew all about what happened back then too. He hadn't lived that far from us, and he'd gone to school with Stephen. They just hadn't gotten to be friends until high school.

"I don't know, Marcy. It's been twenty-six years. Maybe this guy just liked how St. Martin did things and is trying to be like him?" Mike offered.

"Yeah, maybe, but he didn't say it wasn't him when I spoke to him."

"You talked to the killer?" Stephen glanced up at me with bloodshot eyes that were filled with horror.

"He emailed me." I went on to give them a brief overview of that conversation as well.

"Damn it, I've told you not to give out your personal information. How did he find your email?" Stephen set his plate on the table with a loud clatter.

I winced. "It was on my Facebook account. I didn't even think about having it on there."

Stephen ran a hand over his weary face. "You need to make that shit private. Do it right now. And get your email address off of there. You don't have your phone number listed too, do you?"

"Uh..." I knew I did. It was just easier to have it on there for my friends to have it.

"Shit, Marce, are you trying to get yourself killed?" he exclaimed. "Give me your tablet."

"He's not wrong. There are some dangerous people on those sites," Mike added.

I handed my tablet to Stephen and told him my new password. I didn't mind him knowing it, he was my brother, but I'd have to change it again since I'd said it in front of Mike.

"Anyone want more pizza?" Mike asked as he got up.

"I'm good," I answered.

"Grab me another slice," Stephen replied without taking his eyes from my tablet. He went through and changed all my settings to private and made it so that people could only message me on there if they were already friends with me.

"What other social media do you have?" he demanded as he took another drink of his gin.

I gave him all my social media sites, and he made sure everything was set to private and that my email and phone number weren't available to anyone, even those who were friends.

"God, Marce, I thought you were smarter than this. I'm in IT, for God's sake! Do you know what kinds of things happen to people every day because they post this shit?"

He was right. I did know what happened to people because of stuff said or done online. I just never thought about it as pertaining to me since I didn't go on there very often. "Sorry, I didn't think about it."

He nodded. "Look, I don't mean to get all upset about it. This guy contacting you has me worried, but I guess a lot of serial killers like to taunt the cops investigating their crimes. He probably found out you were the one investigating and looked you up. You made it really easy for him."

"Well, you don't have to worry, our tech guys are keeping an eye on my email, and if he contacts me again, they'll try to garner his location from it while I keep him talking. At least that's the plan."

"That's good," Mike said, coming back into the room and sitting down again, this time closer to me, his plate loaded with six more slices. He set one of them on my brother's plate.

"When it's over, I want you to trash that email address and get a new one, okay?" Stephen stared at me.

"Yeah, all right. Now if only it was as easy to get rid of that reporter as it was an email address." I giggled as I attempted to shift a little away from Mike without being too obvious. "The guy knows too much about what's going on in my life."

"He's probably got a source at the police department. Most news media do, even the minor ones," Mike suggested, scooting just a bit closer to me, eating up the room between us.

"He's just a blogger. I don't even know how he makes money doing that."

"Some blogs pull in good money with ad revenue," Mike replied before stuffing half a slice in his mouth.

"I hate to say it, but when he called to get a quote, I looked up his blog," Stephen said. "He's got over a million followers."

"Seriously?" The idea that over a million people were reading about me being a vigilante cop was daunting.

"He is very focused on weeding out corruption in the LAPD. I don't know, maybe he's had run-ins with some bad cops, like the ones who investigated Mom's death." Stephen shrugged and finished off the bottle of gin.

Stephen had always had a problem with cops too; he didn't care for them and had been really upset when I had told him I was going to the police academy. He didn't speak to me for a month after I'd told him. I was certain that he still didn't understand my drive to be a detective. Mom's death had affected us both in different ways. For me, it made me want to put the bad guys away, keep people safe. Stephen, however, wanted nothing to do with law enforcement. I honestly didn't understand why he had such a problem with them.

"Maybe," I acknowledged.

Stephen started to get up, his glass in hand.

"You want to stay here tonight?" I asked, eyeing the now empty bottle he was picking up to take to the kitchen.

"Nah, I'd better not. Gotta get up early for work, and all my gear is at home." He headed for the kitchen, and I followed him. "Besides, Mike's here; you gonna offer him a place to sleep too?" He tossed the gin bottle in the recycles and set his glass in the sink.

"No."

Stephen chuckled as he opened the fridge and pulled out a beer.

"Have another slice?" I pushed the pizza box toward him. I was worried that he wasn't sober enough to drive, but he wasn't slurring his words, so he couldn't be too drunk.

"Okay." He took another piece and munched on it as we returned to the living room.

I sat down on the far side of the sofa, away from Mike. "Do you two want to watch a show with me?" I asked, hoping to keep Stephen with me longer, not just because I was hoping to make sure he was more sober, but also because I dreaded being alone. I'd even put up with Mike if I had to.

"Sure."

"Sounds good," Mike answered, once more inching his way down the cushions toward me.

"Great," I said and picked up the remote, turning on the TV. This was going to be a very long night.

21

TAUNTING A KILLER
MARCY

When I got to the station the next morning, which would normally be my day off, Captain Robinson had me open up my email. There was another message from the killer. I hadn't bothered to look at it the night before, not wanting to deal with the guy after having to deal with Nicholas and then trying to keep Stephen sober and Mike from sitting too close to me on the sofa.

Now, though, was a different story. I braced myself for what I was about to read.

My dearest Marcy,

I have been thinking a great deal about you. You witnessed your mother's death, and I wonder how that made you feel? Do you think it played a part in why you are so successful at killing? Or do you think you were born to it as I was? I've thought quite a bit about that over the years as I've followed your career. It surprised me when you chose law enforcement, but then perhaps it was a smart choice for a woman like you. You can hide in plain sight, can't you? I've also wondered if your mother's murder made you into the killer you are today or if you were always meant to be a killer.

For me, I believe I was born for it. I was created to kill these whores; it is my passion in life. I enjoy it immensely, watching the life leave their eyes... it is powerful, don't you think? Holding someone's life in your hands. There is no greater joy for me. Is it the same for you?

I have been thinking about how I can improve my kills, draw out the experience. I really want to give these whores more of what they deserve. A truly torturous death... I want to bask in the glory of my kill for longer.

Do you ever think of giving your victims a more torturous death? Like the last guy? The pervert who attacked children... he deserved a more excruciating death than a bullet to the head, don't you think?

Perhaps next time you can do that. I am sure it will bring you great joy to make them suffer. We are two peas in a pod, you and I. I look forward to the day we meet face-to-face, and you know it's me.

For now, I must go. I have to prepare for my next move in our game.

Ever yours,
FF

I was appalled. How dare he compare me to him. How dare he think that I enjoyed taking someone's life. I only acted when I had to in order to save myself or someone else. There was no joy in it.

"He seems to think he's got a real connection with you, Kendrick."

I nodded, unable to speak because if I did, I'd probably say some very inappropriate words that shouldn't be said in the workplace.

"You'd better write him back, get him talking some more. Maybe he'll let something slip if you play along."

"Sir, I'm not going to tell this psychopath that I'm like him—I'm not!"

"No, of course not, that wasn't what I meant. I meant talk to him and draw him out some more, tell him whatever you want, but keep him talking."

"Yes, sir," I huffed. I had no idea what to say to this despicable asshole, but I needed to think of something.

My mother's murder made me angry. I felt that she was stolen from me, and I was abandoned. And her murder did push me in the direction of becoming a police officer so I could put people like you behind bars for the evil things you do.

I do not take joy in having to kill anyone, and I try to de-escalate things so I don't have to. Some criminals just don't want to obey the law, and choose suicide by cop instead of going to prison. I would much prefer they rot in a six-by-nine cell for the rest of eternity as they try to get right with God.

*I am absolutely nothing like you. I don't want to torture
anyone. Every person deserves to live life how they choose
within the laws of society. Only a psychopath would
want to torture and kill women, then steal their faces.
Nobody deserves that.*

*I will catch you, and I swear I will make sure you spend
the rest of your life behind bars with no chance for parole.*

Detective Marcy Kendrick

Captain Robinson read what I wrote and then shrugged.
"I suppose taunting him like that might work. Send it."

I took a deep breath and hit send. I waited for about ten
minutes, but there was no reply, and I started to get worried
that I'd gone too far by not playing along. By speaking the
truth. I might have gotten more out of him if I had pretended
to be like him, but it went against everything I believed in.

I decided to send another; maybe I could push more and
get a rise out of him by bashing his manhood.

*Tell me, are you a coward who only preys on helpless
young women because you can't get it up unless you have
them weak and defenseless? Do you think that makes you
a man? Do you think that drugging, raping, and
murdering these women is somehow improving the world?
Who voted you to be their judge, jury, and executioner?*

I didn't bother to sign it. I also didn't wait for the captain
to read it before I hit send. I just closed my eyes and did it.
Part of me worried that I'd pissed him off, but most of me
didn't care. I was disgusted by him, and just reading his

messages made my skin crawl. I wanted to catch him and pin him to a wall like a bug. I wanted him trapped and helpless in a cage with no windows. Locked away from the rest of the world where he couldn't ever hurt anyone again.

It didn't matter if he was the original Face Flayer or someone new. I was going to catch him, and I was going to make sure he never saw the light of day again.

22

ANGEL'S PLAN OF ACTION
ANGEL

E very chance I got, I watched the news for progress on Marcy's case. It didn't seem like there had been much, nor had the media put together that the two murdered women shared a killer. For Marcy's sake, I supposed that was good. It meant there would be less hysteria and outcries for the LAPD to make an arrest quickly.

Whenever there was a serial killer on the loose, the media liked to play up the drama and stir everyone into a frenzy. Death and drama sold more ad dollars. It had been that way for as long as I could remember. The media always liked to push fear because that meant more people would tune in and stay glued to their TV or computer screens for the tiniest update.

I wish I could say that I didn't fall for it, but being stuck in this bed with nothing better to do, it was all I had to stay in the loop of what was going on when Marcy wasn't here. It was a poor substitute for being out there by her side, helping her to catch this guy.

I hated being stuck here. I was going to lose my ever-loving mind if I had to be here much longer. I was tempted to just say screw it, hire a nurse, and go home. The problem with that was that I could lose full mobility of my leg if I did, and then I'd be put on desk duty for the remainder of my career, and I really didn't want that. So here I stayed.

I was wallowing in self-pity when there was a knock at the door. I rolled my head across the pillow to look toward the door. I felt my heartbeat pick up a notch as Marcy stuck her head in.

"Hey, up for some company?" she asked, then shouldered the door open wider and held up two Styrofoam containers. "I brought food."

I smiled. "I'm always up for food that's not connected to the hospital... it's not, right? You didn't get that from the cafeteria here, did you?"

She laughed. "Now, would I do that to you?"

"Definitely."

She rolled her eyes and sat down in the chair next to my bed. She lifted the lid, placed it on the table that sat over my bed, and handed me a fork. "Chinese."

"No chopsticks?"

"Not for you." She pulled out a pair for herself. "Figured being in that bed, a fork might be a better idea."

She was probably right. I stabbed my fork into a piece of chicken and dipped it in the sweet and sour sauce. "This is great. Haven't had it in a while."

"Figured." She twirled her chopsticks around some lo mein noodles and brought them to her mouth. "Told the captain about the emails."

I glanced over at her to gauge her mood. She seemed peeved. "What happened?"

"He's got IT monitoring my email account. There was another message when I got in this morning." Her face paled a little.

"What did he say?" I asked. The guy really had me worried, and I wished for the millionth time I was out of here and back on the job so I could help her.

Marcy shook her head and looked down at her food. "He thinks I'm like him," she murmured, but her voice was off, almost as if she was fragile and going to break apart at any moment.

"You know that's not true." I reached over and touched her hand.

She looked up at me, and our gazes connected. After a moment she nodded. "I know. I told him as much. I went off, but the captain told me to send it, so I did."

"He read your reply?"

"That one he did."

"You sent another?"

She nodded again. "Yeah. Said he was a coward who couldn't get it up, basically challenged his manhood." She winced.

"Did he answer?"

"Nope."

"And you're afraid you pissed him off and pushed him to kill someone else?"

"Yep." She had a look of guilt on her face.

"Stop." I set my fork down and looked at her. "Marcy, he's going to kill again. He's not going to stop until you stop him. My worry is that he's going to come after you. I know you can handle yourself if he does, but that doesn't make me worry less." I decided to shift the conversation in a slightly different direction. "Have you gotten any leads on who this guy is?"

"No. I can't find any real connection between the two women. They had nothing in common, really, no overlap of fans that I could see, at least none that stood out. They didn't have any of the same random guys in their DMs, none of the same guys sending dick pics or rants about them being bitches, and believe me, they both had a good amount of them. Can't even believe how many men out there think women want shots of their dicks or that they'll be ready to bone them when they send them. They're insane."

I'd seen many women complaining about those kinds of guys online. I couldn't understand their thought process myself, and I was a guy. Every time I saw some woman grumbling about it, I wanted go and apologize on behalf of the male species. I didn't, but I wanted to. That was why I tended to stay offline as much as possible. It was a cesspool.

"They are," I agreed. "But none of them were the guy you're looking for."

"No."

"Maybe what you need to be doing is building a profile on the guy," I suggested.

"I don't even know if he's the original guy or some copycat. I had been leaning toward copycat, but then he didn't say he wasn't St. Martin when I asked."

"He didn't say he was though, did he?" I arched a brow at her. "You read me the conversation; as I recall, he only said, *Yes, that would include your mother,* when you asked him about her. And then he added something about her being the worst of all because she brought men home with her children there to see, right?"

"Pretty much, yeah."

"So that doesn't necessarily make him the original killer. He didn't say he killed her, only that she deserved her death."

She frowned.

"I'm not agreeing with the guy, Marcy."

Glancing up at me, she nodded. "I know."

"So one thing you know about this guy is he doesn't like men or women who harm kids."

"True."

"Did St. Martin ever mention anything like that?"

She didn't answer me for a few minutes as she sat in thought. I understood how her mind worked, and I knew she was giving my question her full attention, searching the archives of her brain for an answer. "I don't recall seeing anything pertaining to or not pertaining to kids in the original case files. Mom wasn't the only hooker with kids he killed though. There were two others, so maybe?"

"Okay. Well, you know those original cases backwards and forwards. You're going to figure him out. I have faith in you." I smiled at her.

"I'm glad one of us does." She picked up her chopsticks again and took another bite of her chicken. "Maybe I need to pull those old cases out again and do a comparison. See if that will help me draw any conclusions about this guy."

"I think that's a good idea; glad I came up with it," I teased.

She laughed. I loved hearing her laugh; it was light and feminine and warmed me.

I closed my container of food and set it aside. "How's your brother doing? Did Jordan drop the charges?"

"Yes, thank you. I'm sure he only did it because you talked to him." She sighed and put her container on the side table. "I'm still worried about Stephen. Something's going on with him, but I don't understand what. He's been drinking a lot. He actually drank more than half a bottle of gin at my place last night. And once it was gone, he drank a couple of beers."

"Did you make him stay the night with you?"

"I tried. He wouldn't. I did get him to eat more, and I made the both of them stay and watch a movie with me."

"Both?" I wondered who else had been there as jealousy spiked through me.

"His friend Mike Shepard. Stephen ran into him at the pizza parlor and invited him to hang out with us. Anyway, Stephen seemed okay when they left, and Mike promised he'd drive, but what does that mean for Stephen to be able to drink so much and not have it affect him?"

I didn't recognize the name and decided to look into him later. I set that aside and focused on her brother. "Have you talked to him about it? Maybe suggest he go talk to a counselor about his drinking?"

"No. He doesn't believe in that stuff, counselors or psychiatrists, I mean. I'm not a big fan of them either. The group home made us talk to one after Mom's murder; pretty sure that's what turned both of us off from them."

"I can understand that. Still, this is kind of different. He's hurting himself by doing it, but honestly, his drinking could harm others, too, if he's driving under the influence."

"You're right, I need to talk to him. I will." She reached over and gripped my hand. "Thanks for listening, Angel. You're a good friend."

I smiled, but inwardly I was cringing. I wanted to be more than her friend. I cared about her, more than I should, seeing as she had been married to one of my friends. But I didn't care about that anymore. Ever since my accident I'd been thinking about it, about her. I wanted her in my life. As more than my work partner. As more than a friend. I'd settle for that, for now, because I didn't think she was ready to see me as more, but the moment she was, I was going to tell her how I felt.

"I'm always here for you," I replied.

"I appreciate that." She stood up, picked up her container, and took it over to the trash. "I should probably go, let you get some rest."

"All I do is rest. Pretty much required with my leg like this." I gestured to its elevated status.

"True, but you know what I mean."

"I do." I smiled, but it faded quickly as I thought about her going back out into the world without me. "Be careful, okay?"

"I always am."

"Be extra careful now," I stressed.

She looked at me for a long minute, then nodded. "I will, Angel. I promise."

"Good."

"I'll see you later," she said, and then she was gone.

23

THE STUTTERING PROFESSOR
MARCY

At the precinct the next morning, I got to work on Angel's plan. It didn't matter that it was a Sunday; the captain had authorized me to put in as much overtime on the case as I could until we caught this guy. I pulled out everything pertaining to the original murders again, and started doing a side-by-side comparison. The first two women St. Martin killed very much resembled both Michella and Leanne, which I'd thought of before, but looking at them again, the similarities even included their body types as well, not just their general appearance of hair and eye color.

Beyond that, though, I was struggling. I might be able to figure out what kind of woman he was going to go after next, but there were thousands if not millions of women who had a similar look to St. Martin's third victim.

Feeling frustrated, I turned to the computer and typed Face Flayer into the search engine. I wanted to see what I might find online. The third topic down was a book on serial killers by an author named Professor Henry Strauss. Curious, I clicked on it, and it took me to the book's Amazon page. The book talked about several serial killers; one of the chapters focused on St. Martin.

I wondered if this professor might have some insight into my killer and be able to tell if he was a copycat or actually St. Martin. I glanced at his biography and saw that he lived here in LA and happened to teach at Cal State. That was my next search. I found his department—he taught Criminal Justice and held several master's degrees in law and criminal justice. I was able to find a school email for him and decided to contact him.

Professor Strauss,

My name is Detective Marcy Kendrick, I am a law enforcement officer here in Los Angeles, and I'm working on a case that has ties to a serial killer from twenty-six years ago. You happened to write about the case in your book, and I wondered if we could meet and discuss it as well as my current case. I look forward to hearing from you as soon as possible.

Thank you for your time,
Detective Marcy Kendrick

After sending it, I checked my personal email again to be sure that I hadn't received anything new from the killer, and seeing I hadn't, I decided to go to lunch. It was a bit early, but I was at a standstill for the moment and figured I should grab it while I could. I didn't go far, just to one of the food trucks that were usually parked about a block from the precinct.

I got a couple of tacos and a soda, then returned to my desk to eat. By the time I was finished, I had a reply from the professor.

Detective,

You have me intrigued, though I don't normally meet with people that I am not familiar with. Call it a bit of a phobia if you will. Can you tell me more of which case you are speaking about? Perhaps I can get you the information you need without you having to leave the precinct.

Professor Henry Strauss

I was curious about his phobia of meeting new people. How did that work if he was a professor? Didn't he meet new people all the time? Still, I wrote him back.

Professor,

I appreciate your candor. I'm referring to the serial killer the press named the Face Flayer. I have studied the old case files for years on him, but I need some new insights, especially with regard to my current case. That is one of the reasons I was hoping to meet with you, because I'd like you to take a look at the current case as well and give me your take on it.

Detective Marcy Kendrick

His reply came only two minutes later.

Detective,

I am very familiar with the Face Flayer case. You would not by chance be related to one of his victims, would you? Kendrick was the surname of his last victim, if I recall correctly.

As to your request to meet, I would be willing to if you come to me. If I am in a familiar setting, my phobia isn't as pronounced.

I look forward to your reply,
Professor Henry Strauss

Yes! I couldn't help but give myself a mental high five. I quickly sent him my answer so we could set up a convenient time to get together.

Professor,

As it happens, I am Nancy Kendrick's daughter. My brother and I witnessed her murder as children. That is one of the reasons I became a police officer, and also why I've studied that case.

I have no issue with coming to speak to you in a place you are comfortable in. If you would give me the time and address, I will be there.

Thank you so much,
Detective Marcy Kendrick

Within a minute, he replied with an address and asked that I come around six p.m. this evening. I replied that the time worked for me and that I'd see him then.

To prepare for the meeting, I went through all the case files again and took notes. Wrote out questions I wanted to ask, and prepped the current case files so I could show him. As I did that, I realized I probably needed the captain's permission to bring in a consultant, or at least see a consultant about the case, so I went over to his office to ask.

"Hey, Jason, is he in?"

"He just got back from a meeting with the deputy chief; let me see if he's available." Jason got up, knocked on the door, and stuck his head in. A moment later he looked at me and gestured for me to join him. "Go on in."

"Do you have a lead?" Captain Robinson asked in lieu of a greeting.

"Not exactly. I found a criminal justice professor who wrote about the Face Flayer case in one of his books on serial killers. I've contacted him because I want to get his perception of our killer."

"Like a profiler."

"Yes. Figured I'd better get your 'okay' on showing him the case files."

Robinson paused for a minute and then asked, "Who is he?"

"Professor Henry Strauss. Teaches over at Cal State."

"All right, permission granted. Write it up in the report, as he's a consultant, and make sure he knows he can't have copies of anything, nor can he write about any of this or share it with anyone."

"Of course, sir."

"When is he coming in?"

"He's got some kind of phobia and asked if I'd meet at his home."

"You sure this guy isn't our killer? He knows all about serial killers; he wants to get you alone..."

I pulled my phone out and showed him the address. "This is where I'll be. I'll make sure he knows that you are aware of where I am and who I'm with and why."

Robinson wrote the address down. "Not sure I like you going alone, but I've got nobody extra to send with you right now."

"I'll be fine, sir."

"Make sure that you are, Detective." He stood and opened the door for me.

I returned to my desk and finished prepping for the meeting. Once I had everything in order, I emailed Henry to tell him the captain knew about our meeting and that it was confidential, then left the station. I wanted to grab some dinner before meeting the professor, since I didn't know how long I'd be there.

I drove through an In and Out and headed home to eat and change. I also brushed my teeth, seeing as I'd had onion in my burger.

I didn't want to cause the professor to pass out from my onion breath. At five thirty I got back in my car and set my GPS for the professor's place. He didn't live that far from me, so it was a quick drive.

With the files in my hand, I knocked on his door about five minutes to six.

"S-serg-geant K-kendrick, c-come i-in." Professor Henry Strauss stood about a foot taller than me, had thinning black hair and bright green eyes that shone with intelligence.

"Thank you, Professor Strauss, please, call me Marcy." I

smiled as I entered his home. As I passed by him, I got a whiff of his cologne, which reminded me of an ocean breeze. It was subtle, not overwhelming. I thought it suited him nicely.

"He-henry." He gestured to a small living room off to the right of the foyer. He took a deep breath and then said, "W-would you like some t-tea?"

"That would be nice, thank you." I stood, unsure of where he wanted me to sit.

"P-please, sit on the sofa." He shook his head, and I could see he was getting frustrated. "I-I'll get the t-tea."

I did as he asked, and sat down. He returned a moment later with a whole tea service on a tray. He sat down next to me, poured tea into two china cups that sat on matching saucers.

"Sugar?" He held up a small bowl with actual sugar cubes.

"Sure, just one."

He nodded and used a small pair of tongs to add the sugar cube to my cup, stirred it with a small teaspoon, then handed it to me. He added two sugar cubes to his own cup, stirred it with his own spoon, picked it up, and took a sip.

I took a sip and sighed. The flavor was perfect; it was some sort of apple spice blend. "This is nice."

"I find tea helps to calm my nerves and allows me to relax more." His stutter had indeed calmed some, and he only tripped over a couple of words now.

"If you don't mind me asking, how do you teach with your disability?"

"I don't mind. I teach mostly online. I can t-type everything."

"The wonders of technology. I am glad that you found a

way to work around your disability." I sipped the tea again, then set it down in its saucer on the coffee table. "Can you tell me about your book, about what you learned about the Face Flayer?"

He explained what he'd learned. It was all mostly what I already knew, but then he went into his profile of St. Martin, and I learned some things I hadn't known before. St. Martin's mother had been a prostitute. He never knew his father, and when he was about twelve, his mother started abusing him.

"How did you find that out?" I asked, curious.

"Child protective services were called a number of times. He was taken from her." He got up and walked over to a desk that sat in front of the window. He picked up a stack of papers and then handed them to me.

They were copies of CPS reports. "How did you get these?"

"I was researching his background, spoke to the chief of police. He's a friend."

I understood then. He'd pulled strings and gotten special permission to dig into the backgrounds of the serial killers he was writing about. It made sense.

I asked if he believed that St. Martin was dead, and he went on at length about how that all happened and how they had attempted to find the body, but the river was not only deep, the current was rapid and could have dragged the body for miles. They weren't quick enough to get a dive team down there to find him, so it was hard to say where in the water the body actually was, though he did believe that St. Martin hadn't made it out of the water.

I still wasn't so sure, but he was an expert, and that was his opinion based on the facts. I picked up the case files and copies of the emails between myself and the killer and handed them to him. "These are the current deaths I'm investigating, and my correspondence with this killer. In comparison to the original Face Flayer, what are your thoughts?"

Henry read through them several times before looking up at me. He pointed out that the women were not the same as the sort of women that St. Martin had murdered, though judging by the emails, this killer believed they were. The problem was that if the killer was St. Martin, he wouldn't have chosen Michella and Leanne. He was very specific in his kills. He had chosen women who reminded him of his mother; these women wouldn't have done that.

"So even though my current killer claims they are whores, that isn't what St. Martin would have seen?"

Henry nodded. "He chose women who were low profile. These two were not." He gestured to the case files of Michella and Leanne. He went on to say that it looked more like the current killer was trying to mimic St. Martin because of his fascination with me. "My guess is you are his muse."

That sent a shiver of fear down my back. I rubbed my fingers across my forehead and over my eyes to ease the headache that was forming. "So what do I do? How do I find this man?"

"Keep the dialogue between you going. He is trying to impress you. His end game is different than St. Martin's was. He wants to be stopped by you, but only if you prove you are as ex-exceptional as he believes you are."

As Henry grew more comfortable around me, I noticed his stutter less and less. I wasn't sure if I just wasn't hearing it, or if he just wasn't stuttering as much. I supposed it didn't really matter except that he was comfortable in my company. And despite our topic of conversation, that made me glad.

My thoughts returned to the topic of the serial killer I was after. "I just don't want him to kill anyone else. Is there anything here that can help me identify him?"

Henry reread the emails and then said, "He seems very familiar with you. He may be someone you know." He frowned. "You need to be careful."

His words had the effect of ice water being poured over my head. Someone I knew could be the killer? Could be the one taunting me and murdering these poor women? I couldn't even wrap my mind around that idea.

"Are you all right?" Henry asked, laying a gentle hand on my wrist.

"Yes, just worried. I can't even imagine that someone I know could do something like this."

"Is there anyone close to you with knowledge of the original case?"

I nodded. "Several people, actually. My brother, his friend Mike, my friend Lindsey, my ex-husband who's now the lieutenant, my partner, Captain Robinson, a few others at the precinct."

"Any with the skills to be able to do this to someone?" He again gestured to the case files.

Shrugging, I said, "I honestly don't know. I wouldn't have thought so, but then, I never would have suspected anyone close to me as being the killer either."

Henry paused. "It could be someone who isn't necessarily close to you personally, but someone who knows you well via other means."

"There were articles written after St. Martin's supposed death that mentioned me and my brother as witnesses. And my career has been well documented by the local press too, especially in the last year or so."

"Yes, it could be someone who read about you and then started looking into your life and now feels close to you because of it."

I had to admit that suggestion made me feel better than thinking the killer might be someone I worked with or loved. There was still a little niggling feeling that it was someone closer than his last suggestion though.

The clock on the wall chimed the ten o'clock hour, and I realized I'd been there for four hours. I began to gather up my case files. "I should probably go; it's late."

"This has been nice. I don't often have such lovely company."

I smiled. He was a very kind and intelligent man, and I found him rather attractive as well. On top of that, I was comfortable in his presence, and I felt he was comfortable in mine as well. "I have enjoyed getting to know you too. And I truly appreciate your insight."

Henry smiled brightly, his eyes lighting up with pleasure. "I wouldn't mind getting together again with you."

I shook his hand and felt a comforting warmth emanating from him. "I'd like that, Henry."

We exchanged numbers, and I waved as I returned to my car. I'd felt a real connection between us, a spark. I suddenly found myself thinking about Henry on a personal basis instead of as a consultant and couldn't wipe the smile from my face as I drove home.

24

BEING TAILED
MARCY

I woke up the next morning feeling exhilarated. I felt I was making progress with the case now because Henry had given me an idea last night as I'd thought about our conversation. There were a few other men who'd been looked at as being either the actual Face Flayer or connected to him.

Of course, they'd been ruled out at the time, but they weren't fine upstanding citizens then, and I figured they weren't now either. It was possible that one of them had decided to pick up where St. Martin had left off, if he had indeed died. I just needed to dig into some of the old records and find their names so I could look up current addresses for them.

Once I reached the precinct, I caught the captain up on my consultation with Henry and then settled in at my desk to find the information I was looking for. The first man, Jonathon Kirksey, had been in and out of prison for various crimes, including rape and assault. He was currently living in West Hollywood. The second man, Billy "the squid" Caldwell, was now a boxer, but he too had done time for sexual assault and battery. His address was listed as his mother's place in Cheviot Hills.

I wrote the addresses down, gave Jason a heads-up on where I was heading in case the captain asked, and then went out to my car. I plugged the first address into my GPS and pulled out of the lot.

As I drove, I listened to the police chatter on the radio. Sometimes I liked to turn it off and listen to the radio, but not today. It was almost comforting knowing who was where and what was going on. Part of me wondered if, since the killer had been silent since my last email, another body was going to be found.

I shifted lanes, moving around a slower car, when movement in my rearview mirror caught my attention. About two cars back, a black sedan with tinted windows had also shifted lanes. Normally, I wouldn't have noticed, but something about this car in particular had my instincts kicking in.

I moved back into the lane I had been in, and a second later, the black sedan followed suit. They hadn't sped up to pass the car in front of them, just merely moved into my lane, two cars behind me. I pressed on the gas a little, putting more distance between us, then moved over three lanes. The sedan did the same but continued to stay two cars back. It was odd. I saw a gap in traffic and decided I'd weave around several cars, to see if it was just a fluke or if I really was being tailed.

Sure enough, despite the fact that I'd wound my way through four cars and back and forth between lanes, the sedan followed the exact same path I had taken. My nerves started to fray. Had the killer decided he was done playing with me and now wanted to kill me after all?

I grabbed the transmitter to my police radio and pushed the button. "Dispatch, this is Detective Kendrick, I'm on the 101 heading toward Santa Monica Boulevard, and I have a code 133, possible dangerous person tailing me. I need a code 129. Copy?"

"Copy, Detective Kendrick. Sending backup now. Patrol is en route."

"Thank you." I set the transmitter back in its holder, then pressed on the gas and shifted lanes.

The dispatcher reached out again. "Detective Kendrick, do you copy?"

"Detective Kendrick here," I answered as I kept my eyes flicking between the road in front of me and the rearview mirror.

"Patrol is requesting information on the code 133."

"Black sedan, tinted windows. Possible suspect in a couple of murders, could be armed and dangerous."

"Copy that, Detective."

There was a bit of back and forth between them and patrol as I maneuvered my car to turn off the 101 onto Beverly Boulevard. The black sedan quickly followed. I took another left onto South Vermont Avenue, all the while keeping dispatch in the loop of my location. The speed limit was lower here, so I had to be more careful. I didn't want to hit anyone, but that was why I got off the 101 in the first place, it was really busy, and I hadn't wanted anyone getting hurt.

I made a quick right turn onto West Sixth Street, and the sedan stayed with me, they didn't speed up to be right on my ass, but neither did they give up. I took another right onto North Normandie Avenue, and then I heard the sirens of patrol catching up to us.

The problem was, the guy in the black sedan heard them too, and they immediately turned left onto West Fourth Street.

"Shit." I grabbed the transmitter again. "Dispatch, tell patrol the code 133 turned left on West Fourth. I'm going to make the next left and double back, see if I can spot him."

"Copy that, Detective Kendrick."

I made an immediate left on West Third Street and then another left onto South Ardmore Avenue. I could hear patrol's sirens; they were getting louder. I made a right onto West Fourth Street, keeping my eyes open for the black sedan. I slowed my speed, looking up and down each cross street for any sign of the vehicle.

As I started past South Hobart Avenue, I saw it. "Dispatch, I have a possible location on the vehicle. I'm turning onto South Hobart Avenue."

"Copy that, Detective; patrol is right behind you."

I made an illegal U-turn on West Fourth Street and then turned right onto South Hobart Avenue. I could see the black sedan parked on the side of the road. I slowed my car and parked about a car length behind it. I pulled my weapon as patrol joined me, blocking the car in. I got out and met up with the officer who'd been sent as backup.

"Let me go first, ma'am." He drew his weapon.

"Officer Jones, I appreciate your chivalry, but this guy is dangerous. I'll be backing you up."

He gave me a nod, and we proceeded with caution toward the car. "Doesn't appear to be anyone in the vehicle, ma'am."

I could see that for myself; he didn't have to state the obvious. I looked around the area to see if anyone was watching us as Officer Jones moved to open the car door.

"Don't touch!" I started to comment, seeing he wasn't wearing gloves.

He let go of the door and held his hands up. "Do you think it might be rigged to blow?"

That thought hadn't even crossed my mind. "Not until you said that, no. But if the guy left any prints behind, I don't want to have to rule you out."

"Want me to call the bomb squad to check it out?"

"No, this guy is dangerous, but I don't think he's an expert in explosives." I sighed and reholstered my weapon. "Get crime scene out here. I want every inch of this car gone over."

"Yes, ma'am." Officer Jones headed back to his partner and called it in.

It took an hour for me to clear things with crime scene and get back on the road. They towed the car to the police impound lot, but after running the plates, we knew two things. One, the car had been stolen, and two, there were no prints in the vehicle. Not even the actual owner's. It had been thoroughly wiped down, and the guy had most likely been wearing gloves, which left me exactly nowhere.

The guy was a ghost.

I was starving by the time I reached my destination, but I knew it was still going to be a while before I ate. It wasn't like this guy was going to offer me lunch. Especially since I was there to question him about murders that he might have had a hand in twenty-six years ago.

I knocked on the door and waited, my hand resting on the butt of my gun on my hip. I didn't know if this guy was dangerous, but I would be prepared if he was.

The door cracked open, and a muscular body blocked the door. "Yeah?"

"I'm looking for Jonathon Kirksey?"

"Who's askin'?"

"Detective Marcy Kendrick, LAPD." I tapped my badge, which was attached to my belt.

"What'd you want?"

"I've got some questions about a case from twenty-six—"

"Fuck off!" he shouted as he slammed the door shut.

"Sir! I just need to ask you some questions!" I banged on the door, but he wasn't opening. I couldn't make the guy talk to me. I didn't have a reason to get a warrant or to arrest him and drag him down to the precinct to talk, which left me standing there frustrated.

Sighing, I decided to grab some lunch and try Billy Caldwell. That didn't go any better. When I reached his mother's house, she directed me to the gym where Billy worked out. I found him in the boxing ring, sparring with another guy, and had to wait twenty minutes for him to finish.

I approached him as he was taking off his gloves. "You're pretty good with your fists."

He looked me up and down and then grinned. "You lookin' for an autograph, sweet thing?"

"No." I pulled my blazer aside and tapped my badge. "I'm Detective Marcy Kendrick, and I was hoping to ask you some questions about an old case."

He narrowed his eyes at me. "You got those kinds of questions, you can send them straight to my lawyer."

"But—" I tried to keep his attention as I followed him toward a door.

"Look, lady, I ain't answerin' shit. You want to know somethin', you talk to my lawyer. We're done here. Marco! This lady's leavin'!"

A large muscular man started toward me.

I held my hands up and backed off. "Fine, have it your way. I'll be contacting your lawyer; who is he?"

"Jack Davidson." He smirked. "Good luck." He disappeared through the door.

My shoulders drooped as I turned and walked out of the gym. Jack Davidson was a shark. A very high-profile defense attorney. I wondered how Billy could even afford him, considering he lived with his mother, but then who was I to say what he spent his money on. Maybe he was into some shady shit, and he needed to have a guy like that on retainer.

I returned to the precinct and put in a call to Davidson's law office. I had to leave a message because Davidson was in court.

Sighing, I rubbed my temples. This day had not gone how I'd envisioned it, and all I really wanted to do was go home, pour myself a glass of wine and take a long hot bubble bath. But I still had two hours before my shift ended. I dove back into the case files, trying to find myself another lead to chase.

25

PLAYING WITH MARCY
KILLER

Marcy's last email had made me angry. She'd called me a coward and questioned my manhood. I'd nearly gone over there and beaten the shit out of her, but I refrained. I realized she was only saying that because she was being watched.

I knew after our first conversation that she'd taken it to the police captain. It was what she was trained to do, and she was good at her job. That was one of the things I loved about her. She was dedicated to the job. She'd do anything to keep her position so that she could continue on her quest to rid the world of those who defiled women and children. It was admirable.

I also knew she was in denial about her feelings of killing. I knew she was like me, enjoying the kill, but she couldn't say that. Not where her colleagues might read it and question her. That would be unacceptable. I should have known not to push her on it.

Still, she had needed to be punished for her harsh words toward me. That was why I decided to give her a little scare by following her yesterday. I wanted her to know that I could get to her if I really wanted to. It had been exciting watching her panic as she realized I was trailing her. I wished we'd been able to continue the game a bit longer, but her buddies in blue had been heading to intervene, and I wasn't about to let them catch me.

I'd turned down a couple of streets, parked the car, and walked away. I'd stolen the car, which had taken some doing since it had been a newer model and had an alarm, but I'd quickly shut it down. I'd made sure to use a towel with disinfectant to wipe down the entire car before getting behind the driver's seat. I'd also worn gloves, a black hoodie and sunglasses, just in case the tinting wasn't as strong as I thought it was. I didn't want her getting a look at me, nor did I want to leave any kind of DNA behind.

Everything had gone perfectly.

The car behind me honked, and I jerked from my thoughts. I flipped them off and moved through the intersection. I had a few things to pick up for my next move in my game with Marcy.

This time I had chosen the perfect whore. Her name was Kelly. I supposed it suited her. She was medium in height, about five feet seven, had dark curly hair, brown eyes, and dark skin. She was curvy in all the right places and matched Lemuel's third victim perfectly, including in occupation.

Kelly Norton was a call girl. She was perfect.

I parked my car at the big-box store and went in. I needed to pick up a throwaway phone for this project. It was going to be part of the fun for Marcy, and I was so looking forward to her reaction. I found what I was looking for, headed home, and then went to work getting everything in place.

An hour later I placed my call to Kelly's service.

"Erotic Escorts, how may I help you?"

"Yes, I'd like to request the services of Kelly Norton for this evening," I said.

"Of course, sir. Can you give me your name and where you'd like Ms. Norton to meet you?"

I did as the lady on the phone requested.

"Do you have any special requests for her?"

I gave her my requests and then hung up. Everything was set in place. Kelly was going to meet me at nine at a house in Hollywood Hills that was currently vacant. I'd found a way in through a window in the back. It had put me in the dining room, and then I'd had to hurry to the front door to reset the alarm. It was an older alarm system and easy to cut and reset.

I got my bag of fun ready to go, but tonight I wanted to pay true homage to my mentor and do things the way he'd done them. I wouldn't need my cuffs or ball gag for Kelly. She wouldn't be alive long enough for me to use them. Tonight my bag was packed with other things.

At seven, I headed out to my car and drove to Hollywood Hills. I parked several blocks away. I didn't want my car to be anywhere near the property. The estate was in a gated community, but it wasn't hard to get in when you were on foot. I'd called the guard at the gate earlier that afternoon, pretending to be Jason Bryant's assistant. Bryant was another resident here who often had visitors, from what I'd observed. I'd given the guard Kelly's name. I'd told her all she had to do was show her license and they'd let her through.

Every house had a large lawn, and there was a good acre between homes, so the likelihood of anyone hearing anything happening was probably zero. It was one of the reasons I'd chosen this area. I found the house I had prepped the day before and went in via the back door, which I'd left unlocked for myself. I knew there was a caretaker who came around twice a month, unless the house was occupied, so I'd waited until after they'd visited a few days ago before setting everything up.

Once inside, I changed my clothes. I wanted to look the part of the role I was taking on. I lit a few candles, to set the romantic scene I wanted Kelly to walk into. I wanted her guard down. I wanted her to think she was here to do the job she was hired to do. To fuck me.

She wouldn't get that chance, but I would be fucking her, she just wasn't going to enjoy it. The thought made me smile.

I waited near the front door, watching for her arrival. At two minutes to nine, her car pulled into the driveway. I stared at her as she climbed out of her car in a sparkly gold dress that barely covered her ass, and matching stilettos. She carried a gold clutch bag as she made her way to the door.

I moved back, deeper into the room, and took off the gloves I'd been wearing. I didn't want her thinking I'd been watching for her through the window in the door. She rang the bell, and I let a moment pass before returning to the foyer and opening the door.

"Mr. Br—"

I held up my hand and smiled. "No names, my dear. Come in."

"Whatever, you're the one paying." She shrugged and brushed past me into the house.

"This way." I gestured toward the living room, but didn't touch her.

Her heels click-clacked across the tile of the entryway. "This is a nice setup you've got here. I didn't know you could make this kind of money doing what you do." She smirked at me.

"Care for a glass of champagne?"

"It's your dime. If you want to get me drunk first, I don't give a fuck."

I gave her a tight smile and moved to the bar, where I had the champagne on ice. I popped the cork and poured the bubbly liquid into two glasses, then took her one.

She wrapped her fingers around the delicate crystal stem and smiled.

"Why don't you have a seat while I put on some music?"

"Whatever." She moved to the sofa and sat down.

I'd suggested it because she wouldn't be able to see what I was doing unless she turned around. "I'll just be a moment," I murmured, pulling my gloves back on.

I picked up a long silk scarf as I turned on the stereo behind the bar. I crossed the room quickly, looped the scarf around her neck, and pulled.

She immediately dropped her glass and reached for the scarf as she gasped for air.

But it was too late. I braced my foot on the back of the sofa as I pulled the scarf tight.

Hearing the clear sounds of her struggling to breathe was intoxicating. At some point she'd kicked off her heels, and her legs were now splayed open, her short dress up around her waist. She hadn't stood a chance.

I was going to miss seeing the fear in her eyes, but I wanted this kill to resemble St. Martin's completely, so I was going to follow his MO. I loosened the scarf after a couple of minutes and checked her pulse to be sure she wasn't just faking being dead. She wasn't, of course; I had done my job perfectly.

I set the scarf aside and moved around to the front of the sofa. I stared at her for a moment. She'd been an exquisite beauty. It was no wonder men paid her well for her services, but no more.

I'd probably go back to doing it my way with my next kill, but for this one, I wanted Marcy to know I was making the effort to emulate the man who'd changed her life.

I finished quickly, then got to work taking my trophy. I hummed along to the light jazz music I'd put on the stereo as I sliced away at her facial tissue. I looked at her for a little while before deciding on the best way to pose her, but finally got to work manipulating her body into the right position. Then I added the note. This time I left the same note that St. Martin always left on his whores. *Who's pretty now?* It wasn't as eloquent as I liked to be, but it would do the job I wanted it to do.

When that was done, I went through the house and wiped down the door, the bar, the ice bucket, and the stereo of any prints. Those were the only things I'd touched that could have my prints on them, at least the only things I would be leaving behind, anyway. I picked up the glass Kelly had dropped on the sofa and placed it in my bag. I drank the champagne that was in my glass and then put it and the now empty champagne bottle in the bag as well, along with the cork.

I left the music on, but blew out the candles. I didn't want the house to burn down before my work was discovered.

Everything looked perfect for when Marcy arrived.

Feeling accomplished, I pulled open the back door and left.

26

A CARETAKER'S DISCOVERY

MARCY

I woke up to the sound of Blood Sweat and Tears' "Ride Captain Ride" blaring from my phone. I rolled over and pushed to answer.

"Morning, Captain."

"Kendrick, sorry for the early wake-up call, but we've got another body."

I sat up in bed and rubbed a hand down my face. "Okay, sir. What's the address?" I grabbed the pen and notebook I kept on the side table for days like this.

He rambled off the address, and I wrote it down.

"Give me five minutes to dress, and I'll head out there."

"Patrol has the scene secured, and crime scene is en route."

"Thank you, sir." I hung up and glanced at the clock. It was barely past five thirty in the morning.

I made a quick stop in the bathroom, brushed my hair, then threw on a pair of black pants, a light blue blouse, my black blazer and my socks and shoes. I added my belt with my holster and badge, then secured my weapon to my hip. I was in my car within the five minutes I'd told the captain I'd need.

It took me seventeen minutes to get to the address in Hollywood Hills because there was very little traffic this early in the morning. I pulled up to the house and parked at the curb behind one of the cruisers. I got out and headed up to the house, noticing the coroner's van and crime scene were parked in the long driveway behind a red Toyota.

The front door was open, and an officer stood just inside the door.

"Where's the body?" I asked, pulling on some gloves.

"Just through there, ma'am." She gestured toward the living room. I didn't know the officer, but she seemed a little pale.

"If you're going to barf, take it outside," I murmured as I passed her.

"I'm okay, ma'am." Her voice followed me out of the foyer, but I was already focused on preparing myself for seeing the body.

"What do we have, Damien?"

"You're not going to like it."

"I never do. Is it our guy?"

"I think so," he said cryptically.

"What do you mean, you think? Is it, or isn't it?"

Damien stood up and brought me over to the body and positioned me to see her. "You tell me."

The woman was posed on the sofa, wearing no clothes, the fingers of one hand were inserted into her nether region, and the other was in her mouth. Her face had been removed, just like the other women. The handwritten note that was stapled to her chest read:

Who's pretty now?

I sucked in a breath and stumbled slightly. "It's him... It's St. Martin."

"We don't know that."

I swallowed hard. "Okay, tell me what you know."

"Kelly Norton, age twenty-six. According to the business card in her purse, she works for Erotic Escorts—"

"She's a call girl?" I raised my brows in surprise. That was another match to St. Martin.

"Seems like it. She was killed by strangulation, though not with hands this time, the killer used something, probably something fabric since there's no rope impression, and I don't think it was a garrote. You can see where she's clawed at her throat, trying to remove whatever it was. These other cuts were all made postmortem, and I'm fairly certain the killer had sex with her deceased body."

"This is different than the previous two women. This is exactly what St. Martin did."

Damien nodded. "I've read up on the case files since this guy started killing."

"Anything else you can tell me?"

"I've got something," Lindsey replied. "There's champagne spilled on the carpet, but no glass and no champagne anywhere in the house. There is an ice bucket on the bar that is now filled with water, so my guess is the killer handed her a glass of champagne, and she was seated here on the couch when he strangled her. That would account for the spill." She pointed to the spot on the floor.

"And I've got an impression of a footprint on the back of the sofa," Michael said as his camera flashed.

"Can we discern shoe size from it?" I asked, hopeful.

"Not really. You can see a general shape of a shoe, but it slides, so it's hard to say what size."

I sighed. It wasn't really helpful except to show how he strangled the woman. "Who found the body?"

"Ma'am?" the officer from the foyer called to me.

I turned to see her at the edge of the room. "Yes, Officer Allen?"

"My partner is outside with the woman who found her, ma'am. She lives in the neighborhood and takes care of the house for the owners."

"Okay. Do you have a name?"

"Yes, ma'am. Jennifer Sabéen. The owners of the house are—" she looked down at her notes "—Deborah and Larry Cotton."

"Thank you." I passed by her in the foyer and out through the front door to find her partner and Ms. Sabéen at the edge of the yard near the curb. "Good morning, Officer Jenkins, Ms. Sabéen, I'm Detective Kendrick. I was hoping to have a word with you?"

"Of course," Jennifer replied. She looked as though she'd spent the past hour crying. "Do you know who she is?"

"We do." I gave her a moment and then asked, "When was the last time anyone was living in the house?"

"The Cottons haven't been here for about six months. They only spend a few weeks of the year here. I come over and check on the place, dust and clean about twice a month, and just make sure it's secure."

"Okay, so what brought you over to check on the house this morning?"

"I wasn't. I mean, I wasn't coming here initially. I was out for my morning run. I start work at six, so I like to get up early and go for a run before I have to make breakfast for the family. Anyway, I was running past the house, and I noticed that car in the driveway. It doesn't belong to the Cottons, so I went to investigate. That's when I heard the music."

"What music?" I asked, curious.

"It was pretty loud, some kind of jazz." Jennifer frowned. "I let myself in since I had my keys on me, and I called out to see if Deborah or Larry were there, but then I walked in and saw... and saw..." She shook her head, and her eyes fill with tears. "Who would do something like that?"

I reached out a hand and rubbed her arm in comfort. "I don't know, but we'll find whoever did it. I'm going to leave you with Officer Jenkins here, but I'm going to need you to come to the station and give a formal statement, all right? Oh, and please don't mention the state of the young woman to anyone. We would like to keep it out of the press if we can and save the poor young woman's family from any kind of humiliation."

She nodded.

"Officer Jenkins, I'm heading back to the precinct. Dr. Black and crime scene are in charge of the scene."

"Yes, ma'am."

I climbed in my car and sighed. Visions of my mother's murder flashed before my eyes. Without even looking at the time, I pulled out my phone and dialed Stephen. It rang a couple of times, and I was just about to hang up when he finally answered.

"Uh... what?" he mumbled over the line.

"Stephen?" I frowned.

"Hmmm?"

"Are you okay?"

"Shhure... M'fine."

"It's, like, six in the morning; don't you have to go to work?"

"Whass 'at?"

I pulled my phone from my ear and stared at it as though the problem was with my phone and not my brother. "Have you been drinking?" I asked as I put the phone back to my ear.

"Ffft," he muttered and then hung up.

The last thing I needed was to be worrying about him, and now I couldn't do anything but that. I knew he'd been drinking heavily, and I'd hoped it would somehow magically go away, but of course, it hadn't. I needed to talk to him about going to see someone to get his drinking under control, but I felt like a hypocrite telling him to go to counseling. Still, I couldn't see any way out of it. I needed to do something to help him.

I couldn't do anything about it at the moment though.

At the station, I filled the captain in on the scene and then put in a call to Erotic Escorts. It was still early, and the call went to their voicemail. I left my name and number and told them it was in regard to the murder of one of their escorts and asked for the person in charge to call me. It didn't take long.

"Detective Kendrick," I answered when my desk phone rang.

"Good morning, Detective. This is Maria Consuelo. I run Erotic Escorts. You left a message for me about one of my girls having been murdered?"

"I did, I am sorry, but I wasn't sure if you would call me back if I didn't tell you why I was calling."

"You could be right, so are you saying my escort is all right, then, and this was just a way to get me to call you?"

"Oh, no, I'm afraid not. The body of Kelly Norton was found this morning in a home in Hollywood Hills. I was hoping I could speak to you about how she might have ended up there."

"Oh my God, how awful. I don't understand how this could have happened. I try to screen clients for my girls."

"So you know who the client was?"

"I'm sure I have a record of it at the office. Perhaps you could meet me there?"

"Yes, I'd be happy to; what time?"

"Can you give me an hour?"

"Sure," I agreed, "what's the address?"

She gave me an address in the Hollywood area. When I looked it up, I saw that it was a former hotel turned business offices.

I gave the captain an update, and thirty minutes later I was back in my car, driving toward Hollywood. I arrived a few minutes early and decided to try Stephen again. When I dialed, it went straight to voicemail. Thinking maybe he was on the phone, I decided to try again, but got the same result. I left him a message to call me back as soon as he could, but it did nothing to assuage the worry I was feeling.

My thoughts turned from my brother to the case, which led to thoughts of Henry, and I smiled. He was a nice man, and I suddenly realized how lonely I was. We'd exchanged numbers, but we hadn't spoken or texted each other yet. I decided to rectify that, and before I went in to meet with Maria Consuelo, I sent him a text asking how he was.

I couldn't wait for a reply though. I had a meeting with a madam to get to.

27

A SURPRISING DEVELOPMENT

MARCY

I shoved my phone in my pocket and got out of my car. I stared at the former hotel for a minute, contemplating whom I was about to go see. I had mixed feelings about talking to Maria Consuelo because I knew she was running a prostitution ring. She didn't call it that of course, but everyone knew that "escort service" was just a prettified name for what they did.

My mother had worked for a pimp too, and that was all Maria was. She sent women out to meet and have sex with clients. And we were just ignoring that fact so that we could get information on the client Kelly Norton was sent to be with. And look where that got her. It made me angry that they didn't have any safety protocols in place. Maria said she screened clients, but if that was true, then how did this killer gain access to Kelly?

I would have to ask her that. Squaring my shoulders, I marched into the building and right up to the reception counter. I gave the woman behind the desk a tight smile.

"Hello, I'm Detective Kendrick. I have a meeting with Maria Consuelo."

"Good afternoon, Detective, I'll let her know you're here. If you'll just have a seat over there." She motioned to a waiting area with a coffee table, tall plants, and a rack of magazines. There was an open bar complete with bartender. "Feel free to get a drink while you wait."

I stared at her for a moment, wondering exactly how long I was going to be sitting there waiting. My nerves were already on edge, I didn't want to sit around waiting for this woman to speak to me, but it looked like that was exactly what I was going to have to do.

Gritting my teeth, I went and sat on one of the white leather couches and picked up a magazine from the table. I flipped through it while I impatiently waited.

Five minutes later, the receptionist came over to me. "Ms. Consuelo will see you now, if you'll follow me?"

"Great." I dropped the magazine on the table and stood up.

She led me deeper into the building and down a hall on the left, then knocked on a door before opening it. "Ms. Consuelo? Detective Kendrick is here for you."

"Thank you, Janet. Send her in."

Janet stepped aside and allowed me to pass by her and enter the office, which seemed to be one of the converted hotel suites.

I headed for the woman seated behind the large cherry-wood desk and held out my hand. "Good afternoon, Ms. Consuelo, thank you for seeing me."

Maria stood, shook my hand, and smiled. "Please have a seat, Detective."

As I sat in one of the wingback soft leather chairs, Janet closed the door. Maria retook her seat.

"Can you tell me what happened to Kelly?" she asked once we were alone.

"I can't give you any details of her death specifically. I can only give you enough information to see if it matches your records. She was found in a home in Hollywood Hills, and we are certain that it was homicide, not an accidental death. What can you tell me about Kelly?" I asked, hoping to get more insight into the young woman to see why he chose her, other than the fact that she was the same race as the Face Flayer's third victim.

"Kelly is—*was* one of my most requested ladies. She was great at being whatever the client needed for the night. She went to college, so she was well educated, she could converse on many topics. The client who requested her for last night asked specifically for her, but also asked for her to give him attitude."

"What do you mean?" I wanted a clearer picture of what she was talking about.

"Janet was the one who took the call. She'd asked the same question. The client asked that she be cold and indifferent to him. Like she'd do whatever he'd asked simply because he was paying for it." Maria shrugged. "Some men want the girlfriend experience, but this client didn't want that."

"He wanted her to act like a whore," I suggested.

"I suppose. I don't like to use that term; it's degrading."

I arched a brow. "You don't think the service you provide is degrading?"

"No. It's the oldest profession, and these women provide companionship to men who need it."

"For a fee, of which you take a portion."

"True. But my girls aren't out on the street, strung out on crack or meth. All of them are clean. No drugs, no STDs. If the girls consent to have sex with the client—and trust me, there must be consent, and not all clients request that—a condom is required. We have security they can call if a client gets out of control. I don't understand why Kelly didn't lock herself in a room and call. It's what I've taught all my ladies to do. Get somewhere secure and call for assistance. Why didn't she?"

"I don't think she knew or even had time to call before her client struck," I replied. "If she had, how would your security have reached her there?"

Maria pursed her lips, and something flashed in her eyes, but I couldn't determine whether it was fear or resignation. "We have a few off-duty officers who help out occasionally. They wouldn't have had any trouble getting into the neighborhood."

I blinked and sucked in a breath. "You have cops working for you?"

"What we do isn't illegal, Detective. And as far as I am aware, these officers are allowed to work private security jobs when they aren't on duty for the city."

I set that information aside and returned to the reason I was there. "Did you find out who the client was? You said you had a record of it."

"I did say that, didn't I?" She winced.

"Are you saying you didn't get the client's name? I thought you said you screened these men."

"We do screen the clients; not all are men, by the way," she added.

"Okay, so do you have his name or not?" I was getting

extremely frustrated with her, and my words had a bit of bite to them.

"I do... it's just—" She stopped and looked as if she didn't know what to do.

"Don't make me get a court order," I seethed. I was ready to call in SWAT to raid this place and arrest them all for prostitution.

"Jordan Brasswell," she said softly.

I blinked, thinking I misheard her. "Excuse me?"

"The client was Police Lieutenant Jordan Brasswell."

I leaned back in my chair, completely appalled. It took me a couple of minutes to recover and finish questioning her. "I'm going to need everything you've got on him."

Maria nodded and pressed a button on her phone. "Janet, please bring me the client file on Jordan Brasswell. Including the phone recording."

"I'll be right there, ma'am."

I couldn't believe it. My ex-husband was the copycat killer?

I thought back over the email conversations we had and remembered he'd addressed me as my dearest and other things. Horror filled me over what he'd done. I was stunned, but then a sliver of doubt entered my mind. Jordan wasn't stupid. If he were the actual murderer, he wouldn't use his real name. This had to be the killer messing with me, right?

Janet knocked on the door and entered. She handed a file folder to Maria and then left again.

She tapped the folder. "This is everything we gather from the client when they contact us. We record the conversation for our girls' safety, and so we have a record of what they asked for in case they decide to default on payment."

"You take them to court?" I asked, wondering how the

courts would ever rule in favor of a madam. Prostitution was still illegal in California even if they called this place an escort service and had a license.

"So far, just the threat of taking them to court gets them to reconsider." She acknowledged, and then a serious look crossed her face. "Please, if he did this to Kelly, promise me the thin blue line isn't going to save him?"

I shook my head. "If he did this, he will pay for it, I promise you." My heart was racing, but I'd said that with conviction. There was no way I was going to let him get away with murdering these women if it really was him. I'd told the killer that I wanted him locked in a cage for the rest of his life, and I'd make sure that happened, whether he was Jordan or not.

I stood up, put the file folder under my arm, and shook Maria's hand. "Thank you for your cooperation. If I have any further questions, may I call you?"

"Of course, Detective." She escorted me to the door.

Back in my car, I opened the file folder and looked through it. They had a complete profile on Jordan, including that he was married to that hussy he'd cheated on me with. I had to say that they were thorough and had done their best to check out their clients, but I was ninety percent sure that whoever had hired Kelly wasn't my ex-husband. I set the file aside and drove back to the precinct. I had to take this to the captain because if it got out that Jordan's name was used by the killer, the press would have a field day.

As soon as I entered the station, Jordan was in my face.

"Give me an update on the Hollywood Hills victim. Was it the same killer? Did he leave any evidence?"

My heartbeat sped up as I brushed past him and ignored his questions.

"Kendrick, where are you going? I'm your superior officer; you can't just ignore me," Jordan blustered.

I couldn't answer him. I didn't want anyone overhearing what I had to say. I went straight to the captain's office, only stopping at Jason's desk. "Is he in?"

"Yes, but—" Jason started, but I was already moving past him to the captain's office door.

Jordan was still following me, blathering on about protocol, but I was doing my best to ignore him. I opened the captain's door and went inside with Jordan right on my heels.

Captain Robinson looked up from his computer and frowned at us. "What's the meaning of this?"

I held out the file folder. "I'm sorry to interrupt you, sir, but this is highly important. I met with Maria Consuelo of Erotic Escorts. She gave me the name of the supposed client who met with our latest victim."

Jordan stared at the file in my hand. "Why didn't you just give it to me?"

The captain took the file and opened it. A moment later he looked up at me and then to Jordan. "Close the door, Brasswell, and have a seat. You too, Kendrick."

I sat down, but moved my chair a little bit away from the one Jordan sat in. I had a feeling once he knew what was in that file, he was going to lose his shit.

The captain held the small tape cassette up and asked, "What's this?"

"Ms. Consuelo records the phone calls with clients for monetary protection purposes."

Robinson widened his eyes at that and then pushed the button on his phone to reach Jason. "I need a microcassette player."

"I'll find one, sir."

"Who's the client?" Jordan asked, looking completely confused.

I didn't say a word, but inside I was kind of smirking. Jordan was a class A asshole, and while the killer using his name was a bit juvenile, it did make me want to giggle at the trouble he was causing for Jordan. So maybe inwardly I wasn't as mature about our divorce as I should be, but I was professional enough not to show my amusement.

"Care to explain?" The captain turned the folder toward Jordan and pushed it forward across the desk for him to see.

"I don't—" Jordan's eyes widened. "I didn't kill her! I wasn't there. I swear I have never called for an escort service. This is utter bullshit, Captain. Someone is trying to frame me."

I believed him, of course. Still, it was nice to see him getting humiliated for once instead of him trying to humiliate me.

Jordan glared at me. "You set this up!"

I glared at him. He was unreal. How could he think I would do something like that? The jerk. "I did no such thing, and don't think for a minute I wasn't completely shocked to see you listed as the client. I know you like them young and stupid, but I didn't think you were that desperate."

"Enough," Captain Robinson interjected. He took the file back and looked at Jordan with disgust. "We'll soon know if this is you. If it is, you had better admit to it now because I have no problem arresting you for these murders, lieutenant or not."

"Sir, I swear that I didn't order an escort. I wasn't at that house; I don't even know where the murder took place since I haven't gotten the report yet from Kendrick."

Someone knocked on the door.

"Come in," Captain Robinson called.

Jason entered and handed the captain a small cassette player. "Here you are, sir."

"Thank you." Robinson glanced at the open door.

I followed his gaze and could see a couple of detectives peering into the office. I wondered how loud we'd actually been because they were staring at Jordan.

"Close the door on your way out, Jason," he started and then raised his voice, "and, Detectives, I suggest you get back to work!"

I watched them hurry away and knew they'd be starting rumors about what they'd overheard as Jason left, closing the door behind him. I turned back to the captain as he slid the small cassette into the player and pressed play.

"Erotic Escorts, how may I help you?"

"I'd like to request the services of Kelly Norton for this evening."

"Of course, sir. Can you give me your name and where you'd like Ms. Norton to meet you?"

"Jordan Brasswell. 523 Treasure Drive."

"Give me one moment, sir, to update the file."

"Sure."

There was a slight pause, and you could hear computer keys faintly in the background.

"Do you have any special requests for her?" the receptionist asked.

"I'd like her dressed as scantily as possible, and I want her to have an attitude."

"What do you mean by that, sir?"

"Would you like me to be blunt?"

"If you would, sir. We like our girls to give our clients the experience they are after. It helps if we know exactly what the client is wishing for their escort encounter."

"Very well. I want her to behave like a common street whore. Does that answer your question?"

"Er... yes, sir. If that is how you'd like this encounter to go, I will let Ms. Norton know of your request. She will meet you at 523 Treasure Drive at nine p.m."

"Excellent."

The call ended with a click, and the captain turned off the cassette player.

One thing was clear. The voice on the line was absolutely not Jordan, but it did sound like whoever was calling was trying to sound like him.

There was something about the tone of the caller's voice that caught my attention. It was familiar in a way, but I just couldn't place it.

"That is obviously not me." Jordan pointed at the cassette player.

"Clearly not," the captain agreed. "The question is, who would use your name and try to ruin you in such a way?"

Jordan glared at me.

"I had nothing to do with this, so don't you dare accuse me of it again." I scowled at him, but then an odd thought crossed my mind, and I turned to the captain. "Sir?"

"What is it, Detective?"

"After reading this guy's emails... would you say he's got a crush on me?" I asked, trying to align my thoughts and present them in the right way.

"Yeah, I think you could say that."

"And it's pretty well known that Jordan and I have a history."

Jordan stared at me. "What, so because he *likes* you, he's trying to humiliate me?"

I shrugged. "I'd say he accomplished that, if it was his goal."

"That's bullshit."

But I was pretty sure that Jordan knew I was right, and he was just pissed off about it.

28

CHECKING IN WITH MY CONSULTANT

MARCY

Before I left the station that evening, IT notified me that I had a new email from the killer. I logged on to read it.

My dearest Marcy,

Did you enjoy my surprise? I planned everything perfectly, just for you. I hope you enjoyed it as much as I did. I wish I could have been a fly on the wall when Lieutenant Brasswell had to answer for his "actions"! Was it as exhilarating for you as I imagine it was? I was truly hoping to please you with my offering.

Ever yours,
FF

I immediately wrote him back, asking why he'd done it. Why he'd chosen Lieutenant Brasswell of all people to implicate.

He replied swiftly.

Because Brasswell is a prick who should have kept it in his pants! He didn't deserve you!

I sat in my chair, slightly stunned by his words. Whoever this was knew that Jordan had cheated on me. It wasn't something that I'd made public.

My desk phone rang a minute later, and it was IT telling me that the guy had his IP address bouncing all over the place. They were unable to pin him down. After that, I called it a day and grabbed my things.

Once I was home, I remembered that I'd texted Henry before my meeting with Ms. Consuelo, and I pulled out my phone to see if he had replied, which he had.

> I am doing well, Marcy. How are you? How is the case going?

I sent him a quick message asking if we could meet, as I had some things to share about the case, and he said he'd be happy for me to come over at my earliest convenience. After changing out of my work attire into a pair of jeans, a T-shirt, and my tennis shoes, I headed over to his house.

"Hi," I said when he opened the door.

"Hello, Marcy."

I was surprised that he didn't stutter at all as he greeted me. He must have noticed my surprise.

"It fades the more comfortable I am with someone."

"I'm glad you are getting more comfortable with me." I felt a blush rising to my cheeks, but I wasn't ashamed of it. "I find I enjoy your company. You're smart and handsome, and you make me feel welcome."

It was his turn to blush as he gestured for me to join him in the living room again. "I made tea; would you care for some?"

"I would love a cup."

As he poured, he asked, "So something new has come up with the case?"

I nodded. "We have a third victim, and this time, it appears to have followed St. Martin's kills exactly, even down to the note that was left. The weird thing is, he used our lieutenant's name to hire the call girl."

Henry cocked his head. "The same lieutenant you were formerly married to?"

"The same."

"Interesting."

"You think so?" I hadn't even told him about the email yet. "He sent me another email afterward."

"What did he say?"

I pulled out the copy I'd printed off for him to read from the folder I'd brought. "Here's our exchange." I handed it to him.

"It's as I expected. This man is someone who is very familiar with your life and the people in it. He's fascinated by you and feels a personal connection to you. He's not only playing a game with you, but he's hoping to please you by giving you a thrilling case to investigate. I think he chose to humiliate Lieutenant Brasswell because he thinks Brasswell hurt you."

"I had a similar thought about it even before the email exchange," I agreed. "My only issue is that I didn't make it public knowledge that Jordan cheated on me. How would he have that information?"

"I cannot say for certain; only he can answer that. However, I can make a guess."

"Because he married her almost immediately."

Henry nodded. "I would make that assumption."

I sighed. "What do you make of the whole murder scene, right down to the victim being exactly as St. Martin's kills?"

"Again, I think this is someone who is using your connection to St. Martin."

"So definitely a copycat."

"I believe so, yes."

I sipped my tea and took a moment to enjoy it. "This is good, by the way."

"Thank you." He smiled and set his cup down. "I was wondering... would you like to have dinner with me sometime?"

"I would like that very much," I agreed, smiling brightly at him.

His face lit up. "Tomorrow evening, then?"

"Perfect. Here?" I hesitantly asked.

"If you're okay with that?"

"Of course."

"I am a pretty good cook," he added. There was a twinkle in his eye as he said it, and a small dimple appeared in his cheek that was rather cute.

"I'm looking forward to it." I finished my tea and set it in the saucer. "I should probably go."

He seemed a little sad at my words, but nodded. "You don't have to on my account."

I grinned. "I know. I have some errands I have to run, and I've got to be up early for work."

He stood when I did and sighed. "I understand. It is good to have company. I'm enjoying yours."

"I have enjoyed this as well. And I do appreciate your opinion on the case." I walked to the door. "I'll see you tomorrow."

"I'm looking forward to it." He opened the door for me and waved as I got in my car.

I saw him watching me from the doorway as I drove away. It was kind of nice.

29

STRANGE BEHAVIOR
MARCY

A fter leaving Henry's, I went to the grocery store. I hadn't been in a while, and I was running low on all my favorites. An hour later, after arriving home and being harassed by Nicholas, I put everything away. I had also picked up some fried chicken, mashed potatoes, and corn from the deli counter, which I had to warm up in the microwave since it had gotten cold while I was annoyed by the asshole who thought I was a vigilante cop.

While I ate, I called Angel to fill him in on what had happened with the case.

"He used Jordan's name? I bet he went ballistic," Angel commented, but I could hear the humor in his voice.

"He wasn't happy." I giggled, still enjoying the fact that he'd been somewhat humiliated. "I shouldn't laugh. A woman is dead. Three women. It's not funny."

"No, you're right." He sighed. "And it's also a little scary that the killer knows so much about you."

"Yeah, that part's not funny at all." I took a bite of my

potatoes. "And that reporter isn't helping. He keeps hounding me every time he sees me."

"Still thinks you should be kicked off the police force?"

"Yes. He doesn't care that I saved the life of a child. He just rants at me constantly. I wish he'd find someone new to bother." I took a sip of my soda. "And he's been emailing me too. I've been ignoring them, sending them straight to the trash, but still."

"I thought you made your email private on your Facebook page."

"I did. He must have seen it before I did that." I settled back into the sofa and got comfortable, tucking my feet under me as I leaned into the corner. "Stephen made me promise that as soon as this is over, I trash my email and get a new one."

"That's a good idea. How is he doing?"

"Honestly? I don't know. I should probably call him and check in."

"You haven't talked to him about his drinking yet?"

"No. I've been so caught up in the case I haven't addressed it."

"You need to, Marcy. He could hurt someone."

"You're right. I'll call him."

"Good."

"Talk to you later?"

"I'll be here. Not like I can run away," he joked.

I laughed. "True. Bye, Angel."

"See ya." He hung up.

I waited a beat and then dialed Stephen. The phone rang six times and then went to voicemail. I glanced at the clock. It was after seven; he should be home. I set the phone down and finished my meal, but began to worry that he was in a drunken stupor or passed out and going to choke on vomit like some mega rock star and die.

I called again with the same result and decided I needed to just go over there and make sure he was all right. I cleaned up my dinner, tossing the container in the trash, grabbed my keys and my purse, and left.

It took me nearly thirty minutes to get to his apartment with traffic. I tried calling him again while I drove, hoping he'd answer, but he never did. I parked in his complex's lot and walked up the stairs to his second-floor apartment. I banged on the door, but he didn't answer.

"I'm going to use my key," I warned him loudly as I banged again.

When that was met with silence, I put my key in the lock and went in. My jaw dropped at the state of the place. There were empty bottles of alcohol littering every available surface of the living room, as well as the kitchen counter. Stacks of dirty dishes filled the sink. The trash can was overflowing with glass beer bottles and takeout containers. Laundry was strewn everywhere. The entire place looked like a pigsty.

Stephen had never been a messy person. He'd always kept things neat and tidy, so to see his place like this was shocking. He was nowhere to be found though.

As I looked around, I realized I couldn't leave the place looking like this. I started bagging up all the bottles, gathered all the rest of the trash, and took it out to his dumpster. I returned to his apartment and loaded the dishwasher, then picked up his laundry and started a load. While that was going, I dusted and vacuumed the entire apartment. After that, I moved the clean clothes to the dryer. Finally, I watered his plants and fed his fish, which I was afraid hadn't eaten in days by the way they voraciously swam to the top to get the food I'd sprinkled in.

I sat on the couch and turned on the TV while I waited for his clothes to finish. I was fuming, and I hoped he'd come home so I could yell at him.

Eventually, the dryer beeped, and I was able to pull the clothes out and fold them. I took everything to his bedroom and set the piles of clean clothes on his dresser for him to put away. While I was in there, I made his bed with fresh linens and tossed the dirty ones in the laundry hamper. He could wash those.

When his apartment was back to normal, I turned the TV off and left, locking the door behind me. In the car, I called his phone again, but this time it went straight to voicemail, so I knew that he'd seen that I called. That pissed me off. I left him an irate message demanding he call me, then drove home.

I had to pass by Nicholas again, who seemed to be loitering outside the apartment building just waiting for me.

"Where have you been, Detective? Out shooting more civilians?" he ranted.

"Get bent," I muttered as I hurried past him and up to my apartment. Thankfully, he didn't follow me.

I decided to take a shower and try to relax, but right as I stepped under the water, my phone rang with Stephen's ringtone. "Son of a—" I gritted my teeth, shut off the spray of water, and grabbed a towel, tossing it around me. I picked up the phone and answered it. "You have shitty timing, but I'm glad you called. Are you okay?"

"M'fine."

"You sound weird. Where are you?"

"Sorry, sorry. I'm... I'm at a girlfriend's place. Been here a couple of days."

"Yeah? Coz I went by your place. What happened there? You let some vagrants use your apartment for a party?" I asked, tossing in some sarcasm.

"Huh?"

"Your place was trashed, Stephen. Bottles of booze everywhere, garbage strewn about, stacks of dirty dishes and clothes... what the hell is going on with you?"

"Oh."

"That's it? That's all you're going to say?"

"What do you want from me? I've been—look, I'll explain things in a few days, okay? I've just... I need a few days."

"I cleaned your place and fed your fish."

"Thanks."

"Are you sure you're okay?"

"Yeah. Look, I gotta go. I'll call you soon."

I didn't get a chance to say anything else because he hung up. Sighing, I set the phone down on the bathroom counter and restarted my shower.

I never did get to really relax that night.

30

GANG-RELATED SHOOTING

MARCY

The next morning at the station, Jordan was in a foul mood. He demanded that I find a new lead and squash the rumor floating around the detective pool that he was somehow involved in the death of the *Hooker in Hollywood Hills*, as the press had called Kelly. Of course, they didn't have details of her death, only that she'd been found in a currently unoccupied home.

I had assured him I was doing my best, but I was actually stumped. I started going through possible suspects, even wondering if Jordan was actually committing these murders and using his name and all that had been some sort of red herring, but that was ridiculous. Still, whoever this killer was, they knew me. They knew my childhood history, and they knew my history with Jordan.

There were other cops here at the precinct who were aware of what went down between me and him, and who were also aware that I'd witnessed my mom being murdered by the Face Flayer. It was possible that it could be a cop

doing these murders, but I couldn't identify anyone in particular that it might be.

Stephen's name also popped into my head, but I quickly
dismissed it. My brother had witnessed the same thing I had.
There was no way he'd pick up where St. Martin left off, nor
would he taunt me the way this killer was, nor call me "his
dearest." Sure, Stephen knew about the current cases, but I
didn't think he was capable of harming anyone, let alone
doing what this killer was doing to his victims.

Thinking of Stephen led me to consider Mike Shepard.
His apparent crush on me hadn't faded as I'd hoped. And he
knew about Jordan thanks to Stephen and me talking about
him in front of him. Maybe he'd discovered that Jordan had
married his mistress right after our divorce? Was it possible
his re-entering our lives at the time these murders started
wasn't a coincidence, but by design? Could he be the killer I
was looking for?

I did a little digging into his life, but I couldn't find
anything that would suggest that Mike was this killer. He
didn't even have so much as a parking ticket. Other than his
wife's accusations, Mike was a perfect citizen. Didn't mean
he wasn't the killer, but I figured it was unlikely.

I pulled up the case files again and sat staring at my
computer screen for what seemed like hours as the other
detectives around me were called up to go investigate. I
almost envied them. I was stuck. I didn't know where to look,
and I'd been through these case files so many times that I
knew them backwards and forwards. But the captain wanted
me focused on this case, and that was what I was doing.

So when Jordan yelled my name, I was surprised.

"What?" I looked up as he approached me, prepared for
him to start yelling at me again about finding a lead.

"I need you to investigate a convenience store shooting, just occurred, and I've got nobody else to send. Patrol is heading there now."

I didn't argue. I needed a break from all of this, so I turned my computer off, grabbed my purse and keys, and jumped up.

Jordan handed me a piece of paper with the address on it and then turned his back on me as he returned to his office.

I put the siren on my dashboard and took off. With traffic moving out of my way, I was there within ten minutes. Patrol was already there, marking off the building with police tape. There were people gathered around, watching like we were some kind of circus act there for their entertainment. I lifted the tape and went inside.

I found Officer Kim and asked, "What have we got?"

"Armed robbery. Shopkeeper took a bullet in the stomach; we're pulling surveillance tapes now."

"Anyone else injured?"

"Not that we've found. A couple of shoppers witnessed it; we've got them in the back room, giving statements."

"Okay, shopkeeper going to live?"

"I don't know, he was alive when we got here, but he'd lost a lot of blood."

"What do we know about the perp?"

"White teen, probably around eighteen, short brown hair, stocky build, face tattoo of a blue dragon. The witnesses said it covers the whole right side of his face."

That got my attention. I'd seen someone of that description standing outside the police tape. "Come with me." I gestured to Officer Kim. We stepped outside, and I scanned the crowd.

Kim started looking too, and our gazes landed on the guy I'd seen earlier right about the same time.

The boy's eyes widened, and he took a step back, then pushed through the crowd.

"Call it in!" I demanded as I started after him.

A moment later, I had three officers running along next to and behind me as we chased the guy. I watched him turn down an alley between buildings, and I drew my weapon. "Stop! LAPD!"

He didn't stop; instead he fired at us multiple times. I would swear I felt one of the bullets breeze past my face, but that was probably my imagination. I heard one of the officers behind me stumble, but I didn't have time to stop. I returned fire, so did one of the other officers.

The boy screamed and fell to the ground. "You fucker! You shot me!"

I moved toward him as he curled and rocked on the ground, holding his right shoulder. The gun he'd been holding was on the pavement next to him, and I kicked it away. "You're under arrest." I maneuvered him to his stomach and twisted his arm behind his back, then brought his injured arm back too and cuffed him while he screamed obscenities at me. I looked at the patrol officer who was with me. "Read him his rights, Officer Mendoza. Make sure he doesn't have any other weapons on him."

"Yes, ma'am."

"After that, take him to the hospital to get that wound checked, and then book him on attempted murder, assault with a deadly weapon, and assault of a police officer. He'd damn well better pray that the officer he hit doesn't die, or he'll be up for cop killing too, not just attempted murder." I seethed as I stared at the punk on the ground, who was still cussing me out.

"Yes, ma'am." Mendoza gripped the kid by the bicep and pulled him to his feet as he threatened to sue all of us.

I radioed Kim for a couple more patrol officers to join us and secure the scene for crime scene, then walked back to the entrance of the alleyway where the patrol officer was lying on the ground with the third officer hovering at his side. "How is he?"

"Hanging in there, ma'am," the officer on the ground replied with a crooked smile.

I glanced at his name. "I'm glad to hear it, Officer Braun. Where were you hit?"

"Right side, ma'am."

That was when I noticed his hands pressing on the wound. "ETA on the paramedics?" I asked the other officer, whose name I could now see was Garcia.

"They're en route, ma'am. Should be here any minute."

"Good, stay with him."

Garcia nodded.

Once the other officers arrived to block off the alley, I returned to the convenience store to confer with Officer Kim. I watched Mendoza load the kid in the back of his patrol car.

"Mendoza!" I called out before he could climb into his police cruiser. "Did you get the kid's name?"

He turned. "Dillon Youngsmith. Got his license when I patted him down looking for other weapons. Haven't run it yet though. Also have the money he stole from the shop in the robbery."

"Okay, thanks, send me the report once you've got it."

"Will do, ma'am." He nodded and got in the cruiser.

I headed back to Kim, and we finished up with the witnesses as crime scene arrived.

It was another hour before I got back to the station, and I wasn't looking forward to being confronted by Jordan for shooting another suspect. However, I was pleasantly surprised to find that not only was he already aware of what occurred, IA had already ruled it a clean shoot.

"You aren't going to yell at me?" I asked in shock.

"Not this time," Jordan said. "Officer Braun is going to be fine; the bullet was a through and through, missed all the vital organs."

"Glad to hear it."

"Mendoza sent the report over on the shooter. He's got a long rap sheet. He's part of that new gang that formed last year over on the westside, the Blue Dragons."

"Explains the tattoo." I shook my head. "What about the shopkeeper?"

"They got him into surgery, and he's expected to recover."

"Good."

"You look exhausted, Kendrick. Go home."

He wasn't wrong. It had been a very long day already, but I was looking forward to my date with Henry, and if Jordan wanted to send me home half an hour early, I wasn't going to complain.

"Okay." I checked my desk to be sure everything about the case was still put away and locked up in my desk; then I headed home.

As soon as I entered the building, Nicholas was there with questions. "What happened today? Did you shoot another innocent man?"

I didn't dignify that with an answer. The man was

absurd. None of the people I'd shot were innocent. They'd all been in the act of committing a crime. Including this one.

"What did he do wrong besides run from you when you went after him? Witnesses say he was just standing in the crowd."

I slammed my door in his face and ignored his shouting in the hallway. I turned on the stereo to drown him out and went into my bedroom to strip off my work clothes. Since I had time, I decided to take a bath and then get ready for my date.

When I got out and toweled off, I went to my closet and chose a knee-length red dress with an A-line skirt and a sweetheart neckline. I paired it with a pair of low black heels. Since I couldn't use my holster, I switched my purse to a black one with a conceal-carry pocket. I tossed all my necessities into it and then went into the bathroom to run a brush through my shoulder-length brown hair. I added a little eyeshadow to make the blue of my eyes brighter and a little gloss to my lips.

I turned the stereo off and listened for a moment to see if Nicholas had finally left, and when I didn't hear him ranting in the hallway, I headed out. I wasn't that lucky though because he was back outside, standing about three feet from my car.

"Where are you going looking like that, Detective?" he demanded as if I owed him an answer. "Some party where they award you for how many civilians you shoot?"

I gritted my teeth and ignored him as I climbed in my vehicle. As I pulled out of the lot, I noticed that he was right behind me in his own car. I pressed on the gas and changed lanes, leaving him several cars behind me. I made a quick left turn, then an immediate right. I didn't want him following me all the way to Henry's house. I didn't want him bothering us.

I glanced in the rearview and didn't see him, at least none of the cars behind me looked like his in the twilight of the evening, but it was hard to tell with headlights shining back at me.

I was a nervous wreck by the time I pulled into Henry's driveway and rushed to the door.

31

KISSING THE PROFESSOR
MARCY

"I'm sorry I'm late," I said as Henry opened the door. I looked back over my shoulder to be sure Nicholas wasn't in the vicinity. The last thing I needed was him showing up here.

"Is everything all right?" Henry drew me into the house and closed the door.

"It is now." I sighed. "This idiotic reporter who runs this awful blog has been following me and hounding me with ridiculous questions."

"He followed you?"

I shrugged. "He tried. I'm pretty sure I lost him on the way here. The guy is just really annoying. He thinks I'm this horrible cop who randomly kills suspects."

"Why would he think that?" Henry looked confused.

"I've had more than my fair share of uncooperative suspects in the last year, and I have had to defend myself and others. Same thing happened today. Suspect fired on me and three patrol officers, one of the officers was hit, but he'll be okay. I returned fire and struck the suspect in the shoulder.

Pound must have heard about it because he accused me of shooting innocent civilians. It's just so tiring having to rebut his awful accusations."

"Sounds like you've had a trying day." Henry gave me a sympathetic smile. "Would you like a glass of wine?"

"I would love one," I answered as we moved through the living room and into the kitchen.

Henry pulled the cork from the bottle and poured two glasses of wine, then handed one to me. "Dinner is nearly ready. I hope you like salmon?"

"I do. It smells great."

He smiled and pulled the pan from the oven. "I have the table set in the dining room."

"Need any help?" I asked.

"No, I'll be right there." He began fixing two plates. "Go on in."

I did as he asked, and sat down at the small dining room table that had a pretty blue cloth on it. There was also a candelabra in the center that was lit, and the flames danced at the tips of the candles.

A moment later, Henry set a plate in front of me with salmon, long grain and wild rice, and whole cooked carrots. "This is lovely, Henry."

He set his own plate down, then returned to the kitchen for his wine before sitting across from me. "Thank you."

"How was your day?" I asked, considering he already knew how mine had gone.

"I got some writing done on a new book. I'm covering a few other killers in this one."

"Is it hard to study them and their lives?" I asked as I ate. The salmon had a lemon and dill flavor to it and was really good.

"I do find it difficult at times. Their minds are so disturbed that sometimes it is hard to continue." He tilted his head and gazed at me with curiosity. "What about you though? You actually have to interact with these types of people. How do you handle it?"

I set my fork down and considered how to answer. "Ever since my mother's death, I have had this drive to keep people safe. To make sure that what happened to her doesn't happen to anyone else. I know I can't stop evil people from starting what they do, but I can put a stop to them as soon as I catch them, if that makes sense?"

"It does." He nodded and lifted his glass of wine for a sip. As he set it back down, he asked, "What was your childhood like?"

"It wasn't awful, as some might imagine. I never knew my father, but Mom was always there for me and Stephen. She called me her princess, and I never felt like I was missing out on anything. Stephen is older than me, and I always thought he was her favorite, though."

"Why?"

I pursed my lips as I considered my reasons. "At the time I hadn't thought it fair that he got things I didn't. Looking back, I think it wasn't that she considered him her favorite, but more that he was older, and he took on more responsibilities, so she rewarded that."

He nodded. "It is good you can look back and see it that way."

"Her death was really hard on my brother. He rarely talks about it."

"He witnessed it too, didn't he?"

"Yes. I honestly think he saved my life that night. He kept me safe and hidden from St. Martin. If he hadn't been there,

I would have rushed out to try to help Mom. I know he would have killed me too."

"How old were you?" he asked as he finished his plate.

"Ten. Stephen was fourteen."

"Did a relative take you in after that?"

"No, we were put in a group home." I looked down at my plate and pushed some of the rice around with my fork. "At least we were together until he turned eighteen."

"What did he do then?"

"He got into college. He went into computer technology and works for an IT firm now."

"Impressive."

Thoughts of my last phone call with Stephen floated through my mind, but I pushed them aside and refocused on Henry. "How about you? What was your childhood like?"

"My parents were well off, so they got me the best education their money could buy. I was homeschooled by a private tutor. Graduated early and got into Berkeley. I have always loved learning."

"I would think you'd have to, considering all the research you have to do." I grinned at him.

He picked up his wineglass and looked at me. "Would you like more?"

"Sure, not a lot though, I still have to drive home."

"Let's take this into the living room, then."

I agreed and picked up my plate and glass, carrying them into the kitchen. I set the plate in the sink and held my glass out for him to refill. We walked together into the living room and sat down on the sofa close to each other.

Henry stretched an arm across the back cushions, and I leaned into him. It felt nice. I liked the smell of his cologne; it was the same one from before and reminded me of the ocean. I set my glass down and got a little more comfortable.

We chatted for a while longer about our childhoods and his research, just getting to know one another. I very much enjoyed the way his mind worked. He was an intriguing man.

"Marcy," he murmured as he played with the tips of my hair.

"Yes?" I looked up at him.

"May I kiss you?"

I bit my lip slightly. I'd been hoping he'd ask. I nodded and slid a little closer.

He wrapped his arm around my shoulders, drawing me to him. He moved hesitantly, as if he was unsure, and then gently pressed his lips to mine.

I slid my hand up his chest and to his neck, my fingers toying with the hair brushing his collar. I moved my lips beneath his, extending the kiss. I liked the feeling of warmth that spread through me as we continued kissing, finding a rhythm with one another. He tasted of the wine and something that was uniquely him.

Eventually, he broke the kiss and leaned back into the couch, a smile on his lips.

I felt a blush creeping up my neck as I reached for the wineglass that I'd set on the coffee table. "That was nice," I murmured.

"I'd like to see you again," Henry whispered into my hair as he pulled me closer.

My smile widened. "I'd like that too."

He kissed me again, but this time he didn't extend it. "You look sleepy."

"It has been a long day. I think it's caught up to me."

He smiled and tucked a piece of hair behind my ear. "I like having you here, but I'm guessing you're going to have to go home."

"Unfortunately," I agreed, wrinkling my nose.

"I'd ask you to stay—" he started.

I shook my head. "I wouldn't. Not on a first date."

"I didn't think you would." He grinned.

I picked up my wineglass and finished the small amount of liquid still in it, then stood. Henry stood too, and we took our glasses into the kitchen, and I picked up my purse. "I should go."

He walked me to the door, gave me another kiss, and said, "Drive safely, and text me when you get home."

It was nice to have someone who cared like that. "I will." I moved from the stoop and down his walkway toward my car. I wasn't paying a whole lot of attention, but there was something off about the way my car was sitting in the driveway.

As I got closer, I noticed that the driver's side front tire was flat. Not only was it flat; it had a knife sticking out of it.

32

KILLING EVIL
MARCY

"What's wrong?" Henry called from his doorway.

"Someone slashed my tire," I replied. I was absolutely livid. I couldn't even wrap my head around why someone would do this, or even who it might be.

"What?" Henry joined me in the driveway. He looked at the tire in surprise. "Why would they do that?"

"I don't know. Probably some kid doing it for fun." I sighed. "Well, the joke's on them. I'm going to take this straight to the precinct. Can you help me change the tire?"

Henry nodded and started to reach for the knife.

"No! Don't touch it. It might have prints on it."

"Oh, didn't think of that."

I opened the trunk and started to get the jack out along with the spare.

"Let me." Henry reached in and hefted them both out.

"Thank you, Henry."

He smiled. "You look too beautiful to be doing this. Don't want to ruin your dress."

I blushed and tucked a piece of my hair behind my right ear. "You're right, I'm not exactly dressed for changing tires. Still, I'll help."

He made quick work of getting the tire off and setting it in the trunk for me with the knife up, and then replacing it with the spare. He returned the jack to the trunk and shut it. "I'd kiss you again, but my hands are a bit messy."

I didn't care. I put my hands on his chest and leaned into his lips, kissing him. "Thank you. I'm going to swing by the station to report this, then head home."

"Please be careful."

"I will." I got in my car and waved as I pulled out of the driveway.

At the station, I found the desk sergeant and said, "Hi, Mack, I need to file a report."

Mack was short for Phil Mackenzie, who had worked the desk since before I'd hired on with the LAPD.

"What's happened?" he asked.

I told him about the tire with the knife.

"Was this at your apartment complex? You could have had patrol come out and take a look."

"No, I was on a date."

"That explains the dress. You look nice."

"Thanks."

"So where's the tire now? You didn't change it yourself, did you?"

"No, my date helped. It's in the trunk."

He looked past me and called out, "Curtis, Lopez, take Detective Kendrick's keys and get the vandalized tire from her trunk, would you?"

I held my keys out to them.

"Sure thing."

"Don't touch the knife handle, I want to see if they left prints behind."

Curtis nodded.

"They left the knife behind? Who hates you so much they'd want you to know your tire was slashed by a knife?"

I shrugged. "That, I don't know."

"We'll get everything squared away and get you on your way in a jiffy, Marcy. Don't you worry," Mack said as the two officers went to take care of the tire for me.

"Thanks, Mack."

When that was done, I headed home. I sent Henry a quick text letting him know I'd made it back safely.

I changed my dress for a pair of shorts and a T-shirt, then climbed into bed with my tablet. I read a couple of chapters and then turned out the light, snuggling into my blankets. Despite how sleepy I was, I couldn't drift off. My mind was too wired thinking about the case and who this killer could be.

Unable to sleep, I turned the light back on and picked up my tablet. Maybe if I got my thoughts out, my questions asked, maybe then I'd be able to sleep. With that in mind, I started a new email to the killer.

Who are you really? You seem to know me, to know my life, are you someone I've met? Why are you doing this? What is your end goal? What is driving you to kill these women?

Detective Marcy Kendrick

He probably wouldn't answer me, at least not right away considering it was late, but at least I got my questions down.

It was the part about him knowing so much about me that really bothered me. The fact that I might actually know him. Might have worked with him. Spent time with him. Considered him a friend... it hurt my heart to think that I'd so misjudged someone in my life that they could do this sort of thing to another human being.

I was surprised when my email chimed. Drawing in a sharp breath, I opened it.

My dearest Marcy,

I do what I do because these women are evil. Like your mother. How well did you actually know her?

You were a child, but you didn't see her, didn't see beyond the fact that she was your caregiver. She was a truly evil monster. She hurt people. She used people. She was a vile and evil whore who needed to be put down. And you should be thanking Lemuel St. Martin for freeing you from her evil clutches. How you have not come to that conclusion yourself is appalling. I am hopeful that you will soon understand what I mean.

We are the same, you and I, my darling. We both kill evil where we see it. We are cut from the same cloth and meant to be joined as one, but until you can see that for yourself, our game shall continue, my beloved.

Ever yours,
FF

I stared at his words, not comprehending them at first.

He wrote as if he actually knew my mother, but if he wasn't St. Martin, as he seemed to be implying in this email, then how would he have known her to draw any of those conclusions? Could I be wrong? Could this be some former client of my mom's? Someone who knew about her, about the Face Flayer and about me and Stephen? Could they have just lost their mind and picked up where he left off?

It had been twenty-six years. If one of mom's old clients was still around, why would they choose now to do this? It didn't make sense. So if it wasn't one of her former clients, then who?

I set that aside and refocused on the rest of his email. The part where he spoke about us being the same. About killing evil. Did he really believe that? That these women he'd been murdering were evil? And why did he think I was the same? We weren't. I didn't set out to kill anyone. I stopped evil, yes, but I didn't want them dead. I wanted them behind bars. Sometimes I had to kill, but that didn't mean I enjoyed it. It didn't mean that I sought out their deaths.

I was protecting the lives of the innocent.

Frustrated, I shut down my tablet and turned the light off again.

I only wished I could turn my thoughts off as easily.

33

LEANING ON HENRY

MARCY

Being a Saturday, I was only on call at the precinct since the captain said I needed to take some time off. Meaning if there wasn't a murder connected to my ongoing cases that I was called in for, I had the weekend off. At least technically. It didn't mean I shut down my investigation for the weekend. I couldn't do that since it pretty much ruled my thoughts.

I hadn't slept well after that last email exchange with the copycat killer. I kept chasing ideas of who the perp might be in my mind. I knew there was something there, something I should be seeing, but I wasn't. I wondered if maybe I was too close to it, and a fresh set of eyes might be able to pick out what it was that I was missing.

With that in mind, I printed out this latest exchange, added it to the others, and texted Henry. I asked if he was available to go over the case with me again. I smiled when I got his reply, stating that he'd be happy to have me come over and that he would hold lunch for me.

Feeling a little more relaxed, I grabbed my purse and keys, along with the file, and drove over to his place.

A little while later, I was knocking on Henry's door, and he greeted me with a kiss. I felt relaxed and comfortable being at his place. It was like a weight had been lifted, and I was able to breathe a little more freely. It was a nice change.

"I'm making hamburgers, is that all right?" he asked.

"Sounds perfect." I smiled and set my purse and the file down. "Can I help?"

He nodded, and together we got the patties made, the fries in the oven, and then he took the burgers out to the grill. I'd grabbed a couple of bottles of light beer from the fridge and handed him one as he got the burgers cooking. Being with him felt natural, domestic, and really nice. I could see a future with him despite the fact that we'd only had one date.

Once the burgers and fries were done, we sat down at the table in the backyard and ate in the sunshine. His yard was surrounded by a fence, so it was private, and I didn't have to worry about any reporters shouting questions at me. Despite the privacy, I still felt as though I was being watched. It was an uncomfortable feeling, but I couldn't see anyone in a window, or outside the fenced area moving around spying on us, so I dismissed the feeling and just enjoyed the afternoon.

We talked about our interests and just enjoyed getting to know one another a little bit better. We found that we both enjoyed the same kinds of movies and foods, and we both loved animals, specifically dogs. I had always wanted one, but didn't have time for one because of my job. Henry had previously had a dog, but she'd died six months ago, and he hadn't had the heart to find a new pet yet.

"I'm sorry, how old was Lana?" I asked.

"Sixteen. She developed a cancerous tumor that was inoperable. I miss her."

"I can understand that." I reached a hand over to him, and he threaded his fingers with mine.

I scooted a little closer, and he smiled. We talked a bit more; he shared a few stories about Lana and how much she used to love running around the yard and playing. It was nice to talk about other things than the case that was consuming my life, but I knew I'd be bringing it up soon.

So, after we ate, when we returned to the kitchen, I picked up the file. "So, I had another email exchange with him last night." I handed him the newest page.

Henry read it and then said, "Can I see the others again?"

I handed him the whole file, and we sat down at the kitchen table. He got up once to get a pad of paper and a pen. He then read through them several times, making notes. That was one of the things I really liked about Henry. He put a lot of thought into the profiles he created on these killers. He was very thorough.

After about thirty minutes, he said, "His question here... and the statements he makes... I have to wonder if he actually knew your mother. Did she have any enemies? Or anyone who hated her?"

I thought about it for a minute. "I don't think so. But I was ten, so I didn't know anything about her life other than the fact that she would bring guys around all the time and that they gave her money after spending time with her. She didn't fight with any of them while I was home, except for St. Martin the night he killed her." I frowned. "Stephen might know more; should I call him?"

"Not yet." He studied the emails and the rest of the case

file. He wrote a few more things down, looked at the photos of the notes the killer had left on the bodies, and then back to the emails. "Maybe he's projecting?"

"What do you mean?" I asked.

"Perhaps, like St. Martin, his mother was a prostitute and she abused him. Perhaps, because your mother was a hooker, this killer is equating her with his own mother, with St. Martin's mother. That could be why he's chosen to emulate St. Martin in his killings and why he's latched onto you. He feels a connection with you because your mothers were similar, and he sees you both as being like St. Martin."

His words made sense, in a way. It would mean that the killer was making assumptions about my mom, but in his own world that was what women who were prostitutes did to their children. My mom hadn't abused us; she'd never raised a hand to either me or Stephen. And she'd certainly never tried to do anything sexual to me, nor had I ever seen her do it to Stephen.

So maybe the killer was only guessing based on his own experiences. That made me feel a bit better. Maybe it was just some guy who had learned about me and my connection to St. Martin. That didn't help me identify who he was, but at least I didn't have to suspect the people I knew.

Henry and I spoke about the case a little more, and then we set it aside to do more pleasant things. We made some popcorn and watched a movie, then he asked me to stay for dinner, and one thing led to another, and I soon found myself in his bed.

Falling into bed with a guy so quickly was not normal for me. However, Henry made it feel natural.

"Are you all right?" he asked after we finished making love.

I turned my head on the pillow and gave him a smile. "I'm great. You?"

The concerned look on his face turned to a happy smile, and a twinkle lit his eye. "I'm great too. That was... amazing," he murmured, kissing my temple.

I snuggled into his side and lifted my face to his. "It was. We'll have to do it again sometime."

"Definitely." He wrapped his arms around me and held me close. "Do you have to leave?"

I shook my head against his shoulder. "I can stay if you'd like me to." I tilted my head so I could look into his eyes.

"I'd very much like you to stay." He tipped his lips down to mine, and we kissed again.

Eventually we both drifted off to sleep, and for the first time in months, I didn't have a single nightmare.

34

DIRTY OLD MAN
KILLER

After my last kill, I was riding high. Kelly had been the perfect homage to my mentor, and now that I had replicated his kill so perfectly, I felt I could take things a step further and improve upon his legacy. I wanted to establish myself as being as good as or maybe even better than St. Martin. I wanted these evil whores to know and fear me as they did him.

With that in mind, I searched for a new playing piece that would be a worthy kill for my darling Marcy to investigate. I was torn between a couple of whores. Of course, they would all die by my hand; it was just a matter of what order they would die in. I wanted to make it interesting for Marcy.

As I thought about pleasing my beloved, I wondered what she was doing. She'd surprised me with an email the other night, and I'd responded; however, she hadn't answered my questions. I knew she was in denial about who she was, and that bothered me. I wondered why she couldn't see that we were the same. We both rid this world of evildoers. Granted, she didn't take trophies yet, but if I gave her enough time, I was sure that she would see that she was worthy of doing so. I wondered what she would choose for her trophy. Would it be a body part? No, Marcy would more likely take something that meant something to her kills, perhaps some sort of memorabilia of theirs.

The unfortunate part about my trophies was, if I wasn't careful, they would deteriorate. So I'd found the perfect spot many years ago to preserve and hang mine so that I could enjoy them. My first trophies were there as well, the animal kills I'd made and learned to preserve. I liked to relive each kill as I looked at them hanging on the walls of my secret place. It wasn't too far from my apartment, but it was in an area unlikely to be investigated, as it was a bit hard to get to, which had been its selling point for me. I wished I could show it off to Marcy, but at the moment she wouldn't be accepting of it. She needed time.

My thoughts continually turned to her, and I decided I needed to see her. I had put a tracking device on the under-side of her car shortly before starting our game so that I would know where she was. I pulled up the app I used to track her, and it seemed she was visiting the professor again. I didn't find that odd; she had gone to him for advice about me, of that I was sure. He was a local expert on serial killers in general, so I assumed he would attempt to help her.

I decided I'd have a look in on the two of them and see if they were any closer to discovering who I was. I doubted they would, but it might be fun to see their efforts. I parked the car I was using about two blocks away and walked the remainder of the way.

It was just after one in the afternoon by the time I arrived. The house had several bushes under the front windows that would make a good spot to hide in so I could peer into the house, but right now, with it being daylight, I didn't want any of the neighbors to see me and call the police. I decided to have a look in the back, and moved around the side of the house. The backyard had a tall fence surrounding it, but that wasn't what caught my attention. It was the fact that my Marcy and this so-called expert were in the backyard, sitting close together.

I found it absurd that she would even consider this guy as someone worthy of her attention. I squatted down and peered through the slits of the fence. My blood boiled as the man leaned in and kissed her. She belonged to me and shouldn't be kissing that desperate old man. I wanted to jump the fence and beat the shit out of him, but I decided to bide my time and watch them.

Soon they returned inside. I found the back gate, and I was easily able to get past the lock. I crept up to the house and peered in the window. I could see them inside. My Marcy seated on the couch, her head on his shoulder. Anger filled every ounce of my being.

As the day moved into night, and Marcy didn't leave, I got even more angry. And then they moved to the bedroom, and I watched through the bedroom window as that dirty old man defiled her.

I didn't know how Marcy could stand for that creep to touch her. I wanted to rip him limb from limb, but that would have to wait.

I clenched my fists as I left the yard and returned to my car. I needed my tools, my bag of fun, before I returned to that disgusting place. I sat in my car, watching the tracker I'd put on her vehicle. The longer she stayed, the more irate I got.

Finally, around seven the next morning, I saw the tracker

begin to move. She was leaving. I put my gloves on, grabbed my bag, and headed back to the dirty old man's house.

I was not going to let him steal Marcy from me. I would take my revenge.

When I was done with him, Marcy would know that she was mine and that this was what she had to look forward to if she ever allowed another man to have her.

That didn't mean that I wasn't going to punish her too. I would take everything from her, and she would know that I was the only one she could rely on.

The only one who cared for her.

The only one she could be with.

Forever.

She belonged to me.

I would have her.

And soon.

35

A MISSING LIEUTENANT
MARCY

After spending an amazing night with Henry, I felt incredibly relaxed and happy. I still had the case to work on, but I wasn't focused on it right then. Instead, I was going to the hospital to spend some time with Angel. He had just a few more days before he would be moved to the rehab facility, and he was getting antsy.

I stopped at Bob's BBQ before heading over there, and picked up a couple of barbeque beef brisket sandwiches for us. I planned to spend most of the afternoon with him, playing gin rummy, and I wanted to make sure he was in a good mood.

I knocked on the door and poked my head in. "Hey, I brought barbeque; you hungry?"

"I'm always hungry." He chuckled as he waved me in. "I thought you'd never get here."

"Sorry, I took a nap when I got home and then had to clean my apartment." I grinned as I set his container of sandwiches on the tray table.

"Oh yeah, how was your date?" he asked.

A strange look was in his eye, and if I didn't know better, I would have said his question had a little bit of a bite to it. As though he was jealous, but I knew that couldn't be the case since we weren't like that. Sure, we cared about each other, and there was an attraction there, but we'd never acted on it, and I doubted we ever would.

"It was great. We had a really nice dinner Friday night, then I went back over on Saturday to talk about the case, but we ended up spending the day together." I felt a blush creeping up my neck, and I turned so I wouldn't have to look him in the eye.

"Just the day?"

I huffed. He knew me too well. "Maybe more than that."

He didn't say anything, just gave me a look and folded his arms across his chest.

"Fine, I got home this morning. I've had an amazing weekend so far; are you happy now?" I flounced down into the chair next to his bed.

Angel sighed and looked at the food on the tray table. "You're happy?" He glanced over to me, his gaze connecting with mine.

"I am. He's a great guy."

He smiled. "Then I'm happy for you."

"Thank you." I reached for his hand and squeezed it.

"So how come you aren't over there today?" he asked as he picked up his sandwich.

"He's got a Zoom meeting with his editor this afternoon. I'm planning to see him for dinner though." I could not stop the smile that widened on my lips.

"I am glad for you, Marcy."

He stared into my eyes, and I felt he understood how much I needed to have someone in my life and that we both knew it couldn't be him. Not in that way. There were too many roadblocks in our way. First and foremost being his friendship with Jordan.

I reached into my purse and pulled out the cards. "You ready for me to kick your ass at rummy?"

"Never going to happen, Kendrick. I'm undefeated." He grinned.

We were deep into our game, with him beating me just slightly, when my phone rang. I was still on call, and I wondered if the killer had found another girl because I recognized the ringtone.

"It's the captain," I said as I pulled my phone from my pocket. "Hey, Captain, what's up?"

"Thank God. Where are you?" he said, relief sounding in his voice.

"I'm at the hospital with Angel, we're playing rummy, and he's beating me for the moment, why? What's going on?" I asked, suddenly concerned.

"I don't know how to tell you this..."

"Sir? You're scaring me. What's the matter?"

"We got a call about a deceased male. I sent Hummel and Vance. It's the professor you were consulting with."

"What? I don't understand." A sob formed in my throat, and tears began to pool in my eyes. "Are you saying that Henry is dead?"

"Yes. And I'm afraid he's been murdered by our copycat."

I screamed and dropped the phone because I was shaking so badly. I'd been so happy, and now my whole world had been ripped apart. I felt like someone had just reached into my chest and crushed my heart.

"Marcy, oh my God, what's going on?" Angel asked as he reached for me. "Damn leg," he muttered as he tried to shift in the bed to get to me.

I just stood there, screaming and crying.

A nurse came rushing into the room. "What's going on? Are you all right, Mr. Reyes? Why is she screaming?"

"He's gone..." I mumbled. "The Face Flayer took him from me." My mind was spinning. I couldn't believe it. Just hours ago, I'd been in Henry's arms, loving him. And now he was gone. Murdered. Henry had been a good man. He didn't deserve this.

"Who?" one of the other nurses asked.

"Marcy." Angel reached a hand to me, and I barely recall lifting my arm to him. His fingers grasped mine, and he tugged me closer. He pulled me into his embrace and held me as I cried.

"Should I get a doctor?" the nurse murmured.

I felt Angel shake his head. "She'll be okay; she's just had a shock. Can you hand me her phone? She dropped it when she got the news."

She retrieved my phone and handed it to him.

"Hello?" the captain's voice sounded from my phone.

"Sir? It's Reyes. Yes, she's a bit in shock," Angel said into the phone. "I'll tell her, sir. It's probably going to be a little while though. I don't know that she'd be capable of driving at the moment."

I sniffled and felt my sobs subsiding. I couldn't allow this copycat killer to break me. Henry had been taken from me by this psycho who imagined himself as some sort of Face Flayer fan. It wasn't fair, but then when was life ever fair? I needed to pull myself together and catch this fucker. I needed to be strong so I could put the bastard behind bars where he belonged. I wanted him to pay dearly for those young women and Henry. I wasn't going to stop until I found him.

After a few minutes I lifted my face from Angel's shoulder and wiped my eyes. "Thank you," I murmured.

Angel was like my rock. My protector. He always had my back, and I would always have his. I was glad I'd been with him when I got the news; otherwise I'd have been alone. I was still shaking a bit and realized I was half sitting on Angel's bed as he held me. He had to be uncomfortable crunched up around me like that. I moved, dropping back into the chair next to the bed.

"I'm sorry about your friend," Angel said softly, still holding my hand.

I sniffled again and felt more tears pooling, but I dashed them away quickly. I wasn't going to succumb to another crying jag. I didn't have time for it. I would mourn more after I caught this psychopath. "Thank you," I replied.

"The captain needs you to come to the station. There's something about the manner of death that the captain needs you to take a look at."

"Okay." I made no move to get up. If I stayed right here for another few minutes, then I could pretend that everything was going to be all right.

"Marcy?"

I nodded. "I just need another minute, Angel."

"Damn it, I wish I could get out of here and help you." He slapped the bed next to his hip.

I glanced up at him and squeezed the fingers of the hand I was still holding. "I wish you could too." I took a deep breath and stood. "I'm going to go."

"You okay to drive?"

"Yeah. I'll be okay." I wasn't at all confident in my reply, but I was determined to push on.

"Call me later, or better yet, come by," Angel urged, not letting go of my hand.

I didn't want to let go either. He was like my lifeline. As long as I was holding on to him, I was going to be okay. I wasn't going to lose myself. The problem was I couldn't take him with me. I had to go on my own.

"It's going to be okay, Detective. You can do this." Angel held my hand tight as he stared into my eyes. "You're going to find him and put him behind bars for what he's done."

I swallowed hard, breathing through my nose as I tried to settle myself. I gave him a sharp nod. His words helped me strengthen my resolve. To shore me up so I could finish this. I could break down later. Right now, I had a job to do.

I let go of his hand, and I didn't feel as though I was going to float away on a cloud of grief. I leaned down and kissed his cheek. "Thank you," I whispered before standing back up.

"Always." Angel watched me as I gathered my things and said, "I mean it. Call me or come by, I don't care how late."

"I will." I hurried from the hospital, hopped in my car, and drove to the precinct.

"Kendrick, my office," the captain said the moment he saw me. "Hummel, Vance, join us."

I didn't bother to stop at my desk and drop off my purse. I didn't know if I'd be staying at the station, and I wanted my stuff with me. It was like some kind of assurance that everything would be okay as long as I didn't let go of it. The logical part of my brain knew that wasn't true, but I wasn't operating on logic at the moment.

"Have a seat, Kendrick."

I did as he asked, but I still didn't say anything. I had a million questions, but I couldn't make any of them come out of my mouth.

"I'm going to warn you, Marcy, this death isn't like the others." He stopped and frowned, then went on. "Well, it is, but it's much more brutal. And I think, judging by the way you broke down over the phone, that you and the professor had gotten close?"

"Yes, sir," I whispered and looked down at my hands in my lap. "Henry is—*was* a wonderful man."

"Think you can stand to see the photographs?"

"I want to see them, sir."

"Hummel?" The captain looked at him.

Hummel and Vance were both standing awkwardly in the doorway.

Hummel opened the file and handed me a couple of photos. "I'm sorry, Kendrick."

I took them hesitantly, closing my eyes to steel myself for what I was about to see. When I looked down at Henry's mutilated body, I gasped. The captain was right. This was much more violent, more brutal than what he'd done previously. Henry's chest was covered in stab wounds, and his face was missing, but it was worse than that. The muscle tissue and everything had been ripped from his face as well, and the bone was visible in many places. He hadn't taken his time to remove Henry's face. On top of all of that, Henry's body had been dressed in women's lingerie. A red lace bra was strapped across his mutilated chest, and a matching thong hugged his hips.

I bit my lip to keep from releasing the anguish I felt upon seeing him like this. I took a few calming breaths as I looked through the photos. When I was done scrutinizing them, I handed them back to Hummel and turned to the captain. "Was there a note?"

He nodded reluctantly. "Hummel?"

I turned back to Hummel and watched him shift things in the file.

"You're not going to like it," Vance murmured in a gruff voice.

I grimaced. "I don't like any of his notes, Vance. I don't know why this one would be any different."

"I know, but... this is different," he muttered and looked up at the ceiling.

Hummel handed me the photo of the note, and my eyes widened at the words on it.

I told you. You belong to me, my beloved Detective Marcy.

I started to shake again; the photo slipped from my fingers. It was my fault that Henry was dead. It was my fault that this psycho had murdered him. I'd put him in harm's way by being with him. My thoughts immediately turned to Angel, and I jumped up. "Oh my God, Angel, what if he goes after him?" I couldn't lose him too.

The captain quickly assured me, "We've already thought of that. We sent a detail over to the hospital to keep an eye on him."

I took a steadying breath. "Okay." I breathed some more, trying to calm my racing heart. "So what now, Captain?" I needed a direction. Normally, I would know what to do, but the last two hours had thrown me off my game.

"IT informed me just before you arrived that you received a new email. They tried to track it from the incoming IP address, but it pinged back to a coffee shop, and by the time patrol got there, the shop was closed. They don't think the guy was even there. He's somehow figured out how to manipulate his IP address."

"He's done that before, I think." I rubbed my forehead as if that could make me recall things more accurately. "At least he's done something similar."

"Go see if this asshole has given you any clues on how to find him," the captain ordered.

"Yes, sir." I went to my desk and put my purse on the floor by my feet as I sat down. I turned on my computer and pulled up my email. By the time I clicked on the email, Captain Robinson, Hummel and Vance were hovering around me.

My dearest Marcy,

How did you enjoy my present? I wasn't sure about how I wrapped him, but I think he came out perfectly, don't you? I don't enjoy killing men like this, but he touched you. He touched what is mine. And in case I haven't made that perfectly clear to you by now, I don't share. I will destroy any man who even thinks lewd thoughts about you, my darling. In retrospect, there is another that I have been meaning to take care of for having had the nerve to hurt you. I know you still care about him, but that will go away in time, once I destroy him as well.

I promise you, my love, no other man is worthy of you, and I will make sure to take my vengeance out on anyone who has tried to be with you in the past and any who even think of being with you in the future.

Ever yours,
FF

I was appalled by his words. I knew that he'd killed Henry out of jealousy, but to call him a present and say that he'd wrapped him? The man was sick.

"What does he mean about the retrospect part?" Vance questioned.

I reread the line and drew in a sharp breath. "He's talking about Jordan." I looked up at the captain. "Sir, is the lieutenant here?"

Robinson slowly shook his head. "I haven't seen him today. Hummel? Vance? Have you seen Lieutenant Brasswell today?"

"No, sir. It's a Sunday; wouldn't he be home?" Hummel asked.

"He was scheduled to be on shift today," Robinson replied. "I'm going to check with Robbery. Kendrick, call his house. Hummel, call his cell. Vance, call the academy and see if he's there working with the recruits."

"Yes, sir."

We all got busy making our calls. I dialed his house number, hoping he would answer instead of the hussy who stole him from me.

"Brasswell residence."

I sighed. "Hi, Katie, it's Marcy; is Jordan there? It's important."

"No, and even if he was, he wouldn't want to talk to you," she spat.

I gritted my teeth and tried to get through to her. "Do you know where he is? When I say this is important, I mean it's police business. This isn't a personal call."

"Whatever. He left for work this morning around eight. He was only going to work until noon, but he hasn't gotten back yet."

"You're sure that he was coming into work?"

"Of course he was. He wouldn't lie to me."

I wasn't so sure about that, but the captain had said he was scheduled to come in, and Jordan didn't shirk his duty ever. "I wasn't implying that. We'll see if we can find him here. If he comes home, have him phone the captain immediately."

"Fine, whatever." She hung up.

I hopped up and jogged over to the captain's office. I didn't even stop to talk to Jason, and Jason didn't seem too worried about that either. I supposed he knew we were all in a panic over Jordan.

"Sir?" I said as I poked my head in the door. "He's not at home."

He got up from his desk and joined me in the doorway. "He's not down in Robbery either." He looked across the room. "Anything, Hummel?"

"No answer on his cell, sir. I've left a couple of voicemails telling him it's urgent."

"Vance?"

"He's not been at the academy, sir, and he wasn't expected today."

"Sir, the killer has him," I shared my thoughts.

"Email him back, see if he'll confirm it."

"Yes, sir."

I shot off back to my desk and hit reply on the email.

Did you kidnap my ex-husband? Is he still alive? Please don't hurt him!

I didn't bother to sign it; he knew who I was.

As I waited to hear back, I thought about who this guy could be. All the emails of him using endearments, his murdering Henry... I had to wonder if maybe Mike was the killer. He'd had a crush on me years ago that had apparently never gone away; was it possible he was an obsessive psychopath? Could he be the one doing this?

My email dinged with a reply.

I'm doing this for your own good, my dearest. These men defiled you, and to make you clean again, they cannot exist. You are everything to me, and I will not let another moment go by where this scum can still walk the earth. I love you. Remember that.

Ever yours,
FF

"Sir!" I shouted, alerting the captain. "The killer has him!"

Even as I said that, his words played through my mind, and I had an eerie thought. What if the endearments weren't meant in a romantic nature? What if they were meant in a familial way? Was it possible that Stephen was behind all of this? He hated Jordan. He hated what Jordan had done to me. For a long time, Stephen and I only had each other, he was everything to me, and I was everything to him... was it possible that whatever was causing him to drink so heavily had turned his mind so badly that he'd started murdering women like the man who had murdered our mother?

I shook my head, trying to drive that insane thought from my mind. No. Stephen wouldn't do that, would he?

A small part of me was terrified that he would, and I was terribly afraid to find out that it might be the truth.

36

TERRIFYING THOUGHTS

MARCY

"I'm calling everyone in," Captain Robinson said as he started toward his office, but then a moment later he paused and turned back to me. "I know this is your case, but you've been through a lot today. I need you rested. Go home. Everyone else will search the streets for Brasswell."

"But, sir—" I started to protest.

"No, Kendrick. You're not going to be any help here. And I don't want you alone either, so go over to the hospital and stay with Reyes. We've got officers keeping an eye on things there."

I knew there was no arguing with him. "Yes, sir." I grabbed my purse from the floor in a huff. I wasn't going to the hospital though. I was too worried that Stephen was tied up in all of this, and I had to go make sure that he was okay.

As I climbed into my car, I dialed Stephen's number. It rang several times and then went to voicemail. I continued to call his phone as I drove over to his apartment. I hadn't been here in a few days, and I hoped that he was there and just ignoring my calls.

I parked in the lot and went up the steps. I couldn't hear any noise coming from inside his apartment, so I knocked. There was no answer. I banged on the door and called his name.

Ryan, his next-door neighbor, opened his door. "He hasn't been home in more than a week."

I glanced over at him. "Are you sure?"

"Yeah, pretty sure. Saw you over here a few days ago, but haven't seen Stephen."

"Okay, thanks." I gave him a tight smile, then pulled out my keys. I opened the door and went inside. Everything was exactly how I had left it when I'd been here. His laundry was still stacked on his dresser, the dishes I'd put in the dishwasher were still there. The only conclusion I could make was that he'd not been home at all.

I looked around the apartment once more, thinking maybe I'd missed something, but I hadn't. I quickly fed his fish again; the poor things were going to die if he didn't return soon.

Then I had another terrifying thought. Maybe Stephen would never return because he was the killer, and he was either going to be arrested, or he was going to die.

I still couldn't fully believe that he was the killer, that he would murder people and say he was doing it for me... but it made sense in a sick sort of way. I didn't want it to be true. I prayed that it wasn't.

I made one more round through the apartment and called Stephen one more time, but again got no answer. With a sigh, I let myself out, locking the door behind me.

When I reached my car, my phone rang with Stephen's ringtone.

"Oh, thank God, where are you?" I asked as I opened my car door.

"Marcy?" a muffled voice came across the line.

"Wait? Jordan?"

"... boxcar... bottom... ravine—" His words sounded far away and broken up.

"I don't understand, you're in a boxcar?"

"At... canyon."

"I'll find you!" I shouted. "Just don't hang up!" I had no idea where he was or why he had Stephen's phone, but I was glad he was okay.

A thought occurred to me. "Is Stephen with you?"

"Wh—!" he shouted. "Wh... sk... at?"

"I can't make out what you're saying," I said.

The phone went dead.

"No! Damn it!" I tried calling back, but it went straight to voicemail again. "Stephen! What canyon are you and Jordan in? I couldn't hear him! You two need to call me back!"

Again, my mind played through everything the killer had written to me, and then Jordan's call from Stephen's phone. Add that to Stephen's strange behavior, his hatred of Jordan, and his weeklong absence from his apartment, and I feared the worst. That my brother, my own flesh and blood, was the killer I was after. I wanted to cry. I wanted to scream. I wanted to make him pay for what he'd done. I couldn't believe that he had turned into a monster like St. Martin, but maybe watching Mom's murder had messed with his mind more than he'd let on, and he'd had some sort of psychotic break.

If it was him, I could only hope that he wouldn't make me kill him.

"Please don't make me do it, Stephen." I sent that wish up to the heavens as I stood staring at his apartment building.

37

MAKE A WOMAN OUT OF YOU YET
MARCY

I'd been staring at Stephen's apartment building without seeing the area around it. But then it dawned on me what I was really looking at.

The building overlooked a canyon. It was one of the reasons Stephen had chosen to live here, because he'd be able to go climbing anytime he wanted, being so close to the huge ravine. He had always said that climbing kept him in shape.

I started to run toward the back of the building to get a better look, but realized I needed to be higher up so I could view the whole thing. I needed to see if there was a train car in there. I knew the chasm had been caused by an earthquake years ago, and that at one time there had been train tracks that had traversed the area. There was still a portion of them on the road that ended at the edge of the ravine.

Instead of going to the edge of the canyon, I headed for the building stairs. I climbed all the way to the third floor and went around to the back so I could look out over the canyon. I wasn't wrong. About forty feet down there was an old train car perched on a few boulders. It had been left behind after the quake because they couldn't be bothered to pull it out.

I had to get down to the bottom of that ravine and stop my brother from killing Jordan.

I wondered if Stephen had used his climbing equipment to get Jordan down there. I rushed back down the steps to the second floor and around to his apartment. I slammed open the door, ran to his bedroom closet, and started digging. I found the rigging at the bottom behind a pile of shoes.

"Yes!" I muttered as I dragged it out. Holding everything tightly to my chest, I hurried out of the apartment, not bothering to lock the door.

I quickly stepped into the harness, tightening it, then secured the rope to a lamppost near the edge of the ravine. I'd done some climbing with Stephen before, but I'd never enjoyed it the way he did. Still, I recalled exactly what I needed to do, and I rappelled down the canyon, using my feet to push off the canyon wall and hop my way down to the bottom.

Once I was on the ground, I unhooked the harness and pulled my gun. I wasn't going to take any chances. I did an area search all around the boxcar, which seemed much larger than it had from the third-floor balcony of the apartment building. I didn't find anyone hiding out in the rocky terrain around the boxcar.

I circled the car again, looking to find the best way in; then I noticed it had a sliding door. I was afraid of what I would find on the other side, but I knew I had to go in. I pushed the door partially open and stood with my back to it.

When nobody tried to shoot at me, I rolled my shoulder against the door and pointed my gun into the interior. "LAPD!"

"Marcy?"

"Jordan, where are you?" I called into the dark boxcar. "Are you alone?"

"Yeah, he's not here. I'm on the floor." His words were slightly slurred.

I pushed the door open wider to let in more light. As I did, I noticed the car was filled with animal hides and tannery equipment. The floor had spills of blood, which I hoped belonged to the animals, but as I looked around the walls of the boxcar, I noticed what looked to be the three women's faces framed and hanging on a wall of their own.

"You just going to stand there, or are you going to help me?" Jordan asked.

I forced myself to look away from the wall and to Jordan. He was tied to a chair, lying on his side on the floor, his face beaten and cut. His left eye was swollen shut, and his right was barely open. "Hell, what did he do to you?" I holstered my weapon, then rushed over to him and started untying him.

"I stopped for a coffee, and the next thing I knew, I was here, having my face pummeled," Jordan muttered through his busted lip. "He kept saying he was going to make a woman out of me. The guy is completely off his rocker." He bent down and picked up the phone.

"I don't understand why my brother would do this," I murmured.

"Your brother?" Jordan questioned.

"Isn't he the one who did this? You called me from his phone." I nodded to the one in his hand, but then stopped and stared at it. "Wait... I don't..." I took it from him and looked at it. "This isn't Stephen's." The phone looked familiar, but at the moment I couldn't figure out why. It was an older silver android phone. Stephen's phone was a newer model black iPhone, and he kept it in a black and red marbled case.

"Pretty sure it belongs to the asshole who kidnapped me, not your brother. Why would you think Stephen did this?" Jordan looked at me like I was crazy.

"I'll explain later," I muttered, relieved that I wasn't going to have to arrest my brother. "We need to get you out of here and call in crime scene."

Jordan nodded. He looked exhausted.

"How did you get his phone in the first place?" I asked.

"He set it down on the table there. He said he had to get something and for me not to move. I hopped the chair over to the table, knocked the phone to the floor, and used my nose to dial your number. I couldn't believe it was unlocked and I was able to get the call through."

"Why did it come up as Stephen calling me?"

"I don't know."

"We'll see what IT can make of it."

I helped him out of the boxcar since he was still unsteady on his feet. We made it over to the rope, and I put on the harness, then looped the rope around his waist too and pulled it tight. We began the long climb up the ravine, and by the time we reached the top, my thighs and arms were burning.

As Jordan caught his breath, I called it in.

"Sir, I've found Jordan, he's taken a beating, but he'll be okay. Also, we need crime scene here ASAP." I explained about the boxcar and what I'd seen.

I examined the phone again, which I probably should have bagged immediately, but it had already been contaminated with Jordan's and then my prints.

It suddenly occurred to me where I'd seen the phone. "Sir, I know who the copycat killer is."

38

AND THE CHASE IS ON
MARCY

"Who's the copycat killer, Kendrick? We'll get an APB out on them immediately."

"He's a blogger named Nicholas Pound, he writes a cop watch blog, and he's obsessed with me killing suspects." I couldn't believe he'd never even crossed my mind as being a suspect, but when I noticed the stickers on the back of the phone, it had all clicked into place. "He lives in my building."

"Marcy," Jordan called, "there he is! He's getting into that black sedan."

"Sir, we've got him, send backup." I hung up as Jordan ran over to me. I tossed him the keys to my car and got in the passenger side. I could have driven, but I didn't want to argue with him.

I tossed the siren onto the dash and turned it on.

Nick tore out of the parking lot and down the street.

"Hurry up!" I shouted. "He's getting away."

Jordan started the car. "Seatbelt!" Jordan said, not moving the car as he glared at me.

"For the love of Pete, just go!" I growled as I pulled my seatbelt on. Only Jordan would be worried about seatbelt laws at a time like this!

As soon as it clicked in place, he pulled out of the parking spot and gave chase.

"He just went left on Ventura," I directed as I grabbed my police radio.

"I know." Jordan focused on the road as he navigated through traffic that was set on ignoring our siren.

I called dispatch. "This is Detective Kendrick; we've got a code 133, possibly dangerous person, requesting backup on Ventura Boulevard, heading toward Vineland."

"Copy that, Detective, code 129; backup is on their way."

"He's taking Vineland." I pointed as Nick's car sped past numerous cars. "Speed up, Jordan. You're going to lose him."

"I'm already pressing sixty."

"We're in a fucking police vehicle, the siren is on, go!"

Horns blared as Jordan aggressively maneuvered between cars. I prayed that no pedestrians or bike riders decided to play chicken with us.

Jordan growled and pressed the gas. The car jumped forward as he increased the speed.

I quickly relayed our new direction to dispatch and then had an idea. I pulled out my phone and looked up Nick's cop watch blog. He'd posted about me earlier that morning, going on another rant about what a bad cop I was and that I needed to be barred from the police force. It was full of inaccurate information and straight-up lies about what I'd done, how I'd acted at the convenience store shooting.

I couldn't wrap my head around the idea that he'd written all this garbage about me, but then emailed me saying he admired me. It didn't add up. In whose mind did it make sense? Certainly not mine. Of course, given what he'd done to those women, he was a psychopath, so I supposed that it all made sense in his own head somehow.

I scrolled down to the bottom of his website and found what I was looking for. His tip line.

I decided to call. I knew there was a chance that it would just ring the phone Jordan had found, but maybe not. Maybe he had a second phone; either way, it was worth a shot.

The phone rang for a moment, and then he answered.

"Darling, now isn't a good time," he said.

I could hear his tires screeching as he swerved his car onto Moorpark Street. "Nick, you have to stop; we'll get you help—"

He laughed. "I'm afraid that's not going to work, love. I'm not going to prison."

The way he spoke was much different than how he sounded when he was hounding me with questions. He sounded more refined, like he was some kind of scholar. No matter how he sounded, I called him out on what he'd done. Not just to those women but to Henry too.

"You've murdered people. Three women and Professor Strauss. You knew going to prison would be the outcome. I told you as much in that email."

"Ah, the dirty old man, yes, he had to go." He chuckled, then added, "Honestly, I had hoped for a different sort of outcome, darling, one more beneficial to us both."

His description of Henry hurt my heart. As to the rest of what he'd said, I didn't know if he meant me killing him, which wasn't an option; or if he meant that he hoped the two of us would end up together, which was absurd because that was never going to happen in this lifetime or the next. Either way, I wasn't going to engage with him on either of those things.

Instead, I attempted to get more answers from him. "What I don't understand is why mimic the Face Flayer. What connection do you have to him?"

"I had hoped we'd have more time to play our game, my love. I was really looking forward to taking the trash out of your life. I suppose that isn't going to happen now. Perhaps one day you'll understand how much I love you. Goodbye, my dearest Marcy." He hung up.

"Oh my God!" I screamed as I watched Nick's car take the corner onto Clybourne too fast, and he slid off the road and straight into a tree.

By this time Jordan was going about ninety, and when he slammed on the brakes, the car skidded and hit a car on the side of the road, and we spun into the oncoming lane of traffic.

My head hit the glass of the side window, and my world went black.

39

THE KILLER'S LIFE REVEALED
MARCY

I groaned as I reached a hand to my head. My vision was blurred, and my head was pounding with the worst migraine. I looked at my fingers, which had streaks of blood on them. "Ugh... Jordan?" I questioned; my voice sounded slightly slurred to my ears. "You okay?"

Jordan grunted, and his arm brushed mine as he fumbled for the seatbelt release. "No, can you get out?"

Glancing over at him, I could see blood streaking down his face from where the busted window had cut him. The airbags had deployed, but he'd somehow popped them both, so now they were deflated in our laps. I then noticed the pocketknife in his left hand.

I was still dazed, and it took me a couple of minutes to recall what had been happening prior to the crash. "Shit! Nick—where is he?" I looked through the shattered glass of the windshield, but it was so spiderwebbed that I couldn't make out anything.

Jordan pointed through his open window. "Can you get out?" he asked again.

I nodded and released my seatbelt. My door took a minute to open, and made a lot of noise as I pushed on it, but I was able to climb out. Jordan coughed and struggled with his door, but I didn't wait for him. I needed to get to Nick and make sure he didn't get away.

I stumbled as I ran, drawing my gun from my hip. "LAPD!" I shouted, hoping the bystanders who were watching all of this unfold would get the hell out of the area.

I could hear police sirens in the distance and hoped they were heading to us. Ahead of me, Nick was half in his car and half out, his torso lying on the ground as he dragged himself from the crunched vehicle.

"LAPD, stay down!" I shouted at him as he started to rise. My vision was doubled, so it was like there were two of him moving.

He didn't listen and began to get up.

"Freeze, Nick!" I ordered, but he started moving away from me. I fired off a shot toward the ground. I knew I wasn't going to be able to hit him with my vision as fucked up as it was, and I didn't want my shot hitting anyone else, so I made sure to keep it toward the dirt, which splattered upward upon the bullet's impact.

It was effective because Nick stopped moving, and I tackled him, shoving him face-first into the ground. He didn't make a move to try to push me off him, nor did he try to take my gun. He just lay there beneath me, breathing heavily.

I holstered my weapon as I straddled his back, then pulled his arms behind him. "Nicholas Pound, you're under arrest for the murders of Michella Graves, Leanne Williams, Kelly Norton, and Professor Henry Strauss and the kidnapping and attempted murder of a police officer, Lieutenant

Jordan Brasswell. You have the right to remain silent. Anything you do or say will be held against you in a court of law. You have a right to an attorney. If you cannot afford an attorney, one will be assigned to you. Do you understand these rights as I have said them to you?"

Jordan arrived and tossed me a pair of cuffs.

I latched them onto Nick's wrists, then got up.

Jordan dragged him to his feet.

Nick groaned. "I don't understand what's going on. What happened to me?"

His voice had changed again. It wasn't the refined-sounding man on the phone, nor was it the asshole reporter voice he used when he shouted questions at me. Now he sounded like a kid, someone way younger than his middle-aged self.

Patrol showed up along with a couple of ambulances, and Jordan said, "You need to get checked out. I'll get him seen and into custody."

"But—" I started to protest.

"Go, Marcy; you've got a bad head wound that needs looking at."

"So do you." I stared at him.

"I'm fine; go."

I wanted to roll my eyes, but my whole face hurt, and my head felt like it was going to fall off. I made my way over to one of the paramedics.

He immediately helped me into the ambulance. "Ma'am, we're going to transport you to the hospital for some X-rays. Pretty sure you're badly concussed."

I was seeing black spots, and my vision was still really blurry, so I wasn't going to argue.

"Just lie down here." He guided me back onto the gurney

and pulled the straps over me, securing me to the bed. "It's safety protocol, ma'am. We'll be at the hospital in just a bit."

I closed my eyes, but he quickly shook my shoulder, and I blinked at his two heads. "What?"

"Don't go to sleep, ma'am. I'm going to need you to stay awake."

I tried. I really did. But my eyes refused to obey orders. I came to again in a hospital room. My vision wasn't as bad, at least I wasn't seeing two of everything, but there were still a few floating spots whenever I tried to focus on something.

"I see you're back with us, Detective."

I turned my head slightly and noticed a man in a white coat next to my bed. I assumed he was my attending doctor. "How long was I out?"

"About an hour. I'm Dr. West. We were starting to get worried. Your CT scan showed a slight fracture of the skull, but it will heal with time. We've bandaged your head wound and cleaned the cuts to your arms from the window glass. You've got a bad concussion, and we're going to keep you here for a while."

I started to nod, but then thought better of it, as my head was still pounding. "Okay," I said with a wince.

"I imagine your head feels like someone is banging on it with a hammer?"

"Yes."

"I can give you something for the pain; we wanted to wait until you were conscious before administering anything. Now that you are, and you're coherent, I think we can make you more comfortable."

"Thank you."

He turned to the nurse and gestured for her to give me the shot she had been preparing while he and I spoke. "Now,

I'd like to keep you here overnight for observation. I don't want you turning on the TV, looking at your phone or any kind of computer screen for the next two weeks. Keep your activity to a minimum. Right now, if you want to sleep, that's fine, but we'll be waking you every two hours to check on you. After the next twenty-four hours, if you feel like sleeping, then do so. Sleep will help your brain recover from the injury."

"Okay." I gave him a semblance of a smile that was barely more than a slight curve of my lips upward. It hurt too much to do more than that. "Did Jordan Brasswell come in?" I asked, wondering if they were keeping him here for observation as well.

"Not as far as I am aware."

I frowned. "Can I make a phone call?"

"As long as you aren't staring at your phone, looking at media and the like, that's fine."

I glanced to my right and saw both my weapon and my phone on the tray table. "Can either of you push that to me?"

"Oh, sorry, I'll get it." The nurse scurried around the bed. "I'm Ada. I'll be your nurse while you're here. If you need anything, just hit this button and I'll be right here."

"Thanks." I grabbed my phone.

"I'll be in to check on you again soon, Detective."

"Thank you, Doctor," I acknowledged as he left.

Nurse Ada followed him out, and I dialed Jordan's number. Unfortunately, it went straight to voicemail. Frustrated, I dialed the precinct and reached Jason.

"Jason, it's Kendrick; is the captain in?"

"Detective, what are you doing calling in? You're supposed to be in the hospital," he replied.

"I am in the hospital. Is the captain in?"

"No, 'fraid not, he's with the deputy chief. They're about to give a briefing to the news about the capture of Nicholas Pound. Good work on that, by the way."

"Thanks," I muttered. "Is Jordan—I mean Lieutenant Brasswell there?"

"No, he's with Captain Robinson and the deputy chief."

I pursed my lips and bit back a curse. "Great. Would you tell them to call me ASAP?"

"Will do. You get some rest, now, okay?"

"Sure. Thanks." I hung up. It was completely frustrating to me that not only was I stuck here, I couldn't watch the press conference because of the concussion, and on top of that, I had to wait to know what happened after I'd left. All the work I'd done on the case, and I wasn't going to get to close it.

A knock sounded on the door, and I looked up. "Come in," I called.

Angel shouldered open the door. "Thought you might like a visitor?"

"Angel!" I smiled. "What are you doing out of bed?"

He swung into the room on crutches. "I leave for the rehab facility tomorrow, so they decided I could start moving around on crutches for short periods of time."

"It's good to see you up and around."

"I hear you found Jordan and solved the case." He stayed standing with his weight on the crutches and his other leg.

"I did." I pressed my lips together and then admitted, "I thought maybe it was Mike at first, but then after Jordan called, I thought it had to be Stephen." I glanced at him and didn't see any judgment on his face, so I explained how I'd gotten to that conclusion prior to rescuing Jordan.

"It's possible the guy was setting Stephen up. Maybe that

was how he thought he was going to get away with all of it," Angel suggested.

I nodded. I hadn't considered that. "I still feel bad for thinking that about my brother. And I still have to wonder where the hell he is. He hasn't been home in more than a week."

"I'm sure there is a perfectly logical explanation. You'll just have to be patient and wait for him to fill you in."

I blew out a breath and sighed. "Yeah, I guess."

"I should get back to my room. I'm only supposed to be on these for about fifteen minutes at a time for now, but I had to come see that you were okay." He reached a hand out for mine and squeezed my fingers.

"What time tomorrow are you being moved?"

"Around one."

"I'll come see you before I go."

"I'm counting on it." He swung himself around on the crutches and maneuvered out the door. "Later, Kendrick."

"Bye," I returned, leaning back into the pillows. I sat there feeling utterly bored as my mind swirled with questions over what they were discovering at the crime scenes. I was just about asleep when there was another knock on my door. "Yeah?" I called out.

"You awake, Marcy?"

"Jordan, finally!" I sat up, wide awake all of a sudden. "What happened? What have they found out? Did Nick get booked in okay?"

Jordan stepped into the room and held up his hands, one of them holding my purse, which had been left in my car. "Slow down." He sank into the visitor chair next to the bed and set my purse on the table. "Yes, after being evaluated by the paramedics, we booked him into custody."

"And?"

Jordan began going over everything that they'd found up to this point. It turned out that Nicholas Pound was a schizophrenic who had been off his meds for a little more than a year. After a call to his psychiatrist, Jordan discovered that Nick had had previous psychopathic episodes where he'd mutilated animals. The psychiatrist suspected that the killer personality had been preparing for this murder spree for years. They'd also discovered that his apartment held a plethora of evidence that linked him to all of the murders, as well as to me.

"What do you mean to me?" I asked.

"It was nuts. He had an entire room dedicated to you. Photos of you on the job, at your apartment, at the grocery, just doing all kinds of everyday things. Then there was an entire wall dedicated to your childhood, with pictures and newspaper clippings of all the Face Flayer murders. There were shots of your brother, his face blacked out... it was just bizarre." He shivered. "There were a few of me as well that he'd put big red x's on." He looked pale at that. "The guy was obsessed with you."

I was appalled. He had lived just feet from me, had invaded my privacy on numerous occasions, and I hadn't even realized it. I'd known he was an annoying reporter who had a hard-on for getting me fired, but I hadn't thought he was a psycho. Not until seeing Jordan with his phone. Speaking of that, I asked, "How did he get that phone to call me with Stephen's number?"

"It had a spoofing app. He could make it show any number he wanted."

"So he doesn't have my brother locked away somewhere?" I asked.

Jordan shook his head. "Not that we've found. Why? Is he missing?"

"I don't know, honestly. He's been acting strange for a while now, drinking a lot—well, you know, he got into that fight with you."

"It wasn't so much a fight as him sucker punching me, but yeah, I'd say he's been off."

"Thanks for dropping the charges on that, by the way."

Jordan shrugged. "I suppose I deserved it, sort of. I was being overly harsh with you. You know I only shout at you because I care, right?"

I arched a brow at him. He had a funny way of showing it, if that was true.

"Katie's pregnant," he blurted a moment later. "I wanted you to hear it from me, before—well before it got around the station."

Inside I was seething. I had wanted kids with Jordan, had thought he'd wanted them too, but then I found out about a year before our divorce that he'd gotten a vasectomy and had lied to me every time we "tried" to make a baby. "Oh? Sure it's yours?"

He nodded. "I had it reversed right after our divorce."

That didn't surprise me, but it hurt. "Why did you not want to have kids with me?" I asked softly.

He sighed and ran a hand through his hair. "You didn't want what I wanted, Marcy. I wanted a stay-at-home wife. A mother to my kids. You wanted to be super cop."

He'd never discussed that with me. I didn't say anything. It was all in the past, and I was over him by now.

"I should go."

I gave him a slight nod and watched him walk out the door without another word. I didn't know what this conversation meant for the future of us working together, but at least he'd been more open and honest with me than he ever had while we were married.

As I leaned back against the pillows again, my thoughts returned to my brother. I wondered, if Nick hadn't kidnapped him, then what had happened to him?

I decided to try his phone again, but once more it went straight to voicemail. Sighing, I set the phone aside and drifted off to sleep.

40

THERAPY

MARCY

After being discharged, I went to see Angel. He was in good spirits since he was about to be released from the hospital and into rehab. I was looking forward to him being back on the job with me. I missed having my partner around.

Once I was done with my visit, and Angel was on his way to the rehabilitation facility, I called an Uber and went home. Thanks to Jordan bringing my purse and my keys, I was able to get in without having to call the landlord. The captain had come by the hospital and told me I was on leave for the next four weeks so I could recover. I was actually looking forward to it.

I took a quick shower and then made myself a sandwich. Just as I was about to take a bite, my phone rang on the counter. I grabbed it up and hit answer.

"Stephen! Where the hell have you been? Do you know how worried I've been about you?"

"I'm sorry. I didn't mean to worry you so much. I can

explain everything, but first, I wanted to check on you. I heard that you caught the killer. It was that reporter?"

"It's a long story, but yes, it was Nick. He's in custody and being evaluated to see if he can stand trial."

"I'm glad. Um... can you meet me somewhere?"

I frowned, but I wasn't going to pass up the chance to see for myself that he was okay. "Sure."

He gave me the address and asked if I could be there as soon as possible.

"Yeah, I just need to call for a ride."

"Great, see you in a bit."

I didn't recognize the address, but I called for an Uber and met them outside.

Half an hour later we pulled up in front of an office building, and Stephen was waiting for me outside. He hugged me when I got close, and when he let me go, I looked him over. He looked better than I'd seen him in a long while.

"So, what's here?" I looked at the building and finally saw the small plaque next to the door. It read Dr. Regina Faulkner, Psychiatrist. I glanced from it to Stephen. "Therapy?"

He nodded. "I had a mental breakdown. I didn't want to tell you. I was embarrassed." He looked down at his shoes.

"Why?" I reached out to him, pulling him back into a hug.

"Because I'm your older brother. I'm supposed to have it all together. Be in control. Be responsible."

"That's stupid."

He gave a wry chuckle. "I know that now. I've spent the last two weeks at a therapy clinic. That's why I wasn't getting your calls."

"But you sounded out of it when I did talk to you finally," I said, unsure if he was telling me the full truth.

"I was taking some medication to help me work through some stuff."

"So why am I here?" I asked, gesturing to the building.

"My therapist wants to meet you, and she thinks that it would be a good idea if you listen to some things I have to say."

"Okay." I was hesitant, but I would support him in whatever way I could.

He pulled open the door and led the way in, stopping at reception for a moment, but she just waved us on back. "Dr. Faulkner? This is my sister, Detective Marcy Kendrick."

"Detective, it's a pleasure to meet you; please come in. Have a seat."

I shook her hand and replied, "It's nice to meet you too."

After sitting, she asked Stephen to begin. I sat in shock as my brother explained that he'd begun having nightmares about a year ago of things that he'd blocked in his mind. Things from childhood. Things I never knew about.

"Mom abused me," he said, his voice shaky and unsure. "She treated me like one of her clients."

My eyes widened in horror, and I shook my head in denial, but Stephen wouldn't lie to me. Not about this. "Oh my God, Stephen, I didn't know... I can't... how could she do something like that?" I gasped, feeling my world tilt on its axis. I couldn't wrap my head around what he was saying.

"You're shocked, Detective Kendrick," Dr. Faulkner said. "I understand you had no knowledge of your mother's abusive behavior. You loved your mother, and since her death, you've only thought of her as the wonderful mother that she was to you. Now your brother's revelations are challenging that view of her in your head, and you can't make sense of it, but you will with time."

"I just don't understand how I could have failed to notice," I murmured as tears slid down my cheeks.

"You were still a kid, Marce. I don't blame you." Stephen hugged me.

I sniffled and hugged him back. "Is that everything?"

"No." He glanced toward the doctor.

"Let's allow Stephen to continue, he's made great progress over the last few weeks, and sharing everything today will help him to recover."

Stephen started again and said how after our mother's murder, he had actually been grateful to St. Martin for killing her. Then things he'd said over the last month finally started to make sense in my mind. He'd felt guilty for feeling happy over Mom's death, which had led to his excessive drinking, which led to violent temper outbursts and more nightmares. He'd finally hit rock bottom and realized he needed help when his boss had called him in for being drunk on the job, so he'd taken a leave of absence from work and checked himself into the clinic.

"It wasn't immediate, Marcy. I tried to kill myself, but I hadn't taken enough pills. When I woke up, I knew that I had to do something. I had to get help."

I took his hand in mine, holding on tight as tears filled my eyes. "I'm so glad you realized that. You could have come to me, you know."

"I know. But I was too ashamed."

"You have nothing to be ashamed of. You didn't do anything wrong. That was all on Mom."

"I know that now." He hesitated, then said, "I need to admit something else."

I frowned. "What?"

"I was the one who wrecked Mom's grave."

I sat there in silence, not sure what to say. After everything that he'd said, I could understand why he'd done it, but his doing so had cost me half of my savings.

"I'm sorry, Marce. I was angry and drunk, and that's not an excuse, just an explanation. I'll pay you back. I know it was expensive."

Sighing, I said, "I forgive you."

We sat and talked some more with the psychiatrist there to help the conversation along, and I realized that after everything with this last case, with Mom's case, with Henry's death, I probably needed therapy myself, and despite the fact that I'd hated it as a kid, I thought I might give it a go. At least a form of it.

I started looking into group grief counseling and found a place close to my neighborhood to attend.

As the days passed, more and more had come out about Nicholas Pound. He'd been found criminally insane and unable to stand trial. He'd requested to see me, but so far, I'd refused. I did meet with the psychiatrist who was working with him so that I could close out the case.

It turned out that Nick had three personalities. One was the brash obnoxious reporter, one was the psychotic killer, and the third was a mild-mannered teenager. The third made no sense to me, but the psychiatrist hadn't thought it unusual.

The first two personalities were obsessed with me but for different reasons. Nick had studied the Face Flayer case after learning about me as a cop. For years, he studied everything he could find about me, and the more he studied, the more obsessed he became. When he couldn't reconcile his feelings for me, his personality split, with one being in love with me and the other hating me with an intensity that was beyond normal. The third personality had formed when he was a kid and knew nothing about me at all.

With Nick unable to stand trial, he'd been found guilty and sentenced to life in a mental institution for the criminally insane. I was still afraid that one day he'd find a way to contact me. I was trying to work through that fear on my own.

A little more than a month had passed, and I was back at work, but I hadn't been sent out on any major crime cases since my return, and I was ready to get back to it. Jordan had been calmer around me, which was nice, and Angel was due back at work soon too.

After work, I picked up a bouquet of flowers and went with Angel to the cemetery. He had really been my rock over the last several weeks. He had listened as I'd shared how guilty I felt over Henry's death, and had worked with me to get past it and realize that I couldn't take that guilt.

"The only one guilty of his death is Nick, and he's locked up. You made sure of that, Marcy," he said as we walked toward Henry's grave.

"I know. I don't feel as guilty as I had been feeling, but I'm not sure that the feeling will totally go away."

"I get that. You've got a big heart, and you care about people. Henry was a good person. He didn't deserve what happened to him. Still, from everything you've told me about him, I don't think he would want you to blame yourself or to grieve for him for too long. He'd want you to live your life to the fullest." He tucked a piece of my hair behind my ear. "He'd want you to be happy."

I smiled and glanced down at Henry's grave. "I think

you're right." I laid the flowers down and patted the headstone. "Rest well, Henry."

We stayed for a few more minutes and then started back toward my car. I felt lighter somehow as I looked up at the evening sky. I could see a few stars beginning to twinkle in the dusky light, and it made me feel like everything was going to be better. I glanced over at Angel, who walked beside me on crutches.

"So tomorrow?" I asked, smiling.

"Yep. I'll be back tomorrow. You ready for that, partner?"

"More than ready, Angel. More than ready." I bumped my shoulder to his and grinned. "Wanna grab a burger with me?"

"Thought you'd never ask." He chuckled as he pulled open the passenger door of my car.

I couldn't wait to get back to it with Angel at my side. But that was for tomorrow.

THANK YOU FOR READING

Did you enjoy reading *Skin Deep*? Please consider leaving a review on Amazon. Your review will help other readers to discover the novel.

ABOUT THE AUTHOR

Theo Baxter has followed in the footsteps of his brother, best-selling suspense author Cole Baxter. He enjoys the twists and turns that readers encounter in his stories.

ALSO BY THEO BAXTER

Psychological Thrillers

The Widow's Secret

The Stepfather

Vanished

It's Your Turn Now

The Scorned Wife

Not My Mother

The Lake House

The Honey Trap

The Detective Marcy Kendrick Thriller Series

Skin Deep - Book #1

Blood Line - Book #2

Dark Duty - Book #3

Kill Count - Book #4